I0612088

The Bones Below

Lindy Larsen, Volume 4

Gayle Siebert

Published by Idyllbeck Opportunities, 2022.

Table of Contents

The Bones Below© 2022

Warning: Not intended for persons under the age of 18. May contain coarse language and mature content that may disturb some readers. Reader discretion advised.

Cover Art Design by: Miblart
Author Photo Credit: C. Kelly Photography
Second Edition
Published by Idyllbeck Opportunities

Chapter 1

I hear shouts and look out the window above my desk. There's a flurry of activity in the construction site across the yard. The excavator swings its bucket away and a couple of workers hop down into the shallow trench. Both the foreman and K.C. hurry to join them. With the excavator blocking my view I can't see beyond that. My first thought is that someone's hurt, but no one would be down in the trench, so that can't be it.

I sigh and feel my mood plummet. It must be another ancient Indian burial like the one we ran into when we built the wine tasting room. This means another lengthy delay while archaeologists mark out a restricted area ten times bigger than they need and begin their agonizingly slow excavation. It'll be unsettling for Red, who is Cree and Sensitive; she'll use her entire stock of sage smudging everything she can think of.

I pick up my coffee mug and head outside to investigate. The area they're working in was the manure pile, in use from the time my grandfather built the first barn. Going by the date inscribed in concrete at the doorsill, that was in 1928. There would have been no sign of an Indian burial then. Well, unless there was and they bulldozed everything, put the barn where they wanted it and started piling manure in the most convenient spot. That wouldn't have been unusual then and now, six decades later, it still happens. My mind races off to the worst possible scenario: that our barn, corrals, Bistro and farm store—maybe even our houses—are on an ancient burial site, a real possibility if this is another grave.

Can they move that many ancient bones? Would the Nekaneet elders allow it? They weren't happy about the last burial being moved even though they had a respectful ceremony when the bones were relocated to the cemetery in the Rez. Maybe we could make a deal to continue ranching and wine-making and running our farm store as usual if we set aside a little park. We could put up a marker like the monument for nearby Fort Walsh. We're already a stopping off point for tour buses on their way there. But it would mean more money just to go ahead on a project that's already behind schedule and over budget.

Now K.C. steps out from behind the excavator and looks my way. I lift my mug and he acknowledges me with a little wave. He may be coming up to the house for coffee, but even at this distance the look on his face tells me it's not a welcome break.

"Do I need to call the government guys?" I call out as soon as he's within range.

He shakes his head but says nothing until he's beside me on the porch. "Yeah," he says, "but only if you call the RCMP government guys."

Although the grave has been here a while, it's not ancient, so it's a crime scene rather than anything of historical significance, and the Nekaneet Elders aren't interested. The containment area marked by yellow plastic tape is easily four times larger than that needed for the burial discovered when we built the store. To think I was worried about archaeologists taking up too much space! At least the RCMP Major Crimes and Forensic Identification Service will only need access for a day or two. It's business as usual in the store and Bistro. Well, except for the customers finding excuses to wander over and gawk.

Dwight, my uncle Stu and his wife Red are on one side of the picnic table on my patio. K.C. and I are across from them. Dwight is the NCO in Charge of the Maple Creek RCMP detachment. He's explained what that means a few times. I still don't know the difference between a commissioned officer and a non-commissioned one. They're all cops, after all. But my take-away is that although Dwight is the boss, he has to report to someone somewhere else, which is all I need to know. He's off duty now so all three men are drinking beer while Red and I are into ice cold Wacasko-Wâti rhubarb wine. Red brought a platter of the two-bite size meat-filled pastries from the Bistro with her when she joined us. They're rapidly disappearing.

"They noticed a couple areas they're interested in, so they're going to dig more holes," Dwight tells us. He has been a friend of Stu's since before he went into the RCMP, and has been stationed all over Canada, including the Yukon. Now he's back in his home town, his last posting before retirement.

"What got them interested? I mean, it's not an ancient burial and it's unlikely this was an old graveyard, right?" I ask.

"No, but they're wondering about some of the other odd depressions."

"Odd depressions?"

"Yeah. You know when something's buried, first there's a mound, then after a while the dirt settles and there's a depression."

"Oh, for Pete's sake, Dwight! We got depressions like that all over the place. They can't mean to dig up every one of them!?! They'll be here for years."

I met Dwight a decade ago. I had just inherited Wacasko-Wâti and hadn't yet moved here. Stu and Red were living on it. I thought Dwight was striking in his uniform then, but he must have been a real head turner in his younger days. He's still handsome despite his thinning, mostly gray hair and the deep crow's feet when he grins, like now.

"Hey, don't shoot the messenger. I'm just telling you what I know," Dwight says as he selects another pastry. "I still think you need a better name for these. Calling them rat turds, I'm surprised you sell a single one."

"You know dang well the label in the pastry case says they're meat pie pick-ups and bein' called rat turds ain't slowed you down," Red says, and gives a loud sniff.

"Come on, girl, you know I'm teasing," he says. He loops an arm around Red's shoulders and gives her a squeeze. "How come you're so sensitive tonight?"

"She's upset about them skeletons," Stu answers. "Who ain't?"

"We all are," I confirm. "How long before we hear something more?"

"Right now they're still going back over missing persons cases but it'll be a while before they can give us an idea of how long ago those folks died. Just between you, me and the gatepost, they're both female."

"That's what the spokesperson down there just told the reporters, Dwight," I say.

"Well, tomorrow, they're going to tell them there was jewelry."

"Jewelry? So they weren't killed in a robbery, then," I conclude. "What kind of jewelry? Necklaces? Bracelets? Watches?"

"More than that, I can't tell you," Dwight responds. "And folks, keep in mind that back in the day, it wasn't unusual for family members to be buried on the property."

"But surely they wouldn't bury them with their jewelry," I say. Back in Maple Creek less than a year and already I've run into bodies where they shouldn't be. I hope Dwight's right and these are family burials, like from the original homesteaders a hundred years ago, but have to admit that seems unlikely. I can predict what Dwight's going to say next: he can't comment on an ongoing investigation. It's on the tip of my tongue to ask if he means he doesn't know or that he won't tell us. Instead I say, "But both in the same grave? And then pile manure on them? Not likely a family burial, and it's also not likely they died of natural causes, because—two people died at one time?"

"But they weren't in the same grave," Dwight says. "The second one was discovered when they were recovering the first one and the bank sloughed away."

Chilly implications flood through me. Two bodies buried in the old manure pile at different times. Someone who lived or worked on this ranch killed, and more than once. I've barely had this thought when Dwight says, "Of course that means there may be more bodies. Which is why they want to investigate those depressions."

I get it now. My spirits take a nose dive and I feel myself slump as if my bones have suddenly gone soft.

"Where are these depressions and how much more space are they going to keep us out of?" K.C. asks. "We need to get the indoor ring built before the snow flies, and it's already going to be tight."

"Can't say," Dwight responds, "but likely it'll at least take in that corral. Can you work on another part of it?"

"Not possible, Dwight. Christ!" K.C. raps the table, then gets up and goes to get another beer out of the cooler. "Who's ready for another?"

"No thanks," Dwight says. "I gotta run."

"I'll have one," Stu says. "Damn! See, K.C.? Should of listened when Russ told us not to put yer arena so close to the barn. Put it over behind Lindy's house, he said, where you got yer horse trailers. Already got that new road access fer that. If we listened to him, them folks would still be restin' in peace."

"And we'd still be walkin' over their bones," Red points out. "I felt 'em. I'm glad they been found."

"I'm with you, Red. I can't say I felt them, but I'd rather not be walking over anyone's grave," I say.

"We were all fine before we knew they were there," K.C. points out as he slides back onto his seat beside me. My reproachful look is mild compared to the one Red's giving him. He squeezes my hand and traps it under his on his thigh.

"Anyhow," Dwight says, "we're going to need names of everyone who ever lived or worked here. That means you're going to be the first one to spend time with the detectives, Stu. You know the most about this place, right?"

"Yeah. I used to come here as a kid when Cam—Lindy's dad—was spendin' a few days with his old man. You know Cam's dad brought him to live with my folks when we were babies."

"I didn't think you were related," K.C. says. "Lindy said she adopted you."

"Well, it weren't legal. She just started callin' me Uncle Stu when her Dad told her I was like a brother to him. My dad and Cam's was partners in some business deal that went tits up. Somehow they stayed friends after that, so it must of went okay. No hard feelin's, I mean. and when his dad passed, Cam started livin' here full time, so 'course I spent a lot of time here too. Cam had no cattle and me and him was off rodeoin' a lot. Him more'n me. I stayed here in the winter while he went south. At that time, the hayloft was empty, so Cam sometimes rented it fer church services or the odd barn dance. But fer that and rodeo people usin' this as a stoppin' off place from time to time, there'd be no one but me, Cam and our horses here, and that was no more'n half the time."

"So, sounds like it's going to be a long list," Dwight says.

"Them folks never stayed fer long, though."

"It could be a body dump," I suggest. "You know, killed somewhere else and brought here to be buried."

"That's right," Red contributes, "no one around to notice a fresh dig in the manure pile and pretty quick it wouldn't even look fresh."

"But once you lived here, you would've noticed," Dwight says.

"Maybe not," Stu says. "We dug there ourselves. Took dirt to use in the rhubarb patch and the garden, too, right after Red moved in with me. God-damn! We might of dug up one a them bodies then!"

"Well, obviously you didn't, and we would've noticed any digging around there after we started using the manure spreader," I say, "so it's probable the bodies predate any of us living here full time. That would be 1977."

"That narrows the timeline," Dwight says. "Forensic ID may be able to narrow it down more. Meanwhile, start making that list, Stu."

"I'll do what I can, a'course. But lots of them guys, I might know only their nicknames. and they might of had friends with 'em that I never knew 'bout. and they could of been here when I wasn't."

"Just put down as many names as you can remember, and with as much detail as you can. Such as where they were from. When they might've been here. As for way back, anything at all Cam might've said. Or your folks, if you can think of anything they said."

"They both passed years ago, and even without all the nicknames, this is a big job," Stu grumbles. "You got no idea, Dwight. Lindy's boyfriend went by Painless. Red's real name ain't Red, and Cam went by Gobbler as often as anything." He sighs. "This has got me thinkin' back on them times. Cam was a pain in the ass, but I still miss him."

"I miss him, too," Red says, "like a toothache. I know you ain't s'posed to speak ill of the dead, but far as them bodies and who planted them—I'd put his name at the top of the list." She looks at me and says, "Sorry, Lindy."

I draw a quick breath. I thought I was past being offended or hurt by crit-icism of my father but the knot in my stomach tells me I'm not. Red has been my best friend since the summer I ran away from home to follow the rodeo, but when she speaks her mind like that, she can be a pain in the ass, too. "He had his faults, but he wasn't a murderer," I say.

"How does anyone know what someone is capable of?" K.C. asks. "Ted Bundy is a handsome, outgoing guy, and killed dozens of women. Got away with it for decades."

"You think my Dad was like Ted Bundy?" I snap, and pull my hand out from under his.

"No, Lindy, I never even met him. I'm just saying …"

Red says, "He wasn't like Ted Bundy, Lindy, but he was a mean drunk. You only knew him a few months. You never seen him at his worst."

"You mean you think he would kill a woman—a couple of women—and then just bury them in the manure pile?!? My god, Red!" I burst into angry tears, jump to my feet and scurry down to the barn before I say something that can't be unsaid.

Once I'm in the barn I pick the dandy brush off the ledge outside Chica's stall and go in beside her. She looks up from her hay once, just enough to acknowledge my presence, and without even stopping chewing. I brush vigorously, flicking hair and dust from her already gleaming coat. It's really more for me than for her. My sweet mare. We've become so bonded I almost think of her as my best friend. Certainly she is at this moment. I inhale deeply of her familiar scent and feel my heartbeat returning to normal.

Soon, I hear vehicles leaving the yard. The store is closing and the last customers are driving away. There are no more voices coming from my patio, so I surmise Dwight's cruiser must have been among them and everyone else has gone in. K.C. appears at the far end of the alleyway and I turn to face him as he approaches.

"Hey, Lindy," he says. "You okay?"

I realize I am, and nod. "More or less."

"I'm sorry. You know, about bringing up Ted Bundy," he says.

I slide the stall door open and go back into the alleyway, latching the door behind me. "It's okay," I tell him. "I'm more pissed at Red. I'll get over it. Dunno why I reacted like I did. I know how she feels about Dad. She always disliked him. And it's true you could think you know someone well and find out they, um, were married or had even killed someone."

"Yeah. Folks are not always *what you see is what you get.*" K.C. sighs. He pulls me to him and I melt into his hug. He strokes my back, then kisses my ear, releases me and says, "Let's go up. We got some of today's left over chicken and it's nearly time for Wise Guy. Don't want to miss that."

I nod, take a deep breath, and we leave the barn. I'm a little shaky and my legs feel weak. I put it down to the adrenalin rush subsiding. But maybe it's because I'm worried that Red could be right about my father.

Chapter 2

The conventional wisdom is that any attention is good attention. Whether that's true or not, we're getting a lot of it. News crews and reporters fill our parking area so actual customers have to park on the road. They drink coffee by the gallon, causing us to wonder if our unlimited free refills are going to put us in the poor house. They're in the washrooms so often that I ordered an unscheduled septic tank pump out.

They're an all-around pain the backside, but their stories are running in The Calgary Herald, Edmonton Journal, Prince Albert Daily Herald, Vancouver Sun, and even the Minot Daily News. Morbid curiosity is proving to be a greater draw than any of our advertising. We might be shaken at discovering there were murder victims underfoot all this time, but the rest of humanity treats the graves as a tourist attraction.

The world, or at least our little slice of it, is learning that Wacasko-Wâti is Cree for rat hole, which is what my ex called the ranch, and that provides a bit of levity to an otherwise gruesome story. On the plus side, it keeps the farm store and Bistro busy and the wine is flying off the shelves. Who wouldn't want a bottle with a Wacasko-Wâti label to prove they've been here now that we're infamous?

Felix, Red's nephew and our part-time winemaker, suggested we get new labels printed with skeletons on them and have the sign at our gate changed as well. While I applaud his team spirit, my guts churn at the thought.

K.C. convinced the pert little blonde reporter to do his on-camera interview in front of the sign for his horse trailer dealership instead of over at the containment area. He can be very persuasive. Doesn't hurt his cause that he's also a hunk with a dazzling smile. Even without skeletons on the sign he got calls from a couple of serious buyers because of it.

The boost to our cash flow is great but it can't become old news soon enough to suit me. We're all breathing easier since the Forensic ID Service notified us they'd be finished today. They should be taking down their tents and packing their van now, but instead they're still mumbling and bumbling.

I'm in the Bistro trying to keep the swear words in my head from coming out of my mouth as I wipe up the mess the free coffee drinkers leave in their wake, when I see Dwight's cruiser drive in. Instead of parking in the customer lot, he drives up to the barn and parks beside the Forensic ID vans. I toss the dishcloth in the dirty dish bin, wipe my hands on my apron, and go out on the patio to watch as Dwight chats with someone there. In a few minutes he spots me, crosses the yard and comes to join me. Stu looks up from his bar-beque and closes the lid.

"Hey, buddy," Stu calls out, "come fer coffee?"

"You know it. I'll have my customary cinnamon bun too," Dwight replies. "One of the saskatoon ones, if there's any of those bad boys left."

Dwight follows me inside; I hand him a mug for the self-serve coffee bar and get his cinnamon bun. K.C. must have noticed Dwight's cruiser, as he's coming in the side door right behind Stu.

When we're all settled at a table, Dwight says, "Hate to be the bearer of bad news, folks, but there's going to be a delay."

"Damn!" As swear words go, that's a mild one, so it's not too bad that I said it out loud. "What for?"

"They found another burial."

"What?" Stu exclaims. "They already dug up half the damn ranch! Where's this one?"

"Right over at the far fence. The last depression they wanted to check."

I put my elbows on the table and rest my face in my hands for a second, then look up and ask, "Why not with the others in the manure pile?"

"A question we're asking ourselves," Dwight replies.

"So what now? Take down more corral fencing?"

"Afraid so."

"Them corrals ain't there just fer looks," Stu states. I notice his nostrils are flaring and his eyes are narrowing. He's slow to anger, but I think he's heading in that direction now. "What're we s'posed to do with our cattle? Horses? And that corral that they so far just took down one section of is the one with the loading chute, and we got market weight steers to ship."

I'm surprised at the sharpness of Stu's tone, so out of character for him. He's not himself, thinking about the bones we've been walking over all this time like the rest of us are, I suppose. I say, "I guess we'll have to stand down on a lot of what we use the corrals for. Won't be for that much longer." I turn to Dwight and ask, "It won't be, will it, Dwight? Be that much longer, I mean?"

"Um, no, it shouldn't be." His tone is not reassuring, and he knows it. He focuses his attention on his pastry.

Of course they're going to have to expand the search area. If they find more bodies, no one can predict how much longer it'll take. "The corrals on the other side of that, the smaller one is the riding ring, and the bigger one has the water trough. The one the livestock on the pasture use. We can't do without that," I tell him. "And where is K.C. supposed to teach? And train his client's horses?"

"Can you come up with an alternate plan, K.C.?" Dwight asks.

K.C. appears resigned. He shakes his head slowly. "Looks like I've got no choice. Maybe we put in another trough farther out. Right up at the windmill makes sense. Reconnect the pipes when they're done." He sighs and adds, "If it's not for more'n a couple weeks I can ride my in-training horses out. But that's just the basics. Getting them out to see everything. Need the arena for everything else. Might as well just forget about the goddamn indoor arena."

"Not forever, sweetie," I say, and pat his thigh. I share his frustration. I turn to Dwight and say, "The water's been piped down to the big corral for longer than I've lived here, and we are *not* okay with having to haul water from the windmill down to the barn. If they tear out any of our pipes—!"

"They'll put everything back," Dwight assures us.

"Good goddamn thing we ain't usin' that well fer irrigatin' just now," Stu says. "Maybe the govermint supplies what we need to put in that new trough."

"Not just material. Labor, too," I insist, my tone proof I'm as close to losing my temper as Stu is.

"I'll see what can be done," Dwight says, and shrugs. "It's not up to me, remember. Someone sitting behind a desk back in Regina is calling the shots." He glances at his watch, then turns to me and says, "Can I get a doggie bag for the rest of this bun?"

"Of course," I reply, and go to the kitchen for the box. As I put it in front of him, I say, "Sorry, Dwight. I know it's not your fault, but this is bad enough for our store and Bistro, and now it's going to impact our ranch operations and K.C.'s business, too. I say they give us something or we deny access."

K.C.'s brow is furrowed. I know what he's thinking: they'd still get access but they'd have to go through some hoops, and a delay like that would set our indoor arena project back as well. It's a bluff. Besides, we were going to have to reconfigure parts of the corrals around the new building so if we lay out the replacement fences to suit, it's possible there will be a benefit to us, however small. I say, "Surely they'll see the wisdom of following the course of least resistance."

"I agree," Dwight says, "but wisdom isn't always a factor in their decision making. Don't tell anyone I said that." He grins, gets to his feet and says, "I'll call you as soon as I hear more." He leaves the Bistro, his little Styrofoam container in hand, nodding to a couple of women passing him on their way in as he holds the door for them.

As we watch him go, K.C. shakes his head and says, "Good thing I sold a couple trailers this month or it would be a complete bust. And now the arena build is on hold, and even the corral I teach in has to go? I got clinics coming up that I'll have to cancel and we sure as hell can't take in any boarders now. Jesus H. *fucking* Christ, how can they do this to us?"

The F-word? Unusual, at least in mixed company. His intensity surprises me. I hadn't thought about how much he uses that corral. It's going to be worse for him than for the rest of us and I can't think of anything positive to say. I bite my lower lip.

"Waaalll," Stu drawls, "least it frees us up to do the hay ourselves, so we can save the bucks we normally pay the hay crew."

"It's true we won't need to hire as many guys, but it's a small economy," I point out. "Here's a thought: the loft is almost empty now. If we store this year's hay in the shelters the cattle can't access once the corrals are torn down, we could rent the loft out. Remember, Stu? You said back in the day it was rented to a church for their services. Maybe they'd rent it again."

Stu shrugs and says, "I guess maybe."

"How do we contact them?"

"I, er, well, I dunno but Red knows some churchy people. Ask her."

"I will." I think we're all focusing our thoughts on how to work around the expanded crime scene. I'd like to keep a positive attitude and hope someone comes up with a solution but in the back of my mind lurks a thought I can't banish: a serial killer was connected to this place I love, and we've been walking over graves all this time.

I'm not a believer in spirits, but Red is. She's spiritual and the Nekaneet know her as a Sensitive, yet she was unaware of those burials. Or was she? Is that why she's always wanting to smudge? Have those victims been trying to contact her? Are their spirits the reason I sometimes feel I'm being watched when I'm in the barn late at night? The shadowy movement in my peripheral vision that vanishes when I turn to look? The reason the hairs on the back of my neck bristle?

I'm letting my imagination run wild, and remind myself I don't believe it. But now I wonder if there are ghosts Red's smudging rituals can't banish. They're here now. In my mind, if nowhere else.

Chapter 3

We're on the veranda of a neat brick bungalow in the oldest area of Maple Creek. I press the doorbell. I hear it buzzing inside, but no movement. I press the button again.

A voice inside calls, "I'm coming! I'm coming!" In moments, a man with a Dowager's hump and looking old enough to be the original owner of the house opens the door.

"Good morning," I say. "Mr. Barth?"

"Yeah?" The way he's looking at me and the tone of his voice makes me half expect him to say *who wants to know?*

"I'm Lindy and this is K.C. Our ranch, Wacasko-Wâti—"

"Whatever you're selling, I don't want any," he snaps.

"I, er, we're not selling anything. I got your name from our friend who said she thought you were a member of a church here in town."

"How's that anyone's business?"

Both his question and his tone set me back. K.C. steps in to respond, "No one's business but yours, sir, but Red Bear Robe said you might be able to tell us who rented our hayloft for church services in the past. You remember Red? She did housework for you way back."

"Red Bear Robe?" He scratches his head as if casting his mind back, then says, "You mean Rose?"

"Rose is her sister," I tell him.

"Oh. Rose's sister. Yeah, now I remember. She didn't last long."

"She didn't? How come?"

"Why don't you ask her?" he asks, and adjusts his hearing aid. "What do you want to know?"

"Well, the time we're thinking of might be twenty or thirty years ago. Reason we're interested is that the space is available again and we thought we should offer it to them first, but we don't know how to contact them."

"If they rented it before, how come you don't know?"

"Like K.C. said, it was years ago. It was my Dad who rented it to them," I tell him. "He and my Mom were, um, *divorced,* so I never lived there, but when he passed a few years ago, I inherited the property. He wasn't great at record keeping, so he took the information to the grave."

"He belonged to that church?"

"I didn't know him well, but I doubt it. I think he just wanted the income from the rental."

Now he scratches the growth of white stubble on his chin as he appears to give the matter some thought. He says, "Long time since I even thought about them, and it ain't a pleasant memory. That so-called church, forget what the Sam hill they called themselves, but it was a strange name for a church. Fizzled out years ago, far as I know."

I shrug. "Hope not, since we'd like to rent the space to them again."

"Well, that might be a bad idea. Back then there were rumors about strange doin's at their meetings. If they're still around, I wouldn't have nuthin' to do with them if I were you."

"Strange doings? Like what?" I ask.

"You wouldn't believe it if I told you. Always doubted it myself. Still, you know what they say: where there's smoke, there's fire."

"Oh. Hmm. Well, do you know if there's anyone still around that could put us in touch with that, um, church?"

"I don't. But the senior's home on Aspen Street—Aspen Lodge—some old timers there might of had something to do with it. George Kerfoot could help you out. He lives in the corner unit, Number 1. He's the caretaker, and he knows everything that goes on in that place."

"Okay. Thank you."

"Don't thank me. I ain't doin' you a favor. If you're smart, you'll forget it." He takes a step back, closes the door, and I hear the click of the deadbolt being thrown.

"Well, I guess that's his final word on the subject," I observe. We go back to the truck. K.C. goes around to the far side and I get into the passenger seat. As we drive away, he asks, "Where's Alder Street?"

"It's all the way across town. Fourth Avenue is up ahead. Make a right onto it. It'll take us there," I reply. When we're heading in the right direction on Fourth, I say, "That guy was sure strange."

"What's strange about a guy not welcoming a couple of strangers who could be Jehovah's Witnesses?"

"Well, that. But no, I mean, about Red. And he wouldn't say why she didn't last long. And the 'strange doings'. Don't tell me you don't think that was strange."

"About Red, I mean, back when she did housework for him, maybe she wasn't always the energetic little self-starter she is now. What do you know about her life before you met her?"

"I know she worked at the lunch counter at the White Rose station that used to be out on the highway, and did housework for a few people around town. But she left home when she was in her mid-teens and headed west. Even wound up on the Coast, working on a fishing boat."

"Cool. But that's it?"

"I guess it's not much, but it's more than I know about you from when you were in high school. You've told me stuff from when you were in university, your marriage and so on, but I don't know anything much about when you were in your teens. What do you know about me from that time, for that matter?"

"I know you had a mis-spent youth," he says.

"Well, better than being a goody two shoes like you."

"What, me? Goody two shoes?" He clicks his tongue. "Don't worry, I got into the usual amount of trouble. Took the old man's truck without permission and put it in the ditch. Skipped school. Got caught smoking in the boys' room. Let the girl sitting behind me copy my answers in an algebra test and we both got busted. That kind of thing."

"So now I know you were a lousy driver, a sucker for girls and good at algebra."

"Hey, that truck handled like a pig! But yes to the sucker part. Still am, for that matter. I'm sitting here with you, right?" He gives me a sideways glance and grins. "But for math—we both had the same wrong answers. That's what gave us away."

"Did you at least get a date out of it?"

"Naw, that's the sad part."

"Well, her loss."

"But you? I know you hated your Mom's husband and his kid, drank your Mom's Baileys, skipped school a lot, and had never been near a horse. Dunno if you were a church-goer, though," he admits.

"A little, I guess. I did the communion thing when I was about eight, right on schedule. That was a big deal. I had a lacy white dress and a veil like a bride. I got my own bible, and even my own rosary. My Italian aunts and uncles and cousins all came and brought food. So much food! The men drank home made wine and played bocce. Kids everywhere! It was a good party and I had fun, until my stepsister Jillian and I snuck a bottle of wine. We crawled into our secret hiding place under the lilac bushes to drink it. She pushed my arm just as I was going to take a drink and I spilled it on my dress. When Mom saw me, my nice white dress all grubby from crawling under the bushes and of course the red stains, she had a fit. Wouldn't listen when I told her it was Jillian's fault. She screamed something like *as if stealing wine isn't bad enough, now you lie about Jillian, and those stains will never come out.* My party, and I got sent to my room. She was right about the stains, though. The dress was ruined. Dunno why it mattered, I was never going to wear it again anyway. And you wonder why I hated Jillian? But I deserved punishment I guess, because I was a willing participant in the wine theft. Then when I was maybe thirteen or so, Mom was usually too hung over to get out of bed until noon, and I was such a bag about wasting my valuable time in church, that Arthur and Jillian went without us. That was the end of my churchgoing. You?"

"We were Lutheran and proud of it," he says, "My mom and aunts had nothing good to say about Catholics and there were stories even back then about priests molesting altar boys and nuns having babies. Crazy stuff, like they smother the babies as soon as they're born and plaster the bodies inside the convent walls." We come to another stop sign, and he asks, "Okay, this is Alder. Which way, do you think?"

"Left," I tell him.

He checks for traffic and turns onto Alder. He shifts into third, and says, "Catholics probably tell stories like that about Lutherans, too."

"Except Lutherans don't have altar boys or nuns or even convents, so there's that."

"They have acolytes. And there are Lutheran nuns. They call them Daughters of Mary."

"Oh, yeah? Well, I think the priest stories are true. Like the man said, where there's smoke, there's fire. Also, look at all lawsuits coming out in the States now. Some of those claims go back decades but I'll bet it's been going on as long as they've had altar boys."

"Maybe it's something like that he was talking about. Maybe they ate the babies. Or at least drank their blood. Or maybe just smeared baby blood all over their naked bodies and ate each other."

"You're not taking this seriously."

"But that would be weird, right?"

"Not really. They do it every Saturday night where you come from, don't they?"

"Naw, they don't use real baby blood. And it's only the Scotch people, and even they only do it on Samhain," he replies.

"Kevin Connor Garland is about as Scottish a name as you can get, right? Here! This looks like the place."

K.C. slows the truck. On our right is a long one-storey building with a low sign reading Alder Lodge. He pulls up at the curb in front of the corner suite. "Okay?"

"Okay," I agree. "I'll go. I'm starting to think you're right and this is hopeless. You don't need to come with me for this one. I don't think it'll take long." I get out, walk to the door and ring the bell. It's soon answered by a lean fifty-something man with a shaggy gray fringe around his shiny dome.

"Yes?" He smiles.

I'm encouraged by his smile. "Mr. Kerfoot?"

"I am."

"I got your name from Mr. Barth."

"Ahh, my old bridge partner. How is Bill?"

"Fine, I guess. I only spoke to him for about three minutes, but he looked fine."

"Good. So, how can I help you?"

"Well, I'm looking for a man who was active in a church or religious group with an unusual name, and this would've been at least a couple of decades ago."

"Unusual name? What name was that?"

"I, um, don't know, I was just told it was unusual. Not mainstream like St. John's Lutheran or anything. Know what I mean?" It's a ridiculous question and I'm starting to realize it's also a ridiculous quest.

But he keeps smiling and says, "Yeah, I think I know who you mean. One of our residents fancies himself a preacher. Doesn't call himself a preacher though, just says he's an elder, as if no one could figure that out. This is a seniors' home, after all." He barks a laugh. "When the spirit moves him he likes to preach in the common room, and there's a few who listen to him. Dunno if he can help you out, but he lives in Unit 20 in the back wing. Just follow the sidewalk around to the back." He points the way.

"Thanks." With a nod to K.C., I head around the corner.

The facility is bigger than it looks from the street, built in a U-shape around a lawn and garden area. I follow the walk to the appropriate door and ring the bell. After a moment a man opens the door. A voice from farther inside asks, "Who is it, Fred?"

A short, middle-aged man with a strawberry birthmark on his cheek comes to stand beside the first man and says, "You can go back to your T.V. program now, Fred."

Fred appears puzzled, then his neutral expression returns, and he heads back inside.

"I'm his caregiver," Strawberry birthmark explains. "Alzheimer's. So. What can I do for you?"

"I'm looking for someone who rented space at our ranch for church services a couple of decades ago, and I was told your friend might have been the preacher."

"Might have been Fred, all right," he says. "On his good days, he's a real hellfire and brimstone preacher. Other days he doesn't recognize me. Or he thinks I'm a buddy of his from back in the day. But most days, he just sits in his chair."

"What a terrible disease."

"It sure is. Who knows what life has in store for any of us, right?"

"Yes, sadly. What do you think? Would he be able to tell me who to contact?"

"I doubt it. No one from any church has ever come around to visit, that's all I know. But if you leave your name and number, when he's more, er, *with it*, I'll ask him and call you if he remembers."

"That would be great."

He gets a note pad and a pen, I give him my name and number, and say, "Thanks. Sorry to bother you." I turn and leave.

When I'm back in the truck and we're driving away, K.C. says, "So?"

"Nothing," I reply. "If he's the guy, he's got Alzheimer's. His caregiver said he'd talk to him when he's more lucid, and call me if he knows anything. Otherwise, it's a dead end."

"Oh, well. We just go ahead and advertise the loft. We're better off renting it to someone who wants it full time instead of just for church services anyhow."

"You're right."

"If we can't rent it, it's not the end of the world," he says, and reaches over to pat my thigh. "Hey, you know it's nearly lunch time. How be instead of going home, we go out? Someplace nice, like The Jasper?"

It does sound nice.

The Jasper looks the same as I remember it from the last time I was here, which was on the first nice date I had with Jake. Technically our third date, but the first nice one. We went to my place for dessert because, you know, why buy a slice of pie for three bucks when I get Red's Famous Pies for free? We wound up in bed.

I push that memory away and concentrate on what the beautiful man across the table is asking me. "You remember what day it is?"

"Other than Thursday, you mean?"

He reaches across the table to take my hand. "You really don't remember what day it is?"

"I guess I don't. What are you talking about?"

"On this date two years ago, the most beautiful, wonderful girl in the world walked into my life."

"Oh!" It's on the tip of my tongue to ask her name, but when he looks at me like that, I feel such a rush, all I can do is blush. I cast my mind back and realize today is the anniversary of the day I started my new job in Katawasis Lake.

"Well, actually, we didn't meet that day. And that wasn't even the first time I saw you," K.C. continues. "The first time I saw you was the day before, when I cut you off to get to the highway exit, and you followed me for about ten blocks just so you could stick your arm out the window to flip me the bird."

"Oh, yeah," I sigh. "As I've told you before, you just happened to be going in the same direction I was."

"*Riiiiggght*," he drawls. "Anyhow, when I saw you at the restaurant the next day, I didn't know you were the girl in the truck with the mis-matched fenders or that you were new to Katawasis Lake, just that I hadn't noticed you around town before. I remember looking up and seeing you walk in, the sun on your head making your hair glow like a halo, and I fell in love."

"Pfft! Love at first sight?" By now I've gathered my wits, and shake my head. "Big tough cowboy, with all those women flocking around you at your barn, one look at me and you're in love?"

"It's a cowboy thing. Ain't you been listening to country songs? Right up there with my dog ran away and my truck won't start." He grins, and gives a wink. "Well, that's when I started wondering if I could get you into my bed, anyway." He releases my hand so the waitress can put our drinks in front of us.

"Your order will be just a few more minutes," she tells us, and scurries off.

I sip my wine, and as I settle back and scan the room with mild interest in the dozen or so other diners, I'm struck with a thought. "Hey, K.C.? Why the little trip down memory lane?"

"Um, well," he replies, then reaches for my hand again. "I have something to tell you." He gives my hand a squeeze, looks me in the eye and says, "I'm going to do that clinic at Douglas Lake Ranch after all."

"What? But I thought you turned it down because it was too far away. What's different now?"

"Well, now my business is on hold possibly for the rest of the year. It's true it's a bit of a trip—twelve hour drive on a good day—but they want me for longer than just the clinic because they've got colts they want me to help start. Pay's good. Includes room and board. But it means being away for about a month."

"A month?"

"This time. More might come along. I'll come home when I can. At least I won't be dead weight around Wacasko-Wâti."

"You're not dead weight. You're busy every day."

"I don't do much for Wacasko-Wâti, though," he argues, "I'm just busy doing my thing, mostly. Working on getting the indoor build organized, training clients' horses, and teaching. Now, all that's gone. Can't even take new boarders, even if they didn't care that we don't have our indoor yet, because there's no turnout for them once the corrals are demolished. Nobody's going to want their expensive purebreds turned out with the herd where they might get beat up." He lifts his beer for a sip, then adds, "Besides that, no one is going to come all that way, at least a forty minute drive even for someone living in Maple Creek, when there's any number of places closer where they could keep their horses. Without the indoor, there's nothing other than weekend riding all winter."

"There's lights in the barn and a moonlight ride in the snow can be nice," I murmur. But it's feeble. I can't dispute his logic. It's true he's the one most impacted by so much of our barnyard being a crime scene. It's temporary, but there's no way of knowing how temporary, and we have enough manpower around the place without him. We could find something for him to do, but it would be obvious that it was just busy work, and he's too proud for that. My heart swells both with love for this man and pain at the thought of being separated from him.

"When do you leave?" I ask quietly.

"Monday," he replies.

I force a smile. "I'll miss you, but I understand."

"Good," he says. "Besides, you know what they say. Absence makes the heart grow fonder."

"That's what they say," I agree. But I can't stop thinking of the bastardization of that saying I've often said myself, thinking it was a joke: *absence makes the heart go yonder*. Somehow now it doesn't seem funny.

Chapter 4

We're up on the hill beside the old windmill, its rotor blades spinning lazily in the light breeze, emitting a *screech! screech! screech!* that's enough to set off a migraine. There's been a gas motor running the pump since before I moved here, so the windmill does nothing other than spin and screech.

"We either got to send someone up there with a lube gun or tear the windmill down," I grouse.

"If it bugs you that bad, I volunteer you fer the job," Stu says, and laughs. Obviously the screeching doesn't bother him. This is when being half deaf is an asset rather than a handicap. It's also a useful excuse to ignore anything he doesn't want to hear.

I'm with Stu and a couple of laborers the government provided. We marked out where the new fences go. Earlier, the excavator levelled the spot for the water trough the government is supplying. We've been raking and pushing dirt around ever since, waiting for the tank to show up. Once it's in place, the guys will get to work on the fences.

The forensic people are anxious to get the old fence torn out so they can mark off their new grids and continue working. At every coffee break they discuss the possibility versus the probability they'll find more burials. They seem excited, or hopeful might be the right term, that there are more. Interesting bones to them, maybe, but they were people who met a terrible and violent death. I can't stop thinking about it, hoping against hope that they don't find so much as a button.

The rumble and hiss of jake brakes draws my attention to the road. A tractor with the shiny new tank on its flatdeck is turning into our yard now. "It's here." I point to it.

"You go down and direct him," Stu says. He comes to the pickup, wipes the sweat off his brow on his shirtsleeve and gets the water jug out of the cooler. He screws off the lid and takes a good, long swallow, then says, "I'll git the guys started here and then come down to take over from Barney at the barbeque. You don't need to come back up."

"Good," I agree. It's pay day and I have checks to write, so I'm happy to comply. "Come on, Henry." I put my rake in the bed of the pickup and head down the hill and along the lane past the corrals at a jog, my dog Henry keeping up despite his limp.

As I approach the cab of the idling truck, the driver rolls down his window and asks, "You waiting for this tank?"

"We are," I confirm. "Just head up the hill to the windmill." The windmill is visible from most of the yard, but the lane that leads to it is behind the implement shed, so I point that out.

"Yes, ma'am," the driver says with a nod. He works the gearshift and drives off.

I go inside, settle at my desk, and get on with writing pay checks. Bookkeeping is my main contribution to the ranch, farm store, Bistro and winery as well as the Rocking R. That business began when Stu bought a Brahman bull off the kill truck when he was at an auction to rescue horses. Russ Benson, another old pal of Stu's, is a rough stock contractor for the rodeo circuit. He recognized the bull as a once-famous bucker known as Domino. Russ and Stu started the Rocking R, which is across the road and a mile or so south of Wacasko-Wâti. Besides breeding our own cows so we now have a bunch of our own up-and-coming bucking bulls, Domino provides semen we ship all over the continent. When we set out to diversify, we had no inkling just how diverse we would become.

Pay day is always my busiest day for books, although that will slow down now that we're laying off seasonal workers. These are the last checks for some of them, which means filling out government employment insurance forms. It's time-consuming at the best of times, thanks to part time and temporary workers all with varying hours and rates, so it's nearly five when I'm finally done and have the pay envelopes ready to go.

I look out the window over my desk and see workers drifting in and congregating on the patio at the Bistro. A pickup with the Rocking R logo on the door drives in and parks at Red and Stu's trailer. Charlie and Johnny, old enough to do ranch work at the Rocking R and earn a paycheck and young enough to be excited about it, spill out and race across the yard to join the others waiting for their pay. Russ exits the driver's seat and tilts his head from side to side as if to banish a crick in his neck before joining Stu on the deck.

I gather the envelopes and join the crowd outside the Bistro to pass them out, then go inside the store and through to the kitchen. "Paychecks are here, everyone!" I call out, and drop the envelopes on the pastry case.

Red has a dishcloth and a bin, and looks to be heading out onto the floor to bus tables. "Come on, Red! Russ and Stu have already started Happy Hour, and I'm heading over there now. Leave that and join us."

"I just want to clean up a bit so Marci doesn't have to," she says. "She's already done her shift and is just waitin' on her paycheck before she leaves." She lifts her chin to indicate the woman just coming into the Bistro from the wine tasting room.

"Well, it's my fault she's had to wait. I was late getting checks done. I shouldn't've gone up to the windmill to help the guys. They didn't really need me."

"'Course they needed you. They'd screw up where the fences gotta go otherwise."

"Stu was there."

"Yeah, and you don't think he's capable of screwin' that up?"

I shrug. "He knows where they have to go better than I do."

"Yeah, maybe, if his brain's turned on. Which ain't always the case." She makes a tsk sound and shakes her head slowly.

It's true Stu has often seemed lost in thought lately. I put it down to him having the odd senior's moment. "He's just got a lot on his mind. Anyway, that's what made me late getting the payroll done. But bussing tables is not your job," I scold. "You're the boss and you've probably been on the clock twelve hours by now. So quit, already. Did you see Russ brought your boys home?"

"They already been in here raidin' the cinnamon buns. Chased 'em out to git started on their regular chores."

"Okay, good. So. Baking's finished for the day. Barney's here to take care of any orders. He and Lucy are booked to close tonight." I call across to the burly thirty-something man at the grill and the petite young woman busy washing down the mixer. "Right, guys? Lucy? You close tonight?"

Barney grunts something that must be agreement and continues scraping the grill, mumbling in the monotone he insists is singing.

Lucy looks my way. "Yeah. I was hoping to take off early, though."

"I said I'd cover for her," Barney says.

Will he ever realize Lucy is never going to look at him the way he looks at her? Poor guy. I say, "Well, Lucy, if you can convince Marci to stay until close, you can go as soon as you bus."

"I got time now. I'll bus," Barney offers.

"Okay, then," I agree.

Red takes off her apron, tosses it in the laundry basket, and we leave together. Lucy must have convinced Marci to stay, because she's driving out when Red and I are barely across the parking lot.

Loud voices attract our attention to the men on the deck. They seem to be arguing about our breeding program. "What's going on with them?" I ask.

"Dunno," Red replies. "Sounds like they're arguin' again."

"They seem to argue a lot. I thought they were friends."

"They are. This ain't new, but they been buttin' heads more than usual lately."

"Two alpha males?"

"I wouldn't say Stu's alpha. Fact, he lets Russ push him around too much fer my liking."

The men look up and stop talking when they see us. We go up the stairs to join them and I drop their pay envelopes on the table.

"Sit here, darlin'," Stu says, and pats the chair next him. Red sits where indicated, and I take a chair across the table from her.

"Thanks, pretty girl," Russ says as he takes his pay envelope and slips it into his shirt pocket. "Lucy didn't waste no time leavin'. Hot date?"

I shrug and reply, "Maybe. Remember when you were still frisky enough to go out after a day's work?"

"I'm still plenty frisky, trust me, but there ain't no gals around here worth wastin' money on," he says, "at least 'til you quit turnin' me down."

"Won't happen, Russ," I tell him. I don't point out that I'm in a commit-ted relationship and wouldn't be interested even if I wasn't. I've never been drawn to older men and he's old enough to be my father.

"Well, if you git lonely, you can find me down in yer tack room."

"Why do you stay here, anyway? Had your electricity cut off?"

"Well, lookit this," Russ replies, and holds up his beer. "You wouldn't want me to drink and drive, would you? I got lucky last time I was pulled over. Can't afford to lose my license."

"You think yer gonna git stopped and breathalyzed drivin' from here to yer place? Ain't stopped you from gittin' a skin full at Billie's or up at the Le-gion even though you got a forty-five minute drive home from there," Red says.

"Yeah, well, the Legion ain't got cops hangin' around all the time like you got here."

"I'd say Dwight is at the Legion as often as he's here," Red says. "Come to that, ain't there any gals at the Legion?"

"Nope. All too married or too long in the tooth."

"You seen the length of yer teeth lately?" Red chides.

"I should of said, too ugly. I don't mind well-aged beef, but it's gotta be Grade A."

Stu says, "Aww, now, quit teasin' my buddy. He's got gals everywhere, he just don't brag about it." He gets up and goes inside, returning with two glass-es and a bottle of Wacasko-Wâti rhubarb wine. He fills both glasses before passing them to us and sitting down again.

I lift my glass and say, "Cheers," then take a good long sip. "Mmmm! Per-fect end to the work day." I sigh. "What're you guys up to? We heard you ar-guing about something."

"No, er, we weren't arguin'," Russ says. "Just talkin'."

"Pretty loud talking."

"You know you gotta yell or this asshole pretends he can't hear," Russ says, and takes a long swallow of beer.

"Russ and me're talkin' 'bout who might of stayed here a while back in the day," Stu says. "Fer Dwight's list."

"Oh, sure. Can I see?"

21

Stu hands me the notebook and I glance over the list. "Lots of names. But so many that're only first names or only surnames, and nicknames! You knew all these people, too, Russ?"

"Yeah. I was ridin' the rodeo with Gobbler and Porky. Er, yer dad and him I mean." He indicates Stu with a tilt of his head. "We all went to school together. Fer as long as we actually went to school."

"Did you know my grandfather, then?"

"I did."

"What was he like? I mean, Stu said he was a tall, good-looking man. But he's never said much about what he was like as a person."

"Oh, well, I'd say if you knew yer dad, then you knew Olaf, 'cause yer dad was a chip off the old block. Life of the party. 'Course we all liked to party back then. Emptied many a bottle around a campfire with him. Gals went after him hammer and tongs as much as they went after yer dad. I quit the rodeo long before Stu and yer dad did, though. Didn't see Olaf much after that. Suppose he mighta slowed down in his later years."

I knew what my father was like, but I always pictured my grandfather as a kindly old gentleman, working this ranch that was barely enough to survive on, working elsewhere as we've done in the past to keep it afloat. When my grandmother ran off with the Watkins man, he had no choice but to leave his baby son, my father, with Stu's parents. Now, he was just like my father? No wonder my grandmother left him. I wish I hadn't asked.

"He was good friends with my folks, though, and spent lots of time with Cam. He was a good father, in his way," Stu says. "Gittin' back to the list—damn all them nicknames! Jeee-sus! It was decades ago. How're we s'posed to remember? And fer this bein' a quiet spot out in the middle of nowhere, when you sit down and start to think 'bout it, the list is shore gittin' to be long."

"Maybe that's the point," I say. "Being quiet and away from everything, I mean."

"Whoever killed them gals shore liked it that way," Red says. She frowns and shudders as if the ghosts of the murder victims just materialized around her.

"I don't envy the detectives having to run down all these names. I'll take this to my office to make copies for everyone so we can all add names as we think of them." I tuck the little notebook in my pocket.

Russ drains his beer and gets himself another, a hang dog look on his face. He's well on the way to another night on the couch in the tack room, just as he said. Maybe both Red and I were a little rough on him. In hopes of making amends, I ask, "How's your week been, Russ?"

"Good enough," he responds. He squares his shoulders, lifts his hat and scratches the top of his head before resetting his hat. "I was tellin' Stu I got nothing goin' on I need my bull hauler fer right now, so we can ship yer market weight steers before that corral gits tore out."

"Fencin' won't be done fer a few days, so we got the corrals fer that long anyhow," Stu says. "Them guys'll be around fer a few more days yet. Bitched like hell 'bout havin' to work through the weekend. I told 'em it ain't up to me, some dickhead back in Regina calls the shots and they can bitch to him if they think it'll do any good."

"What's them dirt sifters doin', anyhow?" Russ asks. "Don't seem to be makin' much progress."

"Ay-yuh, it's a slow process alright," Stu says.

"So, fer shippin' them steers, tomorrow's a go?" Russ asks. "Unless there's a problem gittin' 'em sorted and into the chute corral by then?"

"Nope, no problem," Stu confirms. "Wisht K.C. was home. But me and the boys can do it, with a little help from Lindy, if she's willing."

Willing? That's an understatement. "I'd love to!"

"Settled, then." Russ takes a long drink of his beer. "After that, I'm on the road. I got bulls to deliver to Regina and then on down to Minot. Yer boys wanna come. Okay if I take 'em, Red? Won't cost you nuthin'. I'll cover their expenses."

"Sure, I guess. So long's they're back in time fer school. Starts the day after Labor Day."

"Yeah, I ain't goin' all that far. I'll have 'em back long before then. Felix can be my swamper after that."

"If you can work around his rodeo schedule," I say. "Also, don't forget, he's Stu's number one winemaker, and that comes first."

"I'll check with him. Is he around?"

"No," I reply, "he got an advance on his pay because he wanted to head out early. I figured he was off to a rodeo somewhere."

"Could be some new gal he's hot after," Red says. "'Bout time he settled down."

"A young feller's gotta sow his wild oats," Stu says. "Just like we done. Right, Russ?"

"Fer sure," Russ replies

"Like you done?" Red says. "You, Stu?"

"Well, I was Gobbler's wing man, remember."

"I remember. You didn't go at it as hard or keep at it as long as he did."

"You know how much energy it takes to chase that young stuff? I was run ragged. Still, I would of toughed it out. Thank gawd you swooped in and hogtied me."

"I *swooped in?*" Red asks.

"Whoever hogtied who, you're together and that's all that matters," I intercede before they erupt into one of the silly arguments I think they enjoy so they can have makeup sex later. "As for Lucy, hasn't she been dating one of the guys that was on the road crew this summer? I hope she doesn't leave. She's been sloughing off lately but she'd still be hard to replace."

"One more thing you don't need to worry 'bout, Lindy," Stu tells me. "Might never happen but if it does, it ain't the end of the world."

"No use tellin' her not to worry, Stu," Red says. "If it ain't that, it'll be somethin' else. Now that K.C.'s away, she's most likely worryin' 'bout what he's doin' on a Friday night."

"I'm not worried about K.C." My tone isn't convincing even to me. Is the ache I feel mistrust or am I just missing him? "Speaking of K.C., he'll be phoning about now. I gotta go." I finish my wine, fill the glass again and take it with me as I head along the path through the cottonwood grove to my house.

I'm just climbing the steps to my door with my dog right behind me when I realize he has stopped and is facing the yard, tentatively wagging his tail. I hear a vehicle on the road. It slows and turns in. I hope it's not a carload of folks looking for supper now that only Barney and Marci are on, because

I don't want to go back to the Bistro to help out. My heart leaps when I recognize K.C.'s truck. I put my glass down on the railing and trot out to meet him just as he pulls up to my garage, only now noticing there's someone in the passenger seat.

K.C. slides out from behind the wheel, pulls me to him and we kiss as if we haven't seen each other in weeks, which is actually the case.

"I missed you so much," he whispers.

"I missed you, too," I whisper back, breathing in the mixture of horse and aftershave that's the smell of him, and luxuriating in the roughness of his five o'clock shadow against my cheek. We kiss some more. If not for his passenger, I would herd him into the bedroom but instead we pull apart and I say, "You're home early. I wasn't expecting you for a couple of weeks. Not that I'm complaining. How did it, er, come about?"

He gives Henry's ears a scratch, then loops an arm around me and explains, "They got tired of my long face I guess. Anyhow, I took an extra day off, so it's a long weekend for me. I figured I'd surprise you. Hey, I want you to meet someone." He propels me around the front of the truck to the passenger door, and opens it. A pretty, dark-haired young woman with an uncertain smile slides out.

"Trina," K.C. says, "this is Lindy. Lindy, this is Trina."

"Hi, Trina," I say.

"Nice to meet you," Trina says.

K.C. explains, "I ran into Trina at a gas station this side of Medicine Hat. She was alone and hitchin', which you know is not a good idea for a woman, so I couldn't leave her there. I asked how far she was going and she said she didn't really have a destination, just somewhere that there's Indians. Why? Because she was looking for her birth parents, and her mother's name was Beulah Bear Robe. Definitely an Indian name. I told her I know someone with the same last name, and she could come with me to meet her. What are chances of that?"

"My best friend was a Bear Robe!" I exclaim.

"Yup. That's what I told her. Too late for her to go anywhere tonight. I figured we could put her up. I'm sure she's going to want a nice long chat with Red," K.C. says, "but right now, I'm tired and hungry. Grab your bag, Trina. Let's go inside. I've been fantasizing about a couple things for the past hundred miles, and one of them's Stu's barbeque chicken. Hope it's not all gone."

"Too early to be sure today's won't sell out, but there's some left over from yesterday." I tell him.

"Well, that's one fantasy taken care of," he says, then lowers his voice and murmurs, "the other will have to wait until later. But not too much later." He gives me such an intense look I experience a sudden hot surge of desire. I feel my face turning red but manage to collect my wits and lead the way into the house.

Once K.C. and Trina are settled on stools at the island in the kitchen, I set plates and cutlery out for all three of us. I get the chicken and a Tupperware of potato salad out of the fridge, along with a beer for K.C. and a glass of wine for Trina, then take a stool myself. K.C. goes for a thigh and Trina selects a wing.

"So, Trina," I begin once everyone has food in front of them, "you're searching for your birth parents?"

"Yeah. My parents have been hinting that it was time for me to move out. Imagine! They've got a big house. What are the two of them going to do with all that space? Anyway, I thought maybe it was time I looked up my birth parents. I've wondered about them ever since I was old enough to realize my parents are white and I'm not."

"Well, I get it," I assure her. "I ran away and went searching for my birth father myself."

"K.C. told me," she says.

"If you're like me, you've been wondering for years. I knew my father's name but not much more than that, but at least I always knew my birth mother. She is small, with dark hair and eyes. Italian. And as you can see, that's not me. I stuck out like a sore thumb at every family gathering."

"Did you find him? Your birth father?"

"I did."

"Oh, that's great!"

"Well, let's just say it was...*interesting.*" Just minutes ago I had a reminder of what my father was like. I didn't have much time with him, but enough to know they were right, about him chasing women, anyway. Not the memory of their father most people would like to have. I tell her, "I only knew him a few months before he was killed in a plane crash so I didn't have a chance to get to know him well. I still regret that."

"Oh," she says. "Too bad."

"It was a long time ago." I feel teary despite the passing of so many years, but more because my first love was with him and died, too. I don't mention that. Instead I say, "Anyhow, let's hope you're luckier than I was. So. You know Bear Robe is an Indian name. It's really a Blackfoot name and the Nekaneet reserve, which is the closest to here and is what we call 'our' Rez, is Cree. My friend Red's family is from Nekaneet but her mother married a Blackfoot and of course she goes by Pedersen since she got married. Stuff like that makes it next to impossible to locate women."

"But she's a Bear Robe? You mean I've actually found someone with that name?" She's lost interest in the chicken wing. "Do you have a phone number? Maybe I could phone her? Tonight? Or like, now?"

"I can do better than that. She lives in the trailer up by the gate. You drove by it to get to my house. Eat up, and we'll go over for a visit."

Her eyes widen and her breathing is shallow and fast. Adrenalin rush. I'm not surprised at her sudden loss of interest in food.

"You know what? They're probably still sitting out on the deck yakking. Let's go right now," I suggest. "You can finish that later."

"I'll join you in a few minutes," K.C. says, and reaches for a drumstick.

Stu, Russ and Red are indeed still on the deck, drinking beer or wine and snacking on dill pickles and garlic sausage. They turn to watch us as we come toward them. Trina and I climb the steps and I say, "Hey, guys, this is Trina. Trina, that lady with not a scrap of red hair or a single freckle or any other red head feature is my best friend, Red. The guys are Stu and Russ."

"If you git the names confused, just remember the handsome one is Russ," Russ says.

"Also the modest one," I say. Russ actually is handsome as middle-aged men go, but I'll never let on I think so. I smile and continue: "K.C. ran into Trina on his way home."

"Welcome, darlin'," Russ says, looking at her with interest. "There's nuthin' here but dirt and gophers. How'd you git talked into comin' here?"

"Well, she didn't come for the dirt or the gophers," I answer for her. "She's searching for her birth parents. I think maybe Red can help her out." I look at Red and say, "Red, I told her your maiden name is Bear Robe, same as her mother's. Her mother's name is Beulah Bear—"

Red stops me mid sentence and leaps to her feet, sending her chair skidding back to bump against the trailer wall. She utters an anguished sob as in near panic she practically climbs over the two men blocking her path to come out from behind the table, grab Trina's arms and stare up into her face.

"My baby! Oh my god! You're so beautiful!" Red sobs, and wraps her arms around the taller woman. She's unable to say more because she's crying now; once the shock wears off and I realize what I'm witnessing, I am too.

It's taken nearly fifteen years, but I finally know Red's real name. I think I'll keep calling her Red.

Chapter 5

It's going to take time for Trina and all of us to get to know each other, but short term, there are logistics. Red won't hear of Trina renting an apartment in town, and it does seem like the wrong idea at least in the short term, since she's going to be working here and doesn't have a car. Besides, she's family. An actual blood relative for Red after all these years. She's moved into Red's and they've been inseparable ever since. I think I'm a little jealous.

I donated a bed to the cause. It had been in what was my third bedroom but has since become my home office. It's not completely altruistic because the room is small, and I couldn't roll my chair away from the desk without crashing into the file cabinet. Now Stu is busy installing shelves on the wall behind me.

"Should've moved the bed outta here long before now. I'm really going to love having those shelves so I don't have to pile everything on a chair in the corner," I tell him. I've finished entering the invoices for this week's deliveries in accounts payable, made a note in my daytimer to make sure I send the checks so the vendors get them within the thirty days allowed for payment, and now I'm entering Trina's details in the payroll ledger. "I'm just about done here, so I'll be out of your hair in a few minutes."

"Don't rush on my account," Stu says, "I gotta stop now anyhow. Gotta make a run into Home Hardware again 'cause Murphy's Law, I'm short some shelf brackets. Goddammit!"

"It's okay. I've been without shelves all this time so another day won't matter, and you deserve a break anyhow."

"Okay," Stu says as he closes his toolbox. "Say, how's Trina workin' out?"

"Fine, I guess. Remember we were worried that with Lucy wanting her hours cut back, maybe she was getting ready to quit all together? Now if she does, it won't be an issue."

"Trina ain't got food service experience, though." He pats his chest pocket, then remembers he quit snoose a few years ago. "I worried she might not take to it and if she, er, ain't no good, Red won't say nuthin.'"

"She must be doing all right because Red's got her making pie fillings on her own already." I finish my tasks, put my pen down and close the ledger. "Say, Stu, a question?" I begin. "This is kind of sensitive, but I don't feel like I can ask Red."

"Shoot."

"Well, has she told you who Trina's father is? I mean, I thought you might know since you were around back then."

"Nope. She won't say. She might never tell."

"But you remember her from back in the day, don't you? I mean, she was around the rodeo about that time?"

"Well, she's younger'n me, remember. Trina's what, about yer age? I remember yer dad and mom from back then a course, and I knew about it when you were born. But Red? First I noticed her, she was workin' one of the concession stands. She said somethin' like 'hey Porky' when she served me. I thought, who's that cute little number and how come she knows me and I don't know her? Everyone knew yer dad so I figgered that was how she knew me. Cute, but just a kid, and I never knew her name. and later when she was old enough and our age difference didn't matter so much, she had a guy and I had a gal and we were never, um, *unattached* at the same time, you know, until that summer you showed up lookin' fer yer dad. I remember a couple of her boyfriends, but that was long after Trina was born. I never even knew she had a kid."

"She never told you? I mean, after you got together?"

"Nope. Could of knocked me over with a feather when she jumped up and grabbed Trina like that."

"Hmm. I wonder why she kept it secret all these years, especially from you. I thought you were soul mates."

"Well, we shore have had some heart-to-hearts these past couple days. She won't tell me who the guy was neither, but says she thought about that baby every day of her life since. You know they took her away when she was only a few hours old? She held her the whole time and didn't want to let go of her. Goddamn! Red was so young. Fourteen! Barely takin' care of herself.

No help from her folks. She'd of been better off if they lived on the Rez. Least then Rose could of helped her, but even so, she might of been took away. The govermint took Indian kids away from their parents all the time back then. Rose never knew about the baby. Her own sister, and she never even told her. It was too hard, she said. Talkin' 'bout it made it too real." Stu utters a long sigh, then rubs his face before fixing me with an intense gaze and warning, "Don't you let on I told you this."

"Our secret," I agree. I press my lips together and fight back tears thinking of Red, still a child herself, holding her baby for the few brief hours that were all she would ever have with her. How did she manage, alone and pregnant at fourteen? I sigh and mutter, "Jesus H. Christ, who has sex with a thirteen or fourteen year old girl? And then abandons her? Goddamn pedophile, that's who."

"Maybe that's why she won't tell no one."

"Oh, you mean she's protecting someone?"

Stu just shrugs.

"Ahhh! You think it's someone we know, then?"

"Maybe."

I wonder who, among the men I know that are closer to Red's age, could be Trina's father. Doesn't Red realize Trina has a right to know who he is? Still, unless it was a boy her age, it seems someone I know actually is that pedophile. Finally I sigh and say, "What a terrible burden for Red to carry all this time."

"Ay-yuh, she's had hard times, but lookit us now," Stu says. He rotates his bad shoulder to ease an ache, scratches his neck, and asks, "Anything else you need while I'm in town?"

"Not that I can think of. Stu? Don't lollygag too long. That guy who wants to look at the loft is due here at three."

"You need me here fer that?"

"I'd like your impression of him. Especially with K.C. not being here."

"Ain't you had yer ol' buddy Jim check him out?"

"I haven't heard back from him yet."

"Oh, okay, then," he agrees. "Don't worry. I'll be back in plenty a time."

Once he's out the door and I'm alone with my thoughts, I go over what I just learned about Red. It's a few minutes before the tension in my shoulders eases. I turn my thoughts to Jim. Should I call him again to see if he's found out anything yet? I decide against it because if he had, he would have called me.

Jim isn't my 'old buddy'. I've only known him a couple of years, but he's married to my other best friend, Kristy. They live in Calgary, about a four hour drive from Wacasko-Wâti. I met him when he came to investigate insider fraud at the Katawasis Lake Branch of Western Savings and Loan. I was the assistant manager there, and Kristy was my roommate. Despite Jim being ten plus years older, Kristy was smitten from the moment she laid eyes on him, and it didn't take more than a heartbeat for them to connect. Maybe K.C. is right about love at first sight.

After twenty years in the RCMP, Jim started working at what bank rank and file called the Fraud Squad and has kept up his old connections. Dwight has always been good about sharing RCMP stuff with us. He's careful about what he says and it's always strictly off the record. Since he's been in contact with Jim he's been even better. Lately he hasn't even told Jim anything, though. All he's said about the timeline of the murders is that unless they happened in the last couple years, establishing how long remains have been buried is difficult because bones of a person who died ten years ago aren't much different than those of someone dead only five years. A human body can decompose to a skeleton in just one year. So we still know nothing.

I presumed on my friendship with Jim to have him find out all he could about our potential tenant. Fingers crossed he shows up and signs on the dotted line, because the first month's rent would be enough to cover those checks I just set aside. It's not that we're having trouble meeting payroll, but the bills don't always jive with income. I'd rather postpone paying them if I could, to avoid running up our line of credit. My Mom is my major investor and she's been poking her nose in Wacasko-Wâti business way more than I'm happy about. She is very debt-averse, and I will be too, but until our cash flow improves, debt is something I have to live with.

We got a good price for the steers we shipped and the store is doing all right, but winter is coming. Last year, we had to lay Lucy and Marci off, because fewer people drive this far on snowy roads for a meal and the tour buses only run in the summer. We won't be so seasonal if, as we hope, our customer base expands now that we have a liquor license. Billie's Pub does well all year round, after all, and we're not much farther out of town. With K.C. unable to train, the barn we hoped to fill with new boarders is empty, and with sales from the winery, Bistro and farm store likely about to slump, the rental income would be very welcome.

I should quit rolling things around in my mind and go down to the Bistro. But there are only two customer vehicles in the yard right now so, they can manage without me. I'll have a coffee break first.

I take my mug to the kitchen and fill it with hours-old brew that smells like shoe polish. The Bistro is starting to sound like the better option. If I go I'll be stuck there, though, so I take a sip, decide it's drinkable, settle back at my desk, and pull out my copy of the list of people who have been on the property since the 1920's.

I've gone over the list so often I barely notice the names anymore. Today, though, I realize an obvious name is missing. My grandfather's. I pick up a pen and write *Olaf Larsen* at the top of the list right above Dad's name. Unless they tell us the bodies weren't buried until after Dad inherited the ranch, he's what the cops call a person of interest. If dead people can be persons of interest.

Come to think of it, what about my grandmother's name? Women can be murderers. If the killer was small and not very strong, it could explain the location of the burials—not too far to drag the body, and easy digging in the manure pile. It sickens me to think any of my ancestors was a murderer, so I won't dwell on it. It's so much more likely it was a transient hired hand or rodeo bum. Still. Everyone who ever lived or even just visited here should be on the list, my grandmother included. I write her name next to my grandfather's.

My father told me she ran off with the Watkins man, and that's what I want to believe. It must have been a spur of the moment thing. Maybe they only had a small window of opportunity like when my grandfather was out with the hay crew or something, but not gone for long such as to a rodeo, because she wouldn't leave her baby otherwise. But she left in such a hurry she forgot her jewelry box along with her baby. When Red moved in with Stu and gave the old trailer what she called a good shoveling out, Red found it. It's small, lacquered wood and lined in red felt, with a pair of silver earrings and a cameo brooch with a broken clasp inside. Wedged in the lid is a tiny, over-exposed black and white photo of a couple with *Olaf and Myrtle* written across the bottom.

I pick the box off the window ledge above my desk, open the lid and carefully pull out the photo to examine it for the thousandth time. Her hair is light, possibly blonde; she's short and slim, wearing a shapeless dress that lacks trim of any sort and ends mid calf. It must be a warm day because her dress is sleeveless and my grandfather's shirt is unbuttoned. She's tucked into his armpit, smiling up at him. They look to be so much in love, gut-wrenchingly young and innocent, standing at the cab of a stake truck with a company logo partially visible behind them. As happens every time I look at the photo, I'm flooded with a profound sense of loss.

After a moment of feeling sorry for myself, I put the photo back and pick up the earrings. I like them, not just because they were my grandmother's, but also because they remind me of the silver conchos on my saddle, except with a small stone in the middle. Red says the stones are hematite and calls them Grandfather Rocks. They're supposed to make a warrior strong and brave. I'm not a warrior, but who couldn't use help being stronger and braver? I replace my gold hoops with the silver drop earrings and experience a sudden intense connection with the woman I have daydreamed about so often. Why did I wait so long to wear them?

It isn't until later I remember something Stu said that just slid right by me at the time: he knew about it when I was born. If he knew, it's a given Dad knew, yet he claimed I was already in high school before he found out about me. Like what Russ said about my grandfather, it's one of those things I wish I didn't know.

Chapter 6

"So, Jim got back to you?" Stu asks.

"Yeah. Said he couldn't find out much. He's not supposed to be running names for friends, you know."

"Ay-yuh, I s'pose not."

"But anyhow, public records for the numbered holding company list some real estate holdings and an import company. Nothing pops for the guy I've been talking to, except a driver's license with a couple speeding tickets. That's it. Jim seemed more interested in asking me if I've been in touch with Kristy. I think she's been giving him some concerns. Says she's working a lot of nights. A lot of special functions at the Ranchmen's."

Stu makes a *tsk* sound and shakes his head. "Workin' nights, eh? That can be tough on a marriage."

"Yeah. I like them both. I hope whatever troubles they're having, it's nothing too serious."

Stu and I have been waiting under the canopy on my patio for ten minutes or so, when a red Silverado turns into the yard and drives past the cars parked at the store, heading our way. We both stand up and watch the vehicle approach. The truck noses up to the lawn edging and the driver cuts the engine.

"That ain't no work truck," Stu observes.

Climbing out from behind the wheel is a man the term *brown-eyed handsome man* could have been invented for. He appears fit and trim, as tall as I am but only just, dressed in jeans and a western shirt. He's wearing a white felt hat of the kind everyone who goes to the Calgary Stampede buys, and boots so shiny I doubt they've ever been in a stirrup. I now know what I looked like when I showed up at the Stampede looking for my father.

He removes his hat to finger-comb a thick mop of dark hair, then re-settles the hat and looks our way. "Hello," he says. He comes up to Stu and reaches a hand out. "You the boss of this outfit?"

"Nope," Stu says as he shakes the outstretched hand. "I'm Stu. This here's Lindy. She's the boss."

His eyebrows rise in surprise, but after a second, he reaches out to shake my hand. His hand is smooth and warm. He says, "I guess I should've known since it was a gal I spoke to on the phone. I'm Daryl."

"Stu's just being modest. He's the real boss here, or at least he's what keeps this place running. Pleased to meet you, Daryl," I say.

"Likewise. But call me Butch. All my friends do."

I'm puzzled at how you get Butch from Daryl, but I shrug and agree, "Okay. Butch it is."

"I know that look," he says with a grin. "With my last name Cassidy, my buddies started calling me Butch when that movie came out, and it stuck." He chuckles. "I'm still looking for the Sundance Kid. This looks like it might be a good place to find him."

"Could be, at that," Stu agrees.

It's amusing. I don't have to force myself to chuckle along.

Butch takes a deep breath, looks around the yard, and says, "Quite an op-eration you got here. Winery. Farm Store. Café. Big expansion?" He indicates the torn up corral area with a wave.

"Eventually," I agree. "We were in process of building an indoor riding arena when we ran into a problem."

"Permits?" he guesses.

"Nope. Unmarked graves."

"Huh!" He blows out a long breath. "I think I heard something about that. So, this is the place."

"Yeah." I wonder if it tanks the deal. No one could be blamed for not wanting to rent something practically on top of a body dump. The 'whistle as you pass the graveyard at night' uneasiness exists in the boldest of us, and for unmarked graves of murder victims, it's worse. I still shiver when I think about it. But it doesn't seem to bother Butch. With a lift of his chin, he indi-cates the only building in view taller than one storey and asks, "I guess when you say loft, it's the upstairs in that building there?"

"Yeah," I confirm. "It's a little rough since it's a hayloft, but the hay has to be kept dry, so it doesn't leak. Let's go take a look."

Together we cross the yard, enter the barn and climb the staircase just inside the door. Once in the loft, Butch looks around, walks back and forth, and lets out a low whistle. "I expected it to be big, but not quite this big."

"If it's too much space, we could partition it," I suggest.

"No, it's okay. I'd like to take it all." He turns to me. "We might not need it, but we wouldn't want some other outfit in there if we do. But the big sticking point is that we can't be humping our stuff up those stairs. I wasn't expecting the stairs to be so steep and narrow. Or for there to be so many of them. No elevator?"

"Well, we do have a couple of elevators. Not like what you're picturing, though. More like what you'd call conveyors, chain driven. One end at the truck, the other in the big doors there." I point to the ten-foot wide sliding doors at either end of the loft. "You move them where they're needed. Once the bales are at the top, other conveyors move them further in. That might work for you."

"Yeah, sounds like it would. But there's another problem. It's not secure. Anyone wandering into the barn can go up there."

"What if we enclose the stairs and put a door on it?"

"That should do it," he says.

"Okay," I say, "let's go have a coffee and see what we can work out."

We head back down and cross the yard to the Bistro. I had arranged for Red to join us; she looks up from checking the pies in the oven and gives us a nod.

"Man, it smells good in here," Butch observes.

"We've got something in the oven pretty well all day," I explain.

We fill mugs at the self-serve coffee bar, then settle at the table that's reserved for staff. Once Red joins us and is introduced, I say, "So, Butch. We were thinking someone renting the loft would want it for dances or seminars, maybe even church services, but when we spoke by phone, you didn't say what you wanted it for. What do you have in mind?"

"Warehousing, really. And not occasionally, but full time. There will be busy times when stock comes in, gets sorted and then sent out to retailers, but a lot of the time no one would even be here."

"Warehousing? What, exactly?" I press.

"Various things." He takes a sip of coffee and looks around. His gaze settles on Trina, who's at the coffee bar straightening things and wiping the counter. They exchange a smile.

I draw his attention back to the business at hand by asking, "What various things?"

"Well, horse tack things. Giftware too. Coffee mugs with horses on them. Goofy little signs that say stuff like 'don't squat with yer spurs on' and 'cowboys always welcome'. The kind of stuff you find in a tack shop." He makes eye contact with me. "Sorry if I seem evasive, but I only started this job a few weeks ago. I'm not even sure what you'd call my position. Warehouseman I guess, but I'm more involved in the business end of it really. I know what a saddle is but all the other stuff? Unless it's labeled, I'm sunk!" He chuckles and exhales loudly. "I only got this job because my uncle owns the company. Believe it or not, I never drove off the Trans Canada before today."

"Well, Butch, I don't know if this is the best location for you."

Red gives me a look that says she's wondering why I'm trying to talk him out of a deal when the cash flow from a full-time tenant would be such a boon. Then she shrugs and adds weight to my opinion by telling him, "Lindy's got a degree in Business Admin."

"Oh, yeah?" Butch says. "Me too! I just graduated."

"Congratulations," I say. "No offence, but in that case, I would've thought you'd, um—"

"Know better?" He finishes my question for me. "Yeah, I would. My uncle, though. He calls the shots. In the end, it came down to cost, and location. Shouldn't tell you this, but it would be twice as much to rent space half this size in the city. To you this place might seem like it's out in the boonies, and now that I'm here, I'd have to agree. But it's central to the tack shops we service. Regina. Calgary. Swift Current. Medicine Hat. Weyburn. Lethbridge. So this place is about exactly in the middle. I haven't even called on all our customers yet. My uncle says I have to get on that, just as soon as we wrap up warehouse space so we have product to sell. I don't buy any of the stuff. We have buyers for that. And we have jobbers that go around showing samples and taking orders, so I'm not sure why he thinks I have to go meet everyone." He shrugs. "But he's the boss."

It's starting to make sense, so I agree, "Okay, then. Are you thinking of a month-to-month lease?"

"No. I'd like—make that *we'd* like—to lock something in."

"Well, how does a six month lease sound? That should give both of us a chance to make sure it's going to work."

"I'd rather make it three years with an option to renew," he says.

"No, not three years, but we can do six months, with an option to renew after that," I say. "And if it's working out all right for both of us, we can renegotiate then. Who knows? You might realize this is too far from anything and want to relocate by then. So a shorter lease is in your best interests." I don't mention that we might want to get rid of them if they prove to be too high maintenance.

He appears to be giving it some thought; then in a no-nonsense tone, says, "Make it a year with an option to renew annually, and we've got a deal. First and last month's rent payable on signing."

"Triple net?"

"Triple net," he agrees. His forehead creases and a muscle in his jaw clenches, but after a moment, he adds, "So long as the costs are documented."

"We'll document all the costs."

"Fair enough," he says. "I'll get our lawyers to do up a lease and have it couriered to you."

I was sucked in by a similar scam just a few years ago so I'm not about to fall for that again. Instead, I say, "I've got a boilerplate lease from our lawyer."

"How long will that take?"

"Fifteen minutes."

"Okay," he says. "While you're doing that, I'll take another look at the space. Get an idea of how to arrange everything. A crew will be here to put in shelving within a week." He looks at his watch and adds, "See you back here in fifteen."

As we watch him walk away, I notice Trina at the coffee bar, still wiping it down. He gives her a nod and a smile, then leans in and says something too quietly for us to hear as he goes by.

Once he's out the door I ask, "What do you think, guys?".

"I think someone would of rubbed the finish right off that coffee bar if Slick hadn't of left when he did," Red replies. Her tone sends Trina hurrying back into the kitchen. Then she clicks her tongue and says, "You say you got that lease from Jesse?"

"That's right."

"So no worries 'bout any extra words bein' snuck in like the last deal?"

"None."

"Well, if it saves you goin' back to work in town or one of us drivin' school bus again, we can put up with it. Seems like it's a done deal anyhow." She stands, gathers our mugs and takes them to the kitchen, signaling that our coffee break is over.

"There's something about him she doesn't like," I say to Stu as we get up and walk out. "What're your thoughts?"

"So far what I think is the ol' sayin', he's all hat and no cattle," Stu replies. "As fer my wife, she might of seen somethin' in his aura or whatever she does, or maybe she just didn't like the looks him and Trina were exchangin', but me, I just wonder how in hell someone who don't know nuthin' 'bout tack can run a tack business."

"Strange, maybe, but like he said, if everything's labelled he'll do okay and as long as he pays the rent, do we care?"

"Nope. Guess not. But I'll tell you what, he won't be doin' no heavy liftin', not with them pansy soft hands. "But I guess we better git used to seein' his skinny ass 'round here. See ya."

Later, as I stand watching the Silverado with its shiny chrome trim head out to the road, I wonder if I should have thought less about the check in my hand and more about why anyone would want a warehouse forty-five minutes from the nearest town. But then, you could wonder who would build a Bistro here for the same reason, but since the farm is the best place for a farm store and that's how it started, it makes some sense. I mentally calculate whether anything will be left after paying for the new computer I told everyone I needed and that we could afford, and only now look at the address on the check. Pillerton. I've been there once. Practically a ghost town. Why Pillerton?

The ringing of my phone interrupts my thoughts. K.C. usually calls me about this time. I push my misgivings away and hurry in to answer it.

I'm snuggled in bed, luxuriating in the skin-on-skin contact comfort as well as the heat radiating from K.C. as he snores softly and rhythmically. I think about poking him to get him to stop, but for now, it's peaceful and as soothing as Kitty purring on my pillow. Both fill me with contentment. He stirs, and I think he's waking up. I guess he does wake up at least a little bit and for a second or two, because he gives me a squeeze to draw me closer, kisses my head, then begins snoring again.

This trip home was unplanned and a surprise. He called me from Calgary but didn't get home until late. I wanted to talk to him about our new tenant and his plans but there were other things on his mind. I admit I had the same idea he did. We went to bed instead.

It's all about priorities.

Chapter 7

Part of the reason K.C. didn't want to talk when he got home last night was that Douglas Lake laid him off. It was a blow to his ego even though they said they'd call him back again when they had more colts to start. He told them they'd have to work around his own projects because by then, Wacasko-Wâti's indoor arena would be up and running.

If I was surprised that K.C. was back for good after just a few weeks since his last trip home, he was surprised that we already had a new, full-time tenant. We did our best to prepare him for meeting Butch. That is, Red, Stu and I each gave him our take on the guy.

Red reserves judgment for some reason she can't articulate other than to say he's a city slicker, emphasis on *slick*. This is unusual because she always thinks the best of everyone.

Stu told him Butch seems okay, but time will tell. He thinks Red's holdback is because of how quickly he swooped in on Trina, so it wouldn't matter if he was slick or not.

I give K.C. a rundown on how the monthly rental and sharing building and lot maintenance, insurance and taxes will boost our bottom line, important over the winter months especially since we won't have the indoor ring as a draw. I have to tread carefully so it doesn't sound like I'm blaming him. He already feels uncomfortable being pure overhead, short-term problem though that is.

In any case, it doesn't matter. He and Butch hit it off from day one. K.C. is a cowboy, trainer and businessman, and knows pretty well everything there is to know about tack. They strike a deal for K.C. to be a warehouseman, only part time so he's free to work on the myriad details now that the indoor arena build is back on a front burner. It's what a personal empowerment coach would call a win-win: Butch can learn from K.C. and K.C. no longer thinks he's dead weight.

At this time of year people dump perfectly good horses just because they don't want to feed them over winter, so Stu is busy going to auctions. He only bids against the meat buyers, never against ordinary folks, but even at that, the rescue herd is growing fast. I have to bite my tongue or I'd ask Stu to give the auctions a pass, but we have extra hay this year thanks to an unexpectedly decent second cut, and the glut of horses unwanted through no fault of their own will soon pass. Charlie and Johnny have been working with them to see how (and if) they're broke so they can be sold to forever homes. K.C. pitches in, and is great at coaching the boys.

The new corrals will soon be ready, and as long as the weather holds, K.C. can train again. If the corrals remain too muddy for his work, at least we can ship cattle whenever they're market ready and the price is favorable. The foundation for the indoor is in and there's activity around the building site sporadically. Although we haven't heard anything more about the burials so that's still in the back of our minds, life at Wacasko-Wâti has pretty much returned to the way it was before the bones were discovered.

Butch's crew has finished installing their shelving and shipments have been coming in daily. This morning another cube van arrived. It's at the back of the barn now. I go to check it out and see K.C. is with Butch in the loft. Someone is inside the van loading crates onto the elevator. K.C. and Butch grab them when they reach the top, and transfer them onto the second, horizontal, elevator. They seconded a couple of our field workers to offload them at the far end.

Previous shipments only required Butch at the bottom and K.C. at the top. These are wooden crates rather than cardboard boxes and must be heavier than usual, which seems to me to be pretty labor intensive and a poor way to ship anything. But what do I know? I'm an ex-banker/current bookkeeper and/or kitchen worker with no experience shipping anything.

I go to the kitchen for another cup of hours-old coffee and get back to work on payables. When I next look up, I see K.C. and Butch walking toward the Bistro. K.C. looks up, spots me in the window, and waves. I wave back before going to the bathroom, then I head down to the Bistro to join them.

K.C. has his hungry man size bowl of soup de jour, Cream of Mushroom, and a thick slice of fresh salt rising bread slathered with butter. Butch has coffee.

"Not eating lunch today, Butch?" I ask as I come up to the table.

"Yeah, but not soup. It's Caesar salad and a couple rat turds for me today. Trina's warming them up for me." He grins and with a look I can only describe as a smirk, adds, "Pays to have an in with the waitress."

She would warm them for anyone, of course, but I let the comment pass and ignore the smirk. I don't know that it means anything. I've seen it often enough now that I think it might just be his way, like a facial twitch he can't control. I go into the kitchen to see if Butch's salad is ready and to ask for one of my own.

Red is measuring ingredients into the hundred-quart pot we invested in the last time her pie filling boiled over. When it's on the stove it's so tall she has to stand on a stool to stir. She's so focused on her task I doubt she even noticed I came in.

Trina is about to take Butch's salad out when I step in front of her and say, "It's okay, Trina, I'll take that, and I'll get his rat turds while you fix my salad. Mine's got Cajun Blackened chicken, don't forget." That's me, helpful to a fault. "Blacken some chicken, please, Barney!"

"You got it," Barney agrees, and dumps the pre-measured, pre-seasoned chicken pieces on the grill.

I get the warm meat-stuffed pastries out of the microwave, pick up the salad, and smile at Trina as I pass her on my way out. From the look she gives me and her tone when she thanks me, I don't think she appreciates my help. I set Butch's food in front of him and take my seat. "So, Butch," I begin, "big order in today?"

"Not really."

"Really heavy stuff, from the looks of it. It takes two of you to lift the crates?"

"Yeah. Good thing I've got staff, eh?" His smirk when he looks at K.C., as if he's somehow superior because he's technically the boss, rankles. I remind myself it could be an involuntary twitch.

"Good thing K.C. let you borrow a couple of our guys, you mean," I point out, and hope that puts him in his place. He gives a sniff and shrugs. I continue: "I'm curious to see what you've got. Maybe I could come take a look when you unpack."

"Oh, um, sure. You in the market for something? Anything you want, my cost plus ten percent. Super good deal."

"Yeah, super," I agree, "but I don't really need anything right now. Just curious."

"You could use a saddle," K.C. points out. "Especially if you're serious about barrel racing."

"Well, I haven't quite decided about that."

"Yeah, well, you'll need something much smaller and lighter for barrels if you go that route. I'm not sure Chica's cut out to be a barrel racer though, the way she likes to dink along. If you're going to go to the expense of hauling to a rodeo you don't want to be an also-ran just to fill up the class. If you mean it, we should keep an eye out for a Thoroughbred, off-the-track maybe. Stu might spot something in his travels. But then the saddle you have might not fit. Is there an expiry date on that offer, Butch?"

"Naw, never," Butch promises. He looks toward the kitchen and smiles. Trina is coming our way with my salad.

I thank Trina as she puts my salad in front of me and lays the napkin-wrapped cutlery next to it. Butch reaches an arm around behind her. She gasps and gives a start. From her reaction, I think he goosed her. I look up to see Red watching from behind the pastry case but since Trina and Butch are facing her, she couldn't see what he did any better than I could. Trina hurries back to the kitchen, brushing past Red without giving her a look.

"Anyway," I continue, "I'd sure like to see your stock. I've got a little time today, maybe I can help out, too. You know, with organizing. Just helping a neighbor move in."

"Thanks, Lindy, but we're okay."

"But could I at least see your stock?"

"Well, all you're going to see is the stuff that came in earlier," K.C. tells me. "If you're curious about the big crates that came in today, we're not unpacking those."

"Oh? Why not?"

"Well, um, they're from India, cheap stuff," Butch explains. "We're not selling them except by the crate, so there's no point."

"Oh." I guess that makes sense. "So dealers have to order a crate full of saddles, all the same size? Or is there a mix?"

"I, um, well, I don't remember off the top of my head. Long as the buyer knows what he ordered, no need for anyone else to know."

We make eye contact. I don't need to be told I'm the 'anyone else' he's thinking of. Then he smiles and offers, "You can come see the bridles and so on, anytime, but you should wait until the nice stuff comes. Champion. Circle Y. The good stuff with decent silver that's made in the U.S. and Canada. We're selling those in small quantities, so we have to unpack them. K.C. can let you know when we've done that."

"Okay, thanks." I stab a piece of chicken with my fork and pop it in my mouth, enjoying the rush of spices on my tongue. I can't argue with Butch's logic, but I wonder if he wouldn't sell more of those made-in-India saddles if they let shops, at least the smaller ones, order fewer at a time. I almost voice the thought, then I realize I don't need to stick my beak into someone else's business. I say nothing and spear a chunk of romaine with plenty of dressing on it to cool the heat from the chicken, chew and swallow. "Well, I'm ready to take the bank deposit in. Either of you need me to pick up anything while I'm in town?"

Butch and K.C. both mutter their no-thank-yous, shake their heads, and start in on the need for a fork lift, how much more shelving to put up, what part of the loft to cordon off for the office. No one asks for my opinion. I tell myself it's their business and it's not in my purview anyway.

But I can't help feeling I've just been warned to stay away.

Chapter 8

Monday morning three things happen at once: Dwight's cruiser drives in and parks at the Bistro; a red sports car drives in and parks at my patio; and Butch comes up beside me at the coffee bar holding his mug in his left hand because his right hand is swathed in gauze. As I'm setting a Bunn Thermal Server of fresh Columbia Dark in its base, I indicate his hand with a lift of my chin and ask, "What happened?"

"Accident," he replies.

I fill his mug for him, and press him for details. "What kind of accident?"

"I, well, the damn elevator."

"Why were you using it, anyway? I didn't even know you were here this weekend and I didn't see a delivery truck."

"You didn't see me? I've been parking at the back of the barn so the front lot stays open for your customers. It's okay, isn't it? I mean, that I come in the back like your hired hands do?"

"Um, sure. Of course. That's thoughtful of you."

"And there wasn't a new delivery. I was just, I only wanted to rearrange stuff. Moved some stuff around." He exhales sharply. It's nearly a snort. "Okay?"

I draw a sharp breath and wonder if he ever speaks to K.C. in that tone. He's got a point, though. "Of course," I say, and focus on my task.

He's not mechanically inclined and it's always K.C. who gets the elevators going. Still, there's never been a problem before. I suppose it's possible for someone to get their hand caught, maybe get a finger between the chain and the drive gear, but I don't think it would be easy. I'll ask K.C. if there's a modification to make the things idiot proof.

Should I notify the Worker's Compensation Board? Are we protected if he's a tenant and not our employee? That doesn't seem likely, so if WCB doesn't cover him, can he sue us? I'll call Jesse Bird and see what he thinks. I have to talk to him about the renewal of our contract with Palm Dairies anyway. But for now, my attention is elsewhere. I murmur, "Sorry about your hand," and head out the door.

I meet Dwight just as he's coming in. "Hey, Dwight! Coming for coffee?"

"You know it."

"Any news?"

"Yeah. Can you guys join me?"

"Um, maybe. I think so. Just give me a minute. I need to go see who just drove up to my place. Meanwhile, go ahead and get your coffee and cinnamon bun."

"Will do." He goes past me into the Bistro.

As I head across the yard toward my house, it occurs to me Henry didn't bark, and as I approach I understand why not. A familiar figure is on the steps leading to my door and Henry is squirming joyfully as she scratches his ears.

"Hey, Kristy!" I call out. "Nice ride!"

"Better than that old oil-burning Honda, eh?" she replies. "Didn't expect to see me again so soon, did you?"

We share a quick hug as I reply, "No, I sure didn't. What's up? Everything okay?"

"Um, well, no, not really." She heaves a sigh. "I left Jim. And just like when I left my last husband, here I am on your doorstep."

"Oh, no, Kristy! I'm sorry." Worry lines her face. She's not as happy about leaving this husband as she was about leaving the last one. "We can get your things out of the car later. I'm about due for a coffee break anyhow."

We go inside and she climbs on a stool at the island while I get the coffee maker fired up. As I scoop fresh grounds into the filter, I ask, "Did something happen to make you decide today was the day?"

"No, not really. Although we had his boys for the entire weekend. I should say I did. Jim goes to play in a squash tournament and leaves me to clean up after the little assholes. Every time I tell them to put their shit away, they tell me I'm not their mother and she's been telling them they don't have to listen to me."

"Really? What a bag!"

"You know they were already separated before me and Jim got together. It's not like I stole him away."

"I know."

"Anyhow. Now we're nothing but a convenience for his ex so she can have a dirty weekend with her boyfriend. But it's not really just that. Maybe it's just that I'm not good at relationships."

"Oh, Kristy," I tell her, "it can't be over! There's bound to be bumps in the road. Maybe all you need is a break, you know, to get some perspective."

She shakes her head. I realize with my track record I'm a fine one to be giving relationship advice. And right now I need to go and see what Dwight wants to meet about. "You know what, Kristy? We need to have a good heart-to-heart, but can it wait until later?"

"Yeah, sure. You're busy. I understand."

I'm not sure she does, but Dwight's on the clock so I can't keep him too long. I give Kristy's shoulder a rub and say, "Thanks. I have to meet Dwight. He showed up just ahead of you. I'm hoping he has news, like maybe those bodies I told you about have been identified. You can come and sit in on our meeting, or bring your things in and get settled, whatever you'd rather."

"I'm not really in a mood to be with other people. I'll just stay here," she says.

I stand for a moment studying her downturned mouth and slumped shoulders. Not a single Kristy giggle so far, and the most outgoing, gregarious person I've ever known doesn't want to be with other people? She's genuinely hurting. But I really do have to go. "I shouldn't be too long. Help yourself to coffee when it's ready and if you're hungry, go ahead and eat whatever's in the fridge."

"I'll be fine," she assures me.

I hurry back to the Bistro and find Dwight, Stu, Red and K.C. at the staff table. They all have mugs and the men have cinnamon buns or pie in front of them. K.C. has the CO_2 dispenser and is in the process of burying his pie in whipped cream. I get a mug of coffee and take the vacant chair.

"So. Sorry to keep you guys. Kristy just showed up so I wanted to get her settled."

"Didn't know she was comin'," Red says.

"Me neither. Anyway. What did I miss?'

"Nuthin," Stu replies. "We waited on you."

"Okay! Thanks. So, Dwight, you have news?"

"Well, yes and no. Did I tell you they found jewelry with the female skeletons?"

"Yeah, you told us that at the very start of this mess," I say. My tone is a little sharp. I should be excused given the price we've paid, but it's not Dwight's fault. I smile to let him know I don't blame him, and ask, "So, there's more info about the jewelry?"

"Yeah. One thing, anyway. A necklace with a pendant on it, about the size of a quarter. They've got it cleaned up and are having it professionally photographed. They'll put photos out in hopes someone recognizes it. They're pretty confident it'll be helpful because it's quite unique."

"Oh? Unique? In what way?"

"I don't know, Lindy," he replies, "I haven't seen it myself and that's all I was told."

I click my tongue with a *tsk*, then say, "Well, it's not much."

"Oh, but there's more," Dwight continues. "The one female was short, maybe five foot two, and died between the age of twenty and forty. She'd had at least one baby, so they're hoping to locate kids. If she was in her twenties when she died, they'd likely be quite young when their mother went missing. If older, well, they might have photos and so on. It would ID her and also really help nail down the timeline for her death. The other female was taller, about five foot nine, thought to be in her teens."

How is anyone evil enough to do this? Kill multiple people? I'm glad I didn't get myself something to eat because my stomach clenches in a hard knot. How terrified were those people before they met their violent end? Did they know what was happening to them? Going by the look on Red's face, she's experiencing the same thing. I manage to mumble, "Do they know, um, the cause of death?"

"Not yet," he replies, and drains his coffee. "Oh, and the male? He was also twenty to forty years old, white and about five foot ten tall. Maybe a farmer. Missing a finger. So that's something to go on."

"Yeah, that narrows it down to about a thousand," Red says. "I know half a dozen guys with missin' fingers."

"Ropers with missin' thumbs, mostly, right darlin'?" Stu says.

"Not all. Remember Jake Jordan?" Red says.

I draw a quick breath. Jake Jordan was Dan Baxter's partner in the cattle rustling operation, and one of my kidnappers. It's not an exaggeration to say I barely escaped with my life, only possible thanks to the Swiss Army knife that's always in my pocket. Mr. Baxter has a nice scar on his flank to remind him he's fortunate my knife wasn't bigger.

"Well, thanks for the update, Dwight," I say. "If that's all, I'd like to book off for the day now and go see what's up with Kristy."

"You go on ahead," Red says. "Bring her over fer a visit later, if she's up fer it."

"Will do," I agree.

"I gotta take off, too," Dwight says. "Big meeting at F Division Headquarters. They think we need a task force to look into a bunch of new guns showing up on the streets. These guys come across a banned assault rifle some asshole smuggled over the border and figure it's a good time to waste manpower chasing ghosts."

Stu lets out a low whistle. "You mean like someone's runnin' guns into Saskatchewan? Montreal or Vancouver I'd believe, but here?"

"Yeah," Dwight confirms. "I shouldn't make it sound like a small thing. It's more than one rifle. Uzis and hand guns too. Israeli, believe it or not."

"What the hell," K.C. exclaims, "you don't come across those every day. Sounds organized."

"Yeah, so the crooks'll have more fire power than the cops. As for why here instead of a seaport, you know there's been a pipeline from Chicago to Regina for decades. Al Capone ran liquor from Canada during Prohibition. Bought legal booze here and sent it to Chicago on the Soo Line, which is still in operation today. I mean, not the booze, the railroad. Capone made millions. Some of his Canadian cohorts did too. Authorities here didn't care, booze being legal and all, so Capone's guys could work at the rail yards in Pillerton without worrying about being pinched. You heard of the Al Capone Tunnels in Pillerton, right?"

"No. There really is such a thing?"

"You better believe it. Had gambling and prostitution down there, and stored the booze there while it was waiting for the train south. They're making them into a tourist thing."

"Well, I'll be go to hell," Red says. "Lindy, we bin to Pillerton. I think I seen a sign for them tunnels. Right next to the pub, remember?"

"That's why the pub's called Big Al's," I say.

Stu says, "Any time there's tourists to be fleeced, there's someone happy to oblige. Maybe it'll be a stop for the tour buses that come in here on their way to Fort Walsh."

"Well, if the tour buses leave from Regina, Pillerton is a little out of the way. It would be more than a day trip. And you make it sound like we fleece the tourists, too, Stu," I say.

"That ain't what I meant," he assures me. "You seen how many oriental tourists come in here? Canada is a big deal over in Japan. Ask the drivers. They have tours that last fer days. Nice comfy buses, too, reclining seats like on a airplane, tinted windows and all. Nice biffy on board. Nuthin' like them shitty Greyhounds."

"What's that got to do with guns?" Red asks.

"Nuthin'," Stu admits.

"Well, if the tunnels are a tourist trap the gun runners can't use them," I point out. "So where do you start, Dwight?"

"No idea. I'll find out at the meeting."

"The upside? You might get some overtime out of it."

"That I don't need," Dwight replies. He finishes his coffee and gets to his feet. "I'd rather curl a couple more times a week. See you at the rink on Wednesday, Stu?"

"Uhh, no. I ain't gonna curl this year," Stu replies. "S'posin' I could git down in the hack, I'd never git back up again."

"Damn, that's too bad, buddy. Maybe I'll give it up too. Won't be the same without you."

"Maybe I still show up so I can tell you what you done wrong."

"Deal! Good-bye, all," Dwight says, and heads out the door.

We all say our good-byes and leave. I head up to my house. I didn't say anything when Red reminded me about Pillerton, but the mention of that place sets my teeth on edge. On our one and only trip there, we spotted Jake's truck parked on the main drag when he was supposed to be thousands of miles away. Two reminders of him in the space of half an hour.

Besides Jake's truck being where it shouldn't be, being the headquarters of the cult that stole our cattle thanks to a shady loan deal I got sucked into, is a worse memory. They got our farm store business tied up in red tape. Wacasko-Wâti barely survived, and we're still recovering. Even worse than the fraud and although it was never proven, I'll never be persuaded they weren't behind the kidnapping of Red's nephew Felix and me.

Red doesn't blame me for losing our herd or the other financial problems, but she hasn't been shy about voicing her opinion about the kidnapping. In her view it was my fault for being what she calls a stickybeak, always sticking my beak in other people's business and barging ahead with no regard for consequences. K.C. agrees with her on the barging ahead thing, because it got me into a tight spot in Katawasis Lake, too. I've assured them both that I've learned my lesson.

Pillerton is baggage. It's in the past. But maybe a trip there wouldn't be such a bad idea. Maybe it would exorcise some demons. Besides. It's in the middle of ranching and farming country just like we are here. I'll bet they have a tack shop.

Chapter 9

I find Red in the Bistro kitchen, as usual. No sign of Trina, also as usual. I pitch in to help by grabbing one side of the fifty-pound flour sack while Red takes the other. Together we hoist it and hold it in place while it pours into the bin.

"You couldn't wait for Barney to do this?" I ask.

"Can't wait all day," she replies. That's Red. She wants what she wants when she wants it. "If yer here to work on pies this morning, you should have a hairnet on."

"You wouldn't have to wait all day, silly. You know he's due in any minute. And well, um, about the hair net—I wasn't planning on staying. I'd like to take today off."

"I think we can git by without you. Why?"

"Well, I need some one-on-one time with Kristy. She's really suffering with this split from Jim. Something must have happened, but she hasn't told me about it yet. K.C., you know I love him, and Kristy likes him too, but with him and so many other people around, we don't have much privacy, and she was just too worn out to get into much last night. You know, emotionally drained. I thought if the two of us took horses out for a couple hours that would be perfect, but although Kristy likes the horses, she doesn't like riding them. She does like shopping, though, so we're talking about a road trip to Regina. Check out some stores. Would you believe she's never been to the Army and Navy? And you know what great deals they have on designer shoes. Then we could have a nice meal somewhere. If there's a good movie playing, maybe take that in. It means we won't be home until quite late."

She examines my face closely, and says, "You don't have to ask fer permission."

I shouldn't have run off at the mouth like that. Even to me, that much babbling sounded like a con. I know better than to look away, but I'm beginning to squirm when Barney and Marci come in the back entrance. The gust of cold wind that accompanies them blows a clutch of invoices off the counter and gives me an excuse to break eye contact. I bend over and gather up the papers.

"Good morning everyone," Barney bellows. "Goddamn wind might blow some more snow our way. Anyone hear the weather forecast?"

"Stu or K.C. likely heard it. Dunno what K.C.'s up to today but Stu should be coming down pretty quick to start his chickens so you can ask him. If it gets bad you guys can close up early and go home." I give the papers a little wave and say, "I'll get these invoices into my office. See you tomorrow!"

I scurry out the door before Red can ask more questions. She's not my mother or even my big sister, but ever since I met her the summer I ran away from home to follow the rodeo, she acts like it. She means well and some day she'll look at me, realize I'm an adult and knock it off. Or not.

Kristy is in the bathroom lollygagging, or what she calls making herself presentable. I can guess what she thinks of my five-minute slap-dash makeup routine. I tap on the door and ask, "Ready?"

"I'll be just a sec," she replies. Five minutes later she emerges. She's pretty without makeup but I have to admit that made up like she is, she's a head turner. Smoky eyes. Flawless complexion. Curves in the right places don't hurt either. I know from the time I spent at the Tall Trees Pub in Katawasis Lake where she was a waitress that guys hit on her constantly. The members of the Ranchmen's Club are financially a cut above anyone who frequented Tall Trees, and even an elderly obese bald man with halitosis and flatulence might be irresistible if he has bags full of money. I don't want to believe my friend could be that shallow but I wonder if Jim has cause for concern.

"All set," she says, breaking into my thoughts.

I grab my purse and we head out to her car. When we talked about this trip yesterday, we decided to take her Fiero because it's way more fuel efficient than my truck with its big V-8 engine, so it makes sense. Plus, it's fun to drive and she agreed to let me take the wheel. We'll just have to be sure not to buy anything bigger than shoes.

Just east of Moose Jaw, I turn off the Trans Canada Highway onto Number 39. This takes us south of Regina, heading toward Pillerton. Kristy notices we've detoured and wants to know why. I tell her there's a great little pub I want to take her to for lunch.

"Great Caesar salad, I guess," she says.

"I, er, yeah, um, you know it," I reply. I'd like to agree more enthusiastically, but then I've only seen it from the outside, and only that one time, so I'll be caught in a lie if it turns out they don't have Caesars on the menu.

"I can't believe their Caesars are better than what you have at the Bistro, but if you just want to get away from that place for a change, they got Caesar salads at that pub down the road. What's it called? Billie's?"

"Billie's."

"Billie's has Caesar salads. We're not going to Regina—"

"We will—"

"Never mind. Just tell me the real reason for this trip, and don't say the shoe sale at the Army and Navy because you don't give a fat rat's ass about shoes."

That's Kristy. You might think a woman who looks like she does and can come across as an airhead isn't very bright. In fact she's as smart as a whip, and since she looks so unthreatening it's easy to underestimate her. She proved that a couple of years ago when we were the Katawasis Girls, Detectives at Large. When Kristy sets her mind to it, I'd say there isn't a male of any age she wouldn't have eating out of her hand. And just now, I got a reminder that I made a mistake in selling her short. I don't think she's really mad, but she does look a little peeved.

"Lindy!" she says, this time louder. "You told me you wanted to go to Regina because the shopping's better than Maple Creek or Swift Current, and now we're going to bypass Regina? If all you wanted was Caesar salad somewhere other than the Bistro, we could've gone to Billie's."

"No, we'll still go to Regina. Pillerton is just a little side trip. We'll still shop in Regina," I reiterate. "I thought we could use the time to talk about Jim, you know, you and Jim, what's wrong and ..."

"I already told you, Lindy. I'm sick of being Pissy's free babysitting service. That's Jim's ex, Priscilla. Jim calls her Prissy but I call her Pissy," she explains. "Wouldn't be bad if she'd marry her boyfriend so Jim could quit paying alimony and we might actually have money to do a few things, but will she? Of course not. Weird how before me and Jim got together she'd never let him have those kids except on his scheduled weekends, and now we have them all the time. Every weekend, that is. So, we can't go nowhere. Hardly ever go out for a meal, and dancing? Forget it! He says my work schedule makes it impossible but really it's because he doesn't want to spend a dime. He keeps moaning he's broke because of his alimony and child support. Not that it stops him doing what he likes to do. You know, golf tournaments. Squash tournaments. I got nothing to look forward to and I'm bored stiff."

I ruminate on it for a couple of miles, then say, "If you want my two cents' worth—"

"I don't, Lindy. I just have to call my boss at some point to let him know when I have a better idea of when I'll be back at work. So, no bullshit now, admit the real reason for this trip is to go to Pillerton, and tell me why. What do you hope to find there?"

"Okay, no bullshit? I don't really know what I hope to find in Pillerton. Here's the thing. You likely didn't notice, but we have tenants in the loft of the main barn. They're using it for warehouse space."

"And they rent space down a gravel road to a ranch out on the edge of the Badlands for a warehouse?"

"Yeah. Pretty strange, right?"

"I'd say so."

"The other thing is, in our meeting with Dwight yesterday, he mentioned there's illegal guns hitting the streets. The subject of the Al Capone tunnels in Pillerton came up, and it got me thinking. Pillerton is home to Prairie Equity and Wealth Management. They're the shysters who cheated us. And our new tenant's name? Prairie Outfitters, headquartered in Pillerton. Connected to Prairie Equity and Wealth?"

"I'll bet there's thousands of companies out here on the Prairies that call themselves Prairie something," Kristy says.

"Sure. But Pillerton is a very small town, and the other day Prairie Out-fitters got a shipment of wooden crates that were so heavy it took two guys to lift them. Up until then, their stock all came in cardboard boxes that one guy could lift. I asked Butch—he's the front man for the Prairie Outfitters—to let me see what was in the crates and he politely told me it's none of my business."

"So of course you thought, he won't show me what's in the crates, there-fore it's got to be guns," Kristy says.

"Exactly." I glance her way and see her slowly shaking her head. She's not buying it. I hurry to add, "K.C. has been doing some work for Butch and even he hasn't seen what's in them. When I asked him about it, he said something like, who cares, they're just made in India junk. He repeated what Butch said, that they're going to be sold and shipped out with the crates intact, no reason to look inside. I guess his mind is too occupied with the arena construction. He was like that before we left Katawasis Lake, when all he could think about was wrapping up his business and his deal with his landlord."

"I remember. He can really have a one track mind."

"For sure. But I can't stop thinking Butch is hiding something."

"Maybe nothing," she points out.

"Maybe nothing," I agree, "but I can't get it out of my mind." The sky is darkening and there are tiny snowflakes or maybe it's sleet hitting the wind-shield now. I turn on the windshield wipers. The road is starting to look slick, and the wind is buffeting the Fiero. I downshift to negotiate a curve. Back on the straight away I upshift, adjusting my speed for the deteriorating road conditions. "I know it sounds crazy. If I was to mention it to Red, she'd ask why I'm always so suspicious and even though she doesn't like Butch, she'd tell me to mind my own business. Probably not in as nice a way as Butch did, either. And she'd remind me that it's gotten me into trouble before."

"Yeah. But as it turned out, you were right to be suspicious." From the way Kristy is chewing her lip, I think she might be coming around to believ-ing me. "Red doesn't like Butch? How come?"

"I told you Trina is Red's long lost love child? She and Butch are a thing and Red's turned into Mama Bear."

"They're a thing already? I gotta see this guy. What's he like?"

"Well, I guess you'd say he's a hunk. Handsome. Nice smile. Looks like he works out. But please stay out of it, Kristy."

"Of course! But no harm just looking."

"Sure," I agree, although I have no doubt if Kristy gave any indication of interest, Butch would be looking right back and things could go downhill fast. I push the visual out of my head and say, "Besides, cast your mind back to when you met Jim. Didn't take you two long to become a thing." I could point out they were in bed within a couple of hours and they've been together ever since, but that's a touchy subject right now.

"Yeah, well, maybe that was a mistake."

Touchy subject all right. If I thought the reminder would take her back to happier times, it didn't. I bite my lower lip and wonder if I should make some beige comment like *you'll work things out,* but instead decide to channel the discussion back to my reason for wanting to go to Pillerton. "So anyhow, I thought today we could check out a few tack shops and see if they'll confirm buying from Prairie Outfitters. You know. Maybe prove they're legitimate. I'm hoping there's a tack shop in Pillerton. If not, there's definitely at least one in Regina. So that'll be our next destination."

"You mean there isn't a tack shop closer? Like in town or, um, at least in Swift Current?"

"Well, yeah, but ..."

"So we drove past those. Why?"

She would have to think of that, and she has a point. "Well, aside from the sketchy tack wholesaling business, years ago, my father rented the loft to a church of some kind, small time, not mainstream, and they held meetings there. One of the old timers in Maple Creek said there were rumors of what he called strange doings in that church. He wouldn't elaborate, but what if he was talking about ritual sacrifices?"

"Jeez, Lindy!"

"I know it's a stretch. But stranger things have happened. And I think the church in question is headquartered in Pillerton."

"Yup, if an old man mentioned strange doings at a church, I'd think, hey, that must be ritual sacrifices and that church must be the one from that little town I was at one time."

She clicks her tongue. I give her a sideways look but she's looking out the window, shaking her head. I remind myself our shared history began only began a couple years ago, in Katawasis Lake. "Kristy, you remember I told you about Jake. He belonged to a cult from Pillerton. He was the one who got me involved with the money men who fleeced us."

"Oh! So everything leads back to Pillerton."

"Yeah. It's a historical fact Al Capone had an operation there. It would have been going gangbusters in the Twenties. Al Capone has been dead for decades, of course, but what if his business associates kept on without him? What better cover than a fake church?" I glance at Kristy to see how she's receiving this. This is the first time I've said it out loud because Kristy is the only person I know who wouldn't laugh me out of town. "What I'm thinking is, that church could be connected to those bodies. Which could be connected to Prairie Equity and Wealth Management. Which could be connected to Prairie Outfitters, and they're the gun runners."

"So you now they're both murderers *and* gun runners."

"Well, the two do go together."

"What do the cops think?"

"I guess they might be looking into it, but you know how slowly those things roll. They're always understaffed, plus now they're focusing on the guns. Dwight says they'll never stop investigating and I believe that, but I doubt those old bodies are a high priority. If they could put names to them, that would help. Even if we could just say for sure it was that church that rented the loft, it would give them a place to start."

Kristy chews her bottom lip, ruining her lipstick as she mulls it over. I'm starting to worry she thinks it's ridiculous, when she turns to me and giggles. "Damn, Lindy! You know I'm going to have to suck up to that Butch guy to get him to show me what's in the crates. He wouldn't show you, but you wanna bet he'll show me?"

"I would never bet against you, Kristy."

"Coward! Just bet something, you know, to make it interesting."

"Okay. How about this: I lose, I do your laundry for the week. If you lose, you do mine."

"Deal! And if it's just saddles like it supposed to be, at least that puts the Prairie whatzit saddle selling guys out. Then when we find out what that church is up to these days we can rule them in or out. Which leaves us where?"

"Nowhere, I guess."

"But getting to nowhere will be fun!" She pulls her over-sized purse onto her lap, digs through it, and comes up with a small red jackknife. She holds it up and says, "See? I still have my Swiss Army knife! Lindy, I've been so bored! You have no idea how much I've missed you."

She pulls the hem of her t-shirt from her belt, slides her hand up into her underarm and sticks the little knife in her bra. "Now I'm armed and dangerous, just like back in Katawasis Lake. Katawasis Girl-friend, I'm ready." She giggles.

Although I've never been a giggler, I do too.

Touring Pillerton doesn't take more than fifteen minutes. It's hard to believe it was ever a boom town. There are as many derelict houses as there are inhabited ones, and those could use serious maintenance. Even what must have been a mansion in its day, an imposing two-story Colonial, has needed paint so long it's hard to tell what colour it once was. I drive past slowly enough to gawk, intrigued because of its past grandeur. There's someone half-hidden by curtains peering out, so as derelict as the house appears, someone still lives there.

I turn onto Main Street. From my previous visit I remember the center boulevard with its young trees and angle parking in front of the businesses. Big Al's Pub and the entrance to the Al Capone Tunnels is in a three-storey stone building right on the corner. Across from it is a Co-Op Store. Other storefronts down the block are boarded up, but there is a post office, and insurance office, and branch of Western Savings and Loan. Across from them, Prairie Equity and Wealth Management.

"That's the business that cheated us on a loan, Kristy. Jake's truck was parked right there in front when he was supposed to be delivering hay to Vancouver Island, thousands of miles in the opposite direction." There's a late model Lincoln there now, but no other parked vehicles between Prairie Equity and the Pillerton Curling Rink. I make a U-turn at the cenotaph where Main Street ends and head back to park across from Big Al's.

Inside the pub we're greeted with scents of stale beer, cigarette smoke and old building, but the scent of beef on the grill is pervasive and makes my mouth water. Heads turn as we walk through to settle at a banquette-style booth under a street-facing window.

I scan the clientele trying to categorize the few people who have the luxury of being in a bar at eleven a.m. on a weekday. Aside from two men in suits at the bar, most look like they just came in off the farm. We're being watched. I suppose it's natural for strangers in a small town to attract attention but something about these people seems malevolent. I'm just about to mention it to Kristy when I realize she's looking around, smiling at everyone. No one returns her smile, but one of the guys at the bar is practically drooling, looking at her through narrowed, calculating eyes.

"Quit gawking or we're going to have some unwelcome company," I hiss.

"Unwelcome? Who says it's unwelcome?"

"I say. Look how they're all glaring at us. And that guy you're giving the come on to looks positively predatory."

"You're delusional, Lindy. Red's right. You've got a suspicious mind."

"We should go."

"I don't think so. I'm thirsty and hungry and you're imagining things."

"Hmmpf!" I'd argue, but I'm the one who dragged her here after all, so I sit back and pull the wine list out of the bin of napkin-wrapped cutlery, HP Sauce and Heinz ketchup. It's a short list.

A skinny waitress with faded brassy hair and an inch of grey roots comes to our table after letting us wait long enough to get the message that she's busy and we're not important. I order a glass of house white and Kristy says she'll have the same. We ask for menus, and water when she gets a chance.

"Menu's right up there," she tells us, points at the board on the back wall, and leaves.

"She seems nice," I grumble. "I can't read that from here because I didn't think to bring my binoculars."

"I'll go take a look," Kristy says. She gets up, goes to the menu board, and with a swishing of her hips, smiles at the guys at the bar on her way back. "Well, there's the usual four options for burgers, you know: with cheese, with bacon, two patties, and one chicken burger. Then nachos and yay! Your choice of house or Caesar salad," Kristy says.

"That's it?"

"What else could anyone want? How about we share the nachos and each get a salad?"

"Sounds good," I agree.

When Blondie returns with our wine, we give her our orders and I make a second request for water. She's barely left our table when the two men at the bar get up. The older one leaves. The other sashays over and stands at our table looking down at us. "Ladies," he says, "I don't have much time but what I do have, I'd sure like to spend with you."

Before I can decline, Kristy scoots over so he can sit next to her, and says, "Well, that would be real nice."

I try to give her a kick, but ram my toe into the table leg.

Bar guy slides onto the bench, closer to Kristy than he needs to be. From the expression on his face, I'd say he never considered that the answer might be in doubt. "Hi. My name's Donny," he says, and slides his arm up along the upholstery behind Kristy. We tell him our names, and he predictably asks, "Where're you gals from?"

"How do you know we're not from here?" Kristy asks with a giggle.

"Ain't no classy gals like you livin' in Pillerton," he replies.

I've seen that expression of keen interest on male faces many times. It's true he may have been including me when he said 'classy gals' but I'd be surprised if he even knows I'm here, and for possibly the first time in my life, I'm glad.

I excuse myself to go to the ladies room.

Chapter 10

No tack shop. No church. No water. House white like kerosene and the worst Caesar salad I've had in my life. A poster in the foyer of Big Al's pub announcing it as the entrance to the Al Capone tunnels and soliciting donations for the restoration project is all there is to said tunnels. Our side trip to Pillerton is a bust.

I bolt my lousy salad and most of the nachos while Kristy munches a few chips and picks at her salad. As unpalatable as it is, I'm tempted finish it for her in hopes we can cut this miserable lunch short, but I doubt it would make a difference because she is so engaged in deep eye gazing with Donny that I finally slide out of the booth and say, "We gotta hit the road, Kristy. Weather's getting worse and time's a-wastin.'"

She barely acknowledges that she's heard me, just gives me a sideways glance.

"Kristy!"

"Okay! Okay," she says. "I guess we're leaving, Donny." The big oaf finally takes the hint and moves so she can get out. As she stands, she turns to me and says, "I gotta go to the can first."

Another delay. I blow out a sharp breath and say, "Fine. I'll be in the car."

My mistake. Ten minutes later, still no Kristy. Donny probably waylaid her as soon as she came out of the ladies room. I've brushed the snow off the car once and will almost need to do it again if she makes me wait any longer. I'm thinking of charging back in there and hauling her out like an angry wife after a philandering husband, when I check the rearview and see the two of them coming out.

They cross the street together. He's holding her arm, a wise precaution because those three-inch heels she's wearing are about as useful as skates in the accumulating snow. He comes around so he's in position to open the door for her. I don't know if I'm more irritated at Kristy for wearing such stupid shoes or that I have to admit Donny is being thoughtful. Then, I don't know for sure because they're right next to the car so from inside I can't see what they're doing, but I think they kiss before the door opens and Kristy slides in.

She barely has time to settle in the passenger seat before I back out of the parking stall. Donny has the good sense to get up on the sidewalk double quick to avoid having his toes run over. He grins and waves. She giggles and waves back. I scowl and stomp the gas pedal. The Fiero fishtails. I steer out of it, ease off the accelerator and point the Fiero in the direction of the highway.

The snowflakes, bigger now, are blowing across the road in ribbons. Although that fishtailing incident was totally my fault, it's obvious the Fiero isn't great in snow. I wonder if we should head back home instead of continuing on to Regina, but I don't say anything because I don't trust myself to speak until I'm not quite so irritated.

After a few minutes I realize it's my fault. Why did I insist on taking her to that place? Maybe I did let my imagination run away with me. Did I actually believe there would be a church in Pillerton that would do anything more horrifying than sing hymns on Sundays? But then, Kristy didn't have to keep me waiting just so she could flirt with a random stranger.

As if reading my thoughts, she says, "Him and that guy he was with that left right away? They work at that wealth management place. Donny, he has his own secretary, and there's a bunch of guys working under him besides. He said I should move to Pillerton and he'd give me a job as a receptionist."

"Great." I give her a sideways glance. She looks so serious I wonder if she could be considering it. This doesn't improve my mood. "You're not really thinking of doing it, are you? Work at a place that cheated me? I mean, cheated Wacasko-Wâti?"

"No, of course not! Although he says houses are cheap. His company gives out mortgages, and he would make sure I got one. I could own my own house! And besides, it wasn't Donny that cheated you." She sniffs, then adds, "And I wouldn't be living any further away from my very best friend in the whole world than I am now.

I recognize ego stroking when I hear it. Manipulative much? I guess she's always been capable of it. It's one of the reasons she can wrap men around her little finger, after all. But she's thinking about buying a house? "I remember him giving you the sales pitch. Just didn't realize you'd actually take him seriously."

"Why not? He's different than the other guys in that place. You must've noticed that. Shirt and tie. Nice suit."

"Yeah? That's impressive enough you let him slip you the tongue?"

"It wasn't a tongue kiss."

Well, there it is. Confirmation. She actually kissed the guy. I tell myself not to be judgmental. It was just Kristy being Kristy. Minutes pass before my jaw relaxes enough to let me speak, and I say, "Talk is cheap. A house in your price range would likely be one of those run-down little shit boxes, what do they call them? Fixer uppers? Money pits? If you want to move, there's affordable houses in Maple Creek, too, and you can find insurance agents and bankers in three piece suits having lunch at The Jasper any day of the week. At least there, the food is good," I grumble. That may have been a little snotty. I continue in a contrite tone, "You were so busy hanging on his every word you barely ate. You must still be hungry."

She asks, "Did you notice his ring?"

She hadn't been listening. She was just letting me talk. "His ring?"

"Yeah. Big, expensive looking. Kinda antique looking. You must've noticed it."

"I guess I did. It just didn't make a big impression on me like it seems to have made on you."

"Well, yeah. I asked him about it and he said it's from a group he belongs to. He said it's like Masons. You know what that is?"

"I've heard of them. Don't know much about—"

"He's pretty high up in it. And here's the thing: it's like they've got their own religion. He says pretty soon they're going to make him an Elder. And if I moved here, he says he would be able to get me into the, um, congregation and I'd be an important member because of him being my sponsor." She giggles. "Have you ever heard a come on like that before? It was so obvious. Fuck me and I'll make your whole world good."

I've heard her use the F-word before so that's not what piques my interest, it's the fact Donny told her he was going to be made an Elder. "What's the name of that church again?"

"He didn't say church, he said religion. It's different than a church. They don't have, um, pagan celebrations like Christmas or Easter and instead of sermons they have meetings. That big old house behind the pub you were so interested in? That's where they have their meetings. So that could be the cult you're looking for."

She's right. It's another reminder of what a great Katawasis Girls asset she is. Still, I worry she might be open to a relationship with that Donny guy. "You're actually thinking of moving *and* joining a cult? Just because of some guy you met in a bar?"

"Well, no. I'd miss Christmas," she says, shaking her head. "But then, maybe. I mean, I'll be thirty next month and what have I done with my life so far? I've just been drifting along from one minimum-wage job with no future to another, bouncing from one guy to another. Look at where I am now! I've just left my third husband!"

"But you and Jim—I mean, he's—"

"Yeah, Jim!" She interjects. "Best you can say about me and Jim is that I'm his built-in booty call. He doesn't even have to buy me a drink."

I didn't realize her complaints about Jim and her marriage were this serious. Only now do I understand she's going through more than a marital crisis. Turning thirty can do that. But surely she's not really considering such an enormous life change as to move five hundred miles after an hour's conversation with a stranger. There's no use discussing it now, though, because she's going to be at Wacasko-Wâti for a few days at least, and we can talk it out once we've both had a chance to digest everything.

"How much further?" she asks. I take this as a good sign: moving to Pillerton isn't top of mind for her right now.

"The bypass is just ahead. Another ten minutes or so and we'll be right downtown. We'll go to the Army and Navy first. Besides designer shoes, they have snow boots. Maybe get yourself some. After that we have to go a few blocks further north, and there's Eaton's. Not as big as the one in Calgary, but it does have a great bargain section. What do you think about booking into a motel? Then we could shop without worrying about the time, and have a nice dinner without worrying about the drive home. Maybe see a movie."

"Great idea," she agrees. She digs through her purse, comes out with a compact, and touches up her powder and lipstick.

My mind isn't on my grooming, but on Kristy's report of her conversation with Donny. Could Donny be connected to Butch somehow? Like maybe they both belong to that not-church? Is Butch's tack business actually legit? I ask, "What do you want to shop for, I mean, besides the boots I mentioned, which is something you're going to need right away? Jeans maybe? Tack shops are a great place to get jeans."

"Well, jeans I guess. And I can't wait to see those designer shoes. Other than that, I'm just gonna see if anything grabs me."

"Besides Donny, you mean," I tease.

She giggles. "Yeah, besides Donny!"

She's a great spy and doesn't even realize it. Maybe the side trip to Pillerton wasn't a bust after all.

We end up checking into a hotel downtown, then shop until we're tired, returning to the hotel for dinner in the hotel restaurant. After supper, we go to see *Who Framed Roger Rabbit* at the theatre down the street. I guess the movie is okay, definitely different, and the way they put animated cartoon characters in with real actors is pretty impressive. After a nightcap in the hotel cocktail bar where thankfully there are no interesting men for Kristy to tease, we get to bed at a reasonable hour.

In the morning, after a quick breakfast we hit the road. Or the street, actually, as we still haven't been to a tack shop.

"How do you know there even is one out this far?" Kristy asks..

"I looked up the address, and there's a street map in the back of the phonebook," I reply.

We come to a two-storey building set back behind a decent-sized parking lot, with "Cow Town" in tall red letters on the front. The parking lot has a few pickups and cars in it with no snow on them, so it's open, even though it's just 9:30.

We go inside and wander around for a bit. Kristy follows the sign that indicates the women's section is upstairs, while I go to the customer service desk. There's a blonde woman with her back to me busy with paperwork on a shelf there. The clerk behind the cash register asks, "What can I help you with today?"

I check her name tag and say, "Well, um, Brenda? I'm going to have a look around, for sure. I've never been here before because it's a four hour drive from where I live, but a friend of mine told me about this place and said I should be sure to check it out when I was in Regina." I give her my best smile and say, "He says you carry Big Horn and Circle Y."

"We sure do," she replies. "You looking for a saddle?"

"Maybe. Not until after Christmas, though. My friend said you'd be getting new stock in the spring, too. He's a wholesaler. Hey! Maybe you know him? Butch Cassidy?" The instant I say his name I realize most people would think I was pulling their leg. The blonde woman turns around and I half expect the two of them to laugh.

Instead, Brenda says, "We know him. Is he your boyfriend?" Brenda asks.

"No, he's just a friend."

"I bet you'd like to change that!"

"I, er, no, I have a boyfriend. They, um, work together, so..."

"So he's up for grabs then," Blondie concludes. She grins and says, "Good stuff!"

"We only met him a few weeks ago," Brenda says. "The jobber was in with samples a while ago. Butch just came in to introduce himself, bought some jeans and then asked us to meet him at The Paddock after work and bought us dinner. Nice, eh? He even promised Elaine a ride on his motorcycle."

"Easy on the eyes," the blonde who's apparently named Elaine, says. "I'm gonna take him up on it, too."

"I hope he comes back for more jeans," Brenda says, "because I'm pretty sure he'll need some help in the fitting room!"

We all chuckle at her nudge-nudge, wink-wink comment. I'm surprised he has a motorcycle, but that's not unusual and doesn't make him a gun runner. So, it's confirmed. My tenant is legit, at least as far as the tack wholesaling goes. I should feel relieved. But there's still the question of those big, heavy crates he doesn't want opened.

Chapter 11

"There was sure a helluva lot of bangin' and clankin' goin' on out in the yard last night. I barely slept a wink," Red grumbles. "Yer gonna hafta tell that guy we got a no noise after nine p.m. rule around here."

"I didn't hear anything," I reply.

"Neither did I," Stu says, then mutters under his breath, "didn't bother Trina neither."

"She deserves a sleep-in," Red snaps. "She didn't get in till late."

I didn't ask where Trina was but since she's not at the kitchen table with us and no lights were on in the Bistro when K.C. and I came over, I'm guessing she's still in bed. Red frowns at Stu and seems about to say something about his veiled criticism of Trina. I circumvent that by saying, "Where'd Trina go that she was out late?" I ask. There's not much to do in Maple Creek after midnight, so I don't think she could be out all that late. Or maybe I've just forgotten it's possible to make out in trucks.

"She went to some kinda church thing with Slick," Red replies.

Butch, religious? That's unexpected. "What church thing?"

"I don't know. She don't seem to know. It wasn't like a church service, she said, just a prayer meetin.'"

"I didn't realize Trina was religious," I say. I'd like to know more, but the look on Red's face warns me against pursuing it.

"About the racket last night," Red says, "you be sure and tell him we ain't gonna put up with it."

"I will. But I can't believe I slept through it." It's really no surprise because I was out like a light. Could it be because of the activity in bed last night that left me so sated I could've slept through a tornado? I should take an overnight trip away from the ranch without K.C. more often. I doubt we got more sleep than Red did but I'm not complaining! "What was Butch doing?" I ask.

"If Butch was with Trina, it couldn't have been him," K.C. points out.

"His guys, then," Red says. "He has to tell his guys they can't be makin' noise after nine."

"I'll mention it to him," K.C. offers. "What was going on that made banging noise?"

"I dunno fer sure but something with the elevator from the sounds of it," Stu says.

"Why'd you say that?" Red demands. "You were snorin' like a D8 Cat and slept right through it and you just admitted you didn't hear nuthin'."

"I'm just tellin' 'em what you told me," Stu explains. He gets up from the table to fetch the carafe from the coffeemaker. "Have another coffee, darlin'," he says. "It ain't like you to be draggin' yer ass like this no matter if you ain't slept at all. Maybe you just need another shot of caffeine." He tops up all our mugs before sitting back down.

"Speaking of the elevator, after Butch hurt his hand on it I was wondering if there's some modification that should be made so it's safer."

"It's plenty safe, Lindy," K.C. replies. "Can't make it completely idiot-proof. You have to pay attention when you're running machinery. He must've been gawking at Trina instead of watching what he was doing."

"Well," Red says, "he does a lot of that. Although with Kristy around now, dimes to donuts he'll go after her. And I'll be damn glad if he does."

"Red! That would hurt Trina, and on top of that, Kristy is married," I say. "And if you didn't like him, er, bothering Trina, why would you be glad if he bothered Kristy? My friend? She's pretty vulnerable right now, you know, what with, um ..."

"Yeah, I know, and I'm sorry, Lindy," Red says. "I just meant if he was to drop Trina the second another girl showed up, he'd be showin' his true colors and Trina could count herself lucky to be outta that situation before it got serious. And I think Kristy can give as good as she gets in the man department."

"She is one pretty little gal, that's fer sure," Stu says. When Red frowns at him, he hastens to add, "Good worker, too. Pitches in every time she comes fer a visit."

"Don't see her out there this morning," Red points out.

It's on the tip of my tongue to remind her she's a guest and if Trina is entitled to sleep in when she's an actual employee and should have been down getting the kitchen ready for the day an hour ago, surely Kristy is. But Red has become so sensitive to criticism of Trina I decide against it.

Stu has already overstepped. He seems to realize it, turns to K.C. and asks, "What're you up to today, K.C.?"

"Put a couple more hours on those warmblood colts from Pringle's," K.C. replies, "then after lunch, have to run into town to pick up feed. You free to come along?"

"Ay-yuh, guess so," Stu says.

"Anyone else?" K.C. asks. "Lindy?"

"Maybe," I reply. "If I spend all morning trying to learn that computer not to mention staring at flashing green letters all that time, I'll be needing a break by lunch. We could swing by the Detachment and see if we can catch Dwight in the office."

"We could at that," Stu says. "He ain't been around fer a while. S'pose he's busy but I'd like an update."

"How about you, Red?" K.C. asks.

"Some of us have work to do around here," she snipes. She gets up, dumps her coffee in the sink, and in seconds is out the door.

There's an awkward silence in the wake of her abrupt departure. I say, "She's been so on edge. Not like her to be so, er—"

"She really don't like Butch," Stu explains. "Prob'ly thinks she has to ride herd on her kid or he'll kidnap her."

"Hmmm," I demure. From where I sit, I doubt kidnapping would be necessary. More likely her reason for staying home is that since Lucy quit, Trina slacking off means more work for Red. I make a mental note to call Lucy to see if I can convince her to come back at least a couple days a week.

"Okay then, let's git the show on the road," Stu says.

As we're outside going our separate ways, we encounter Kristy on her way to the Bistro. She's got her makeup on and is in jeans and a Tall Trees Pub t-shirt with a neckline low enough to display her cleavage to good advantage. She's been wearing less revealing t-shirts that don't advertise a prior employer up to now but this is pretty typical Kristy style and I wonder if she's chosen that shirt in particular because she plans to meet Butch today. He must have slept in the warehouse because his truck is parked by the barn door. If he was late dropping Trina off last night, that makes sense.

"Good morning, everyone!" Kristy says. "Hope there's something for me to do in there!"

We all return her greeting, and I say, "Report to Red. I'm sure she'll find something for you. But have you had breakfast?"

"No, not yet. I'm just going to grab a coffee and a pastry from the day old bin," she says.

"I doubt the coffee's ready yet," I tell her.

"Well, that'll be my first job, then," she says, and giggles.

"Okay. Hey, we're going to town after lunch. Come with us?"

"Umm, thanks, but I don't think so. If Red doesn't have enough for me to do, I think I'll just relax."

Relax? I know the real reason. "Well, if you change your mind, let me know."

Just then Butch comes out of the barn, apparently heading for the Bistro. He looks up and gives a little wave. If the coffee isn't ready, he'll have to find something to entertain himself until it is. I don't think that'll be a problem.

We go to the feed store first. While the men deal with buying and loading the feed, I enjoy a little meander around the store, pick up kibble and treats for the dogs and Kitty, and catch up on the local gossip with the clerks.

Next we head for the RCMP Detachment. There's no way of knowing if Dwight's there because the cruisers in the lot all look the same, so I go inside to ask. The receptionist calls him to let him know we'd like to see him and in minutes, he comes through the door into the lobby.

"Hey, Lindy! Good to see you," he says. "Know what? Your timing's great. I'm due for a break. How about I meet you at Robin's?"

"Sounds good," I agree, and head back outside.

When we're at a table in the donut shop with our coffee and pastry of choice and Stu and Dwight have finished chatting about curling, I say, "We were hoping you'd be able to tell us more about the bodies. We'll all rest easier when they're identified. But a bigger deal would be if you got the killer."

"May already be dead," K.C. points out.

"Alive or dead. Don't give a shit either way. Anything to git justice or what they call closure so the spirits botherin' my wife'll rest," Stu says.

"Yeah, about that," Dwight says. "I haven't been out your way or you know I'd stop in, but there's really no news. The man you told me about at the extendacare was interviewed. With his caregiver present in case he was needed, because with his Alzheimer's, there's good days and bad days. But he confirmed he's an Elder in a cult called The Children of Noah, headquartered in a pissant little town called Pillerton."

"Pillerton! I was there a couple days ago and didn't see anything like a church. Kristy met someone who told her he belongs to what we're calling a 'not-church' so I guess you could say cult, and they use an old house for their meetings."

K.C. squirms in his chair and gives me an intense look. I know he's going to want me to explain what I was doing in Pillerton when I said I was going to Regina, since I've assured him I no longer stick my nose into things that are best left to others. I wonder if there's any chance he'll forget about it by the time we're alone.

Dwight continues, "Not-church? Good enough. His caretaker is a member of that not-church too and he put us in touch with the big cheese in Pillerton, but so far, nothing there. Too long ago, no one keeps records, the secretary is a volunteer so they take what they can get, good or bad, and no one stays in that position for long, so on and so forth."

"Well, the guy Kristy talked to works at Prairie Equity and Wealth Management in Pillerton. His name is Donny. Maybe someone could show up at the office and have a chat with him. You know. Lean on him."

"Lean on him? You watch too many cop shows," Dwight chuckles. "But it's a good idea." After a bite of donut washed down with coffee, he says, "As for identifying the females, there's a couple runaways that are possibilities, both from decades ago. They're getting dental records and trying to piece together how either of them might've found their way to Maple Creek. It's a wide area and a given the decades-long time span there are thousands of runaways or missing persons. Thousands."

"Thousands? Really?"

"Really. It's a tedious process. I wouldn't be surprised if they were never identified. At least they're done at your place."

"Thankfully," K.C. says.

"In future, if we dig up bones, we're just going to bury them again," I say. One of my barrettes has worked loose and a lock of hair falls forward. I tuck it behind my ear, reset the barrette, and continue, "That way we won't run into this prob—" I stop in the middle of what was going to be a stupid joke because Dwight is giving me the strangest look. "I don't mean it, Dwight. If we find more burials, we'll report it. You know that."

"Of course. Um, where'd you get those earrings, Lindy?" Dwight asks.

"Oh, these?" I touch the silver disk and reply, "They were in a little wooden box Red found when she first moved in with Stu. There was also a photo of my grandfather and grandmother in the box, so she figured they must've belonged to my grandmother, and gave them to me. Why?"

"Lindy, remember I told you there was a necklace in the burial? And they got it cleaned up so they could photograph it?"

"Umm, yeah?

"So, the pendant's bigger but otherwise it looks exactly like those earrings. They could be part of the same set."

I draw a deep breath and can almost feel the blood draining from my face. "There must be something ... I don't think they're worth anything ... I mean, they're real silver and they're old but they're not that unusual I don't think."

"The necklace actually *is* unusual. There's a maker's mark stamped on it and they were able to trace it. It was made in Germany. Actually, not Germany itself but a German settlement in Russia. Back in 1890 or thereabouts. Can you let me have them, at least until we can get someone to confirm if they could be part of a set or not?"

I'm flooded with a mixture of emotions as I remove the earring. I can't bring myself to check for a mark so I just drop it in Dwight's hand. He examines it and then looks at me, his expression so intense words aren't needed. I remove the second earring and hand it to Dwight.

Chapter 12

There's still snow on the ground from Tuesday's storm but it's a sunny, mild morning. I've been neglecting Chica, not that the pampered little princess cares if I ride as long as she has food, pasture all day and a warm stall at night, but she's been freeloading long enough. I want to ride. K.C. does too, and since riding out is part of educating the horses he has in training, he saddles one of them while I saddle Chica. Cisco and Tippy, Wacasko-Wâti's Border Collies, sense a trail ride is in the works and mill around underfoot generally making a nuisance of themselves.

They're in front of us as we head out the door. Henry, who sat quietly out of the way and watched while we tacked up, has to be called. He's so reluctant I change my mind about insisting he come with us, and send him home. He's never been an active dog and now with his damaged shoulder and limp, plus advancing age, if he wants to sleep on the porch, he's welcome to.

We ride along one of the lanes through the saskatoon fields and out into our south pasture, then head down a seasonal creek bed in a ravine that eventually leads to the Avonlea Badlands. With the snowmelt, there's water trickling along and the trail is sloppy. For the last ten minutes or so we've had to ride single file to avoid the worst of the muck. K.C. is behind me. It's the first trail ride for the youngster he's on and he's settling nicely, thanks to Chica being steady and quiet. He's not brave, so he's happiest following the older horse.

The going is becoming sloppier, so when we come to a wye in the trail that leads up and out of the ravine, we take it. At the top the soil is not as muddy, and the land flattens out. It's wide enough for us to ride side by side. The fence and road are several hundred meters off and the trail home follows it, so we head in that direction.

"But my father's side of the family is Norwegian," I insist, picking up the threads of our earlier conversation. "My grandmother wasn't from Russia or Germany or wherever the earrings supposedly came from. I guess those earrings must go with that necklace, but someone must have given them to her and then gave the necklace to someone else. Maybe it was that Watkins man! Maybe he seduced farm women all over his territory and gave them each trinkets but was too cheap to give a complete set to any one woman. That can't be my grandmother literally under my feet all this time! Red thinks it is and that she must've been murdered because otherwise why was she never reported missing? I say it makes sense. If you knew your wife ran off, would you report her missing?"

"Hell no! It would've been an answer to a prayer and I'd bust out in song! Instead I had to give her ninety percent of everything to get rid of her." He chuckles. "As for the earrings, just because they're from Russia or Germany doesn't mean your grandmother was. There's Germans living around here too, and lots of them east of Regina. Balgonie. Edenwold. Around there. And your grandfather could've bought them from a German."

He's right. There are many ways jewelry originating in a German settlement in Russia could find its way to a rancher's wife in southwestern Saskatchewan. Thing is, I don't want to believe it.

"Okay, say it is her," I allow, "it doesn't mean my grandfather killed her. More likely the killer is the Watkins man. Right?"

"I don't know, Lindy. So she abandoned her baby and drove off with the Watkins man, then he killed her and brought her body back to bury her in the manure pile?"

He has a point. "Well, maybe he killed her and buried her when my grandfather was away and he only assumed she left with him. Anyhow, I still don't think it's her. I think she drove off with the Watkins man and lived happily ever after."

"The fairy tale ending," K.C. says. "I guess we'll never know. But leaving the baby?"

"Lots of women leave their kids with the husband. She left with the Watkins man and that's the reason my grandfather never reported her as missing," I insist. As if saying it one more time will change his mind. "Oh, never mind. I know I'm being stupid."

"You're not being stupid, babe," K.C. says. "A bonehead, maybe, but not stupid. I understand. You wanted to know about your biological family badly enough that you ran away from home to find your father when you were only seventeen. Of course you don't want to believe ..."

He lets what he was going to say drift off. I don't want to say it out loud either. My grandfather was a murderer. Not just a murderer, but a serial killer. My grandfather! Is it in me, too? The killer gene? Is that why I didn't think twice about stabbing Dan? I study K.C.'s face. He's frowning. Is the same thought running through his head? I've told him about that stabbing incident. Even though I don't like talking about it, maybe I should tell him how, exactly, it came to that. "K.C., you know I—"

Before I complete the sentence, he exclaims, "What the ...?" and nudges his horse into a canter, dogs in hot pursuit. I didn't think he was going to push the colt to take the lead this soon. Chica is taken off guard, too; she dances around, anxious to keep up. I let her have her head.

We canter the last few hundred yards and rein in at a wide opening in the fence. Two posts have been pulled out and lie in the tangle of barbwire next to the opening. K.C. utters a stream of angry curses.

"Who would do this?" K.C. demands. "Hope the hell no stock got out. What kind of an asshole would do this?"

He wasn't here when the rustlers were active, so his mind doesn't immediately make that leap. Mine does. "Maybe stock did get out, K.C. I should say, they didn't get out, they were taken out."

He utters a hiss, then shakes his head. "You think it's rustlers again?"

"Looks like it. There's tracks, not fresh, but definite tire tracks. What other reason could anyone have for doing this?"

"No idea."

"Well, we've been hit by rustlers before, although not this close to home. I can't believe no one noticed! It would still be my guess. And if there are cattle missing, we should've noticed that, too."

"Who checks the herds? Charlie and Johnny, usually, right? Are you sure they would they notice?"

"I'm sure. They're young but they're good hands," I respond. Then I think about it for another moment, and amend my answer. "I'm pretty sure, anyway. But they might not notice if it was just a few, like what would fit in a stock trailer, and if they did think some were missing, they might've just figured they were down a ravine or in the bushes somewhere, and would turn up. We'll have to do a head count."

"First we have to get this fence fixed, so we'd better boogie on home," K.C. says, and we point our horses in the direction of the farmyard.

When we trot up onto the tarmac, rein in and dismount, I spot Charlie at the wheelbarrow in the alleyway, manure fork in hand. "Hey, Charlie," I call out, "you notice any cows missing when you checked on the herd?"

"Nope," he replies. "Why?"

"The fence has been cut."

"What?" Charlie stands like a statue for a heartbeat, then leans the fork against the wheelbarrow. "I'll go tell Dad." He trots off. He's back with Stu close behind him while K.C. and I are still untacking.

"What's up?" Stu wants to know. "Charlie said someone cut the fence?"

"Looks like we've got rustlers again, Stu," I tell him.

"Yeah. Fence cut less than a quarter mile out," K.C., finished putting his horse away, joins the conversation. "Looks like a truck came down off the road into the pasture there."

"We're going to have to check to see how many cows are missing," I say.

"Aside from that, we can't leave that hole in the fence, so the first order of business is to get that fixed. Damn lucky no stock got out on the road," K.C. says.

"Could be hunters. Or snowmobilers, what with the fresh snow. Wouldn't be the first time," Stu says. "I hope that's what it was. He suddenly looks like a balloon that the air's been leaking out of for a couple of days. He sinks to the bench in front of the tack room, hands on knees, and heaves a sigh. "I sure hope that's what it was."

"I hope so too," I say. "For the fence, though, how about K.C. and Charlie deal with that? You and Johnny go see where the herd is. Get a head count. That part's not urgent. We can do it tomorrow."

"Not real urgent," he agrees, "but if we got stock missin', we gotta git it reported. So yeah, we'll at least start a head count today." He blows out a long breath before heaving himself to his feet. "Goddamn! No rest fer the wicked."

"Or for the righteous," I tell him, and give his arm a pat. "Okay, then. I'll finish the barn chores so Charlie can go with K.C., and if Johnny's not finished feeding, I'll take that over, too."

"I can do the fence myself," K.C. says, "so both boys can go with you, Stu. If they take the other two horses I was planning on riding today, it'll kill two birds with one stone."

"Good," Stu says to K.C., and then to Charlie, "Okay son, you go tell Mom what's goin' on. Me and Johnny'll catch them colts and start saddlin' up."

"It's okay, Dad," Charlie says, "We ain't been out to check on the herd yet today so we were gonna do that pretty quick anyhow. We'll catch the colts and saddle Shorty fer you while you go tell Mom what's goin' on."

Daylight is fast fading and the riders aren't back yet. Trina and Kristy are working in the Bistro, so K.C. and Red are with me on my patio. We've got a fire in the firepit and wine, beer and potato chips at hand, awaiting the return of Stu and the boys. I'd say we're relaxing, but we're too on edge for that, wondering how much stock we've lost.

"I should take a horse out and see what's keeping them," K.C. says.

"I'm sure they won't be much longer, and it'll soon be dark. If the herd is scattered and they couldn't get a good count, we'll all go out tomorrow," I suggest. "There's something else. I was waiting for Stu to come back so I could tell everyone at once, but may as well tell you guys now."

"What's that?" K.C. asks.

"I'm worried about Henry."

"Oh? Why? I know you think he sleeps too much, but I think he's just being his usual lazy self."

"Lazy, yeah, but he bit Butch."

"I'll be go to hell!" Red exclaims. "How'd that happen?"

"The story is a little fuzzy. Here's the Reader's Digest version: Kristy came up to the house to freshen up. Henry was on the porch. She heard shouts and snarls and came out to see what was going on in time to see Butch had Henry by the collar, holding him half up off the ground. She thought he was going to kick him. Maybe already had kicked him. She put herself between Butch and the dog somehow. Told him to leave the dog alone. Butch told her the dog attacked him. No warning. Bit his leg. Drew blood."

"Well, I'd bet money Butch done somethin' to deserve it," Red says. "Besides, what's he doin' comin' up to yer place anyhow?"

"Looking for me, I guess. But I'm surprised he didn't know I wasn't in. I thought he saw us ride out."

"Prob'ly did, knew Kristy was up here alone and likely he was comin' after her," Red concludes. "I don't blame Henry. He's a damn good judge of character if you ask me. And like I said, I bet Slick done somethin' to deserve gittin' bit."

"I can't believe he'd attack someone out of the blue like that. No warning even? Only other time he ever bit anyone, he was protecting you," K.C. says.

"But he knows Butch. He's not a stranger in a balaclava."

"Like I said, he done somethin' or was intendin' somethin' and Henry didn't like the look of it," Red says.

"Well, I'll have to check with Butch and see how bad it is. Kristy said she could see teeth marks and some blood, and offered him a Band-Aid. He said something like he didn't need a goddamned Band-Aid, he needed stitches." I exhale a long breath. "This, on top of getting hurt on the elevator. I hope he doesn't sue us."

Before we can discuss it further, we see the riders coming over the brow of the hill behind the windmill and go down to greet them.

When he spots us, Charlie calls out, "Don't look like there's none missin'!"

They dismount at the hitching rail beside the barn and as they're switching bridles for halters, Charlie says, "You go ahead on up, Dad. Me and Johnny'll git yer horse put away."

"No cattle missin'?" Red asks. "What was the point of tearin' out the fence, then?"

"You got me," Stu replies. He loops an arm around her and plants a kiss on her head. "Hope you got a cold beer."

We head back to my patio. Red gets a beer out of the cooler, hands it to Stu, and we all settle. I say, "About the cattle—none missing—really?"

"None missing," Stu replies, and helps himself to a handful of chips. "Horse herd's down that big ravine. Still quite a bit of grazing there. When we rode up, they headed farther down the ravine into a stand of aspen. The pond down there's got water in it again. Lots of hoofprints. and the cows ain't far from the horses, right where the boys seen 'em every day this week, nearly at the south east corner of the pasture. The cows're just waitin' fer them fall calves to show up. Pretty uneasy, though, and the bull was real touchy."

Charlie and Johnny join us. Johnny says, "Dad, you tell 'em about the kill?"

"Not yet," Stu replies.

"Kill?" I ask.

"Yeah," Stu says, and munches the chips. "Cat tracks all around it."

"Damn! Thought they killed off all the cougars around here decades ago."

"I thought I seen cougar tracks the odd time," Charlie says.

"Talk around the feed store is that they've been spotted in the Badlands. Maybe this one is just a little out of its territory," I suggest. "Didn't think they would attack anything as big as a cow, though."

"Not a cow," Stu says, "a newborn calf. Musta bin last night, 'cause the boys were out there yesterday and seen nuthin'. Momma still hanging around the carcass, and the bull run us off when we tried to git closer."

"Probably the cat is still around the kill, or if not nearby, it'll come back," I say. "We got heifers that'll be calving for the first time and might need help, plus maybe rustlers and now a cougar? I should've let you move the fall calvers into the near pasture when you wanted to. I wanted them left out longer so we wouldn't have to start feeding hay so soon, and now we've lost a calf."

"Don't beat yerself up, Lindy," Stu says, "you just done what bean counters do. We'll git 'em moved tomorrow. Meantime, what's fer supper and when can we eat? Me'n the boys're gonna take fresh horses out fer night patrol. Don't wanna lose another calf. Plus we can start pushin' the herd this way."

"Hash, and it'll be fifteen minutes," Red replies. "I'll make biscuits, if you think you can wait that long."

"Ay-yuh, you know I'll wait fer fresh biscuits."

"Okay." Red gets to her feet and hurries away down the path through the grove.

K.C. says, "We should set up shifts. One shift goes out after supper, and the second shift spells them at midnight. How about you and the boys take the first shift. Lindy and I'll take the second."

"Sounds good," Stu agrees.

K.C. says, "Okay. By the way, we need to notify Wildlife Conservation about the kill. They might want to confirm it's a cat, maybe have a look at the carcass"

"We should let the RCMP know about the fence, too," I say. "If we've got rustlers again, they need to drive around more. Be visible around here. So the assholes don't think they can come and go as they please."

"Good luck with that at the best of times, and you know that task force they're workin' is keepin' 'em so busy Dwight ain't even got time to stop in here fer coffee," Stu points out. "Besides, what're you gonna tell 'em? Rustlers tore out some of the fence but didn't take no cattle? Poor excuse fer rustlers. We git the herd moved into the home pasture tomorrow. End of problem." He swigs the rest of his beer, belches, and says to Johnny, "Grab me another one a these, would ya son?"

"End of that problem," I agree. "But there's still Butch."

"What about Butch?"

"Henry bit him."

"Oh? How'd that come about?" he asks, and takes the fresh beer Johnny hands him.

I explain, and finish the story with, "I hope he doesn't sue us."

Stu gets to his feet and says, "Well, if Kristy thought all it needed was a Band-Aid, it ain't nuthin'. I know he's a wimp, but if he went to a doctor, all they'd do would be put some iodine on it, which we coulda done here if he'd hung around. Don't worry, Lindy, he'll cowboy up. This ain't gonna be a problem." He pats my shoulder, then turns to the boys and says, "Let's go chow down, boys. We got a busy night ahead of us."

As I watch them head off along the path through the grove, I take a deep breath and ask K.C., "What do you think, sweetie?"

"Well, I think we apologize and maybe give him a couple steaks and a bottle of wine. If nothing else, Butch doesn't want to look like a wimp. Not in front of you girls."

"How's he going to explain coming up here after Kristy?"

"You don't know he was after Kristy. He could've been looking for you. Once he's had a chance to think it over, he'll realize he acted like a sissy and he won't want to remind anyone. I'll bet he's hoping Kristy doesn't tell anyone and if we ask him about it, he'll slough it off. Don't let Red's low opinion of him rub off on you, babe. He's not that bad. And like Stu said, he'll cowboy up."

"I hope you're right."

"I may not always be right, but I'm never wrong." He chuckles, then stands and says, "Come on, babe. Pretty sure my wife doesn't know how to make biscuits and I doubt there's hash, but let's grab a baloney sandwich and hit the sack for a couple hours. We got a busy night ahead, too."

I follow K.C. inside. Whenever we disagree, he always spouts that little joke about how he's never wrong as if it settles any argument. I guess it's cute. He's spent more time with Butch than anyone except Trina, and he's smart besides. But is he right about Butch? I want to believe him, but I can't quite get there.

And he called me his wife.

Chapter 13

The late calvers are in the home pasture, happily eating hay that costs money to put up instead of grass that's free. The conservation officers came and confirmed the cougar kill, and I suppose they made a report to someone, but that's all they did. I wouldn't expect them to hunt the animal anyway. It'll likely go back to where it came from now that the calves aren't so close to its range, so it doesn't need to be relocated and shouldn't be killed unless it becomes more of a nuisance. I don't want it killed, either, so I hope it stays away.

K.C. was right about one thing. Butch didn't make an appearance for days after the Henry incident, and when he did, he just went about his business as if nothing happened. I need to talk to him about the late night noise as well as the dog bite, but I've procrastinated, hoping he would initiate the conversation.

Finally I'm tired of waiting for him to say something. I go up into the loft to seek him out. He's not at the service counter so I go behind it to look down the rows of stacked boxes and crates. I'm sure he's up here, but I don't see anyone. I call out, "Hey, Butch! You here?"

After mumbled cursing, he comes out from behind the stack of crates at the far end of the loft. From the look on his face, you'd think he'd just been caught with his hand in his pants. "Hey, Lindy," he replies, picking up a clipboard off a shelf as he hurries to me.

"Everything okay?" I ask.

"Oh, you heard me swearing? I caught my thumb between two crates. It's okay though." He holds his hand up as if to show me, but it's not the thumb I see. The tip of his index finger is missing. When he realizes that's what I'm looking at, he shoves his hand in his pocket and says, "I gotta be more careful. So. What's up?"

"If you're busy, I can come back."

"Well, I am busy, because I got a stack of orders to put together. You need something?" he asks. Together we go back to the front counter, where he drops the clipboard.

"Well, not that I need something, but Kristy mentioned Henry bit you. I just wanted to make sure everything's all right."

"Oh, Kristy told you?" He picks up a pen and scribbles something on a paper. "It was nothing, really."

"But you had to get stitches?"

"Is that what Kristy said? Nawww! For a couple little scratches?"

"But she said you left in a hurry because you wanted to go to the doctor."

"Jeez, Kristy! That silly girl! Where'd she get an idea like that?" He shakes his head and clicks his tongue. "But that dog should be tied up before he bites someone else."

"No! I mean, I'm not going to tie him up. I don't know why he bit you, but he's never bitten anyone else." It's not true, of course, but fending off an intruder gives Henry a pass in my view and I'm not going to tell Butch about it.

"Well, if he bites someone again, you'll have to put him down."

"He's not a biter, Butch. He is not going to be put down."

"Your decision. But that dog is a menace. The next cowboy he bites might just shoot him before he sues you."

"I told you, Henry is not a biter." I realize my voice has risen several decibels. I don't blame Henry for biting him. I could almost bite him myself at this moment. If he doesn't notice smoke starting to come out of my ears, he's dumber than I thought. I choke back more angry comments, tell myself to stay calm and on point, and say instead, "I'm sorry he bit you. I was worried, because she said you left in a hurry and thought you needed stitches. But I see you're okay."

"Well, I still got a bruise and I'll have a scar, but I'm okay. I left in a hurry because I had a meeting and I was running late."

"So you were late for a meeting. That's why you left in such a hurry."

"Yeah, I was late for a meeting," he reiterates.

"In that case, why were you on my porch?"

"Looking for you, obviously," he says. "Why else?" No grin now. He knows his excuse is flawed, but he can't back down. He squares his shoulders, readying for conflict.

I take a breath, put on my most winning smile, and in a sugar-sweet tone say, "I was wondering that myself. You saw us ride out."

"Did I know how long you'd be gone, for chrissakes? When you weren't in the Bistro, I went up to your house. That *is* where your office is, right?"

"Of course. Okay, you wanted to see me. Why?"

"I got a couple ideas I want to run by you."

"Go ahead."

"Well, we, er, have giftware, horsey type stuff, for tack shops. That stuff would do well in your farm store, too."

Do I want giftware in the store? It actually sounds like a good idea. But if he wanted to talk to me about that a week ago, why didn't he come see me before now? Why did it only come up when I sought him out? The cliché 'don't poke the bear' comes to mind. I have to leave or I'll keep poking. So I say, "Sure. I'll take a look at what you have, sometime when you're not so busy. I'll let you get back to work now."

"Well, don't put it off. It's already late to order Christmas stuff now." He stiffens. His eyes narrow. "Oh, and something else we need to get straight. What about the fence?"

"The fence?"

"Yeah. We went to a lot of trouble to open it up, and now it's closed up again?"

"What?"

"The fence. You know what a fence is?"

I draw a sharp breath. So many responses swim through my head but before I reply, he says, "Who put the posts and the wire up again?"

I take a deep breath and say, "You mean it was you? Your guys? *You* cut our fence?"

"How'd you think we got the big truck to the back of the barn?"

"Well, I thought through the front yard like always, but you—"

"I asked you if it was okay for us to come in the back and you said it was. No way the big trucks can make the turn to get through the little gate when they're coming from the north, so the guys made a bigger opening, and now they have to tear it out again? Time is money with these guys. You should know that, what with your business degree and all."

"But... But you! You know the fence is there to keep the stock in?" Now I'm close to shouting.

"There were no cows around."

"It's a big pasture, and you don't know they wouldn't be there the next day for shit's sake!" I am shouting now. In fact it could be more of a shriek.

"Oh, isn't that just like a woman. All excited now. I knew I should've talked to K.C. about this. Take a pill. No cows got out, did they?"

Just like a woman? Take a pill? Forget biting, although I've never thrown anything in anger, it's lucky I don't have anything at hand to throw at him now. I want to tell him to keep his Christmas junk. I want to tell him the lease is forfeited and he should get all his stuff including the Christmas junk the hell out of here. But I'm about to break into angry sobs which would be *just like a woman*. I turn on my heel and leave.

I feel his eyes burning holes in my back, then hear him mutter something under his breath. There's a clattery *thump,* as if he picked up the clipboard and slammed it down again. I don't remember ever being this angry, and *he's* mad?

Halfway down the stairs I remember I didn't talk to him about Red's noise complaint. As much as I hate to admit it, he's right. K.C. will have to be the one to talk to him.

K.C. doesn't have a chance to talk to Butch until late in the afternoon. When he comes in for supper, he comes to give me a hug before he even goes to wash up. "Butch knows you were mad, and even hinted he might've said things that crossed the line, but if I thought he might apologize, I guess I don't know him very well. You and him have a personality conflict, is how he put it. He's an asshole, babe. But for the time being, he's our asshole *tenant*. I got things smoothed over."

"Oh? How?"

"Well, I said we'd make the existing gate bigger. We'll do the work but he'll have to pay for the new gate. And he's going to tell his drivers that if they're late getting here, they can come in and park at the back of the barn, but that's it. No door slamming. No yelling. And above all, no running the elevators. I said if I heard so much as a sneeze after nine o'clock I'd sic Henry on them." He laughs and releases me, heading for the bedroom.

"Oh great!" I call after him. "Now he's really going to want to shoot him!"

At the door, he turns and says, "Naw, don't worry. I told him the dog is too lazy to get off the porch most days, but you love him more than you love me so if anyone hurts Henry, I can't be responsible for what you might do. I may have mentioned you once stabbed someone for less."

"What?!?"

He laughs as he disappears inside.

Kristy and I are in our jammies eating popcorn. K.C. just left to do night check, and we're waiting for him to come back before we start the video.

"So, Fatal Attraction. Hope this isn't too scary," Kristy says as she examines the sleeve for the video.

"It's supposed to be a thriller, not a horror story," I say. "So, Kristy, I went up to the loft this afternoon and talked to Butch about Henry biting him. He claims he never said he was going to get stitches."

"I know."

"You know?"

"Yeah. I heard him. The lying bastard!"

"You heard him?"

"Yeah, I was there. Went to ask him how his leg was and things accidentally got *steamy*. Did you know he's got a cot for when he sleeps here?"

"I guess I didn't think about it."

"So, what did you think he was doing back there?"

"You mean you and Butch were—um, you know—?"

"No, we weren't *you know*," she says, and laughs. "We hadn't gotten that far."

"Oh my god!"

"Yeah. Of course it's all hush-hush. He doesn't want Trina to find out, and I'm happy to keep it that way because like I told him, I'm married, and as cute as he is, it wouldn't be worth cheating on Jim, because he has a tiny dick and he—"

"Okay, Kristy!"

"I was just going to say, he's so in love with himself I bet he's one of those *wham bam, thank you ma'am* guys."

"But you got far enough to measure his dick?"

"Well, not with a ruler, if that's what you're thinking. It's just that it reminded me of a pickle."

"A dill pickle?"

"Well, not a big one."

"A gherkin?"

"Bigger than a gherkin. But I like that word! Let's go with that." She giggles. "But yeah. Thanks for coming along when you did. When he came back from talking to you, I said it was just as well, it was a mistake, it was a close call, I had to get back and all that. He said I could meet him somewhere, we could get a good thing going, no one needs to know about it blah blah. I may have agreed to meet him some other time. 'Course that time will never come."

"And you're just now telling me about this?"

"Obviously! I couldn't talk about this in front of K.C.! Not just the tiny dick thing, but remember we talked about me getting Butch to show me what's in those crates? I didn't know if K.C. was in the loop. We decided back in Katawasis Lake that our club was women only, right? Katawasis Girls, right?"

"Katawasis Girls," I agree, and take a deep breath. "I guess we should keep K.C. out of it. He's too close to Butch."

"Okay!" Kristy giggles. "So. Those crates you were interested in? Saddles. Just saddles."

"Oh. That's good," I say, even though I feel deflated at being proven wrong.

"Yup, saddles. Black ones and brown ones. Funny thing is, I thought they'd smell nice, like a new purse or a new jacket, but they don't. Butch says it's because they're from India and they use dog shit to tan their leather, and he doesn't want to open those crates because it would stink up the whole place. Imagine! He thinks they smell worse than the stalls below."

"For the record, horse stalls don't smell bad," I say.

"Right," Kristy says. She stuffs a handful of popcorn in her mouth, chews, and after she swallows, says, "You don't look very happy. What did you expect?"

"I don't know. The guns Dwight's task force is looking for? Counterfeit money? Or real money, like for laundering? Bodies? At least drugs? I don't know." This, on top of what the clerks at Cow Town said. I tell myself I should be glad our tenant isn't hiding anything. As nice as it is to have the rent check, I almost wish he was running guns, because then we wouldn't need a better excuse than a personality conflict, which makes it sound like a failure on my part, to get rid of him.

I take a couple of deep breaths and think of what Kristy did just because her crazy friend wanted to know what was in those crates. Her talents are wasted waiting tables. "Jeez, Kristy, you're the best, you know? You're better than Charlie's Angels. I mean it."

"Hey, you know what? Katawasis Girls are like Charlie's Angels, only with Swiss Army knives instead of guns. You can be Sabrina. A blonde Sabrina. I'll be Jill," Kristy says, "I just need a blonde wig."

"Why not go by hair colour? You be Sabrina and I'll be Jill."

"Nope, I want to be Jill!" She giggles. "I said it first!"

"Okay, you can be Jill. I hope your damn wig is itchy. And why are those particular crates wood instead of cardboard? You wouldn't think a few saddles would weigh so much. Are you sure that's all that was in there?"

"Yup. Nothing else."

Just then the door opens and K.C. comes in, slamming the door shut behind him. The gust of cold air that accompanies him hits the hall thermostat and the furnace comes on with a whoosh.

"Shit, it's cold tonight!" he calls out. "Start the movie. I'm just gonna get into my sweats, grab a beer and I'll be with you before the credits are done."

I insert the cassette in the VCR, pick up the remote, and start the movie. I'm dying to ask Kristy more about the crates and make a plan to get them emptied to make sure there's nothing else in there that would add more weight, but it will have to wait until Kristy and I are alone again.

"Talk later," I say.

Chapter 14

Next morning, I'm in the Bistro getting the coffee bar organized, and Red is just getting the first batch of cinnamon buns out of the oven when the first customers of the day, four men in cotton duck overalls and jackets, come in:. A work crew.

"Good morning!" I greet them, " we're not officially open just yet so not everything's ready, but if you're here for coffee, your timing is perfect."

"Good morning," the short, older man replies. "Perfect timing is the company motto."

"Where're you guys off to this morning?"

"New chicken barn down the road. Pouring the floor today."

"Oh, you must mean Farmer Ben's. We get our eggs from them."

"You got it. So we gotta be there when the concrete truck arrives. Glad you're ready for us."

It isn't until they've got their to-go coffees and warm cinnamon buns in take-away containers and are leaving, that Kristy appears. They stop in their tracks to watch her as she passes. She smiles and says hello to each of them. Kristy in her element.

I do a double take when I see that she's wearing her new spike-heeled winter boots, dark panty hose under a short, tight skirt, and rabbit fur bomber jacket over her customary low-cut t-shirt. She's not dressed for a shift in the Bistro.

"Good morning, Lindy," she says as she comes up beside me, takes a mug and fills it.

"Good morning," I reply. "Going somewhere?"

"Yeah, I sure am!"

"Heading home?"

"Home? You mean, Calgary? Shit no! I'm going to Pillerton."

Pillerton? I'm speechless, something that doesn't happen often. I stop wiping the counter and turn to give her my full attention.

"Donny invited me for the weekend. We're going to a BTO concert in Regina tonight, then there's a party his company is putting on tomorrow night. I'll be back on Sunday."

"When did this all happen?"

"I just phoned him this morning to tell him I'd decided to accept his offer. I know what you're thinking! His company maybe done some bad things, but he wouldn't be so high up in a church if he was a criminal, would he? I didn't agree to sleep with him," she quickly assures me. "Although I might! I just haven't decided yet." She giggles again as she adds cream to her coffee. "Having coffee?"

"Um, sure," I agree, and fill a mug. She gets a cinnamon bun and we go to sit at the staff table. "So," I say, "you've been talking to Donny?"

"Yeah. I gave him your number. Hope you don't mind."

"A little late to ask me now, don't you think?"

If she notices my sour tone, it doesn't slow her down. "He called me a few times. I've been putting him off, but *Bachman Turner Overdrive?* He's got *tickets!?!* Couldn't pass that up."

"I suppose not," I say, although I don't actually agree, because I can think of multiple reasons why it's a bad idea, not the least of which is my suspicion his boss is the guy who had our herd seized not that long ago. But maybe she's right and Donny had nothing to do with it. I force a smile and suggest, "Maybe you can check out some more tack shops."

"I dunno, Lindy ..."

"Kidding," I assure her, and take a long drink of coffee before adding, "you'll be too busy. And it would be pointless anyway."

Kristy looks at her watch, then grabs a napkin to wrap the remains of her cinnamon bun and gets up. "Guess I don't have time for this after all. I better hit the road. I'm meeting him at Big Al's for lunch. I'll just take this to go. Can I get you to mark it on my sheet?"

"Sure, um, okay," I agree, although she works for nothing so I'm not about to make her pay. "So, you'll be back Sunday?"

"I will."

"Have you left a number I can reach you at in case he murders you?"

She goes to the coffee bar where she transfers her coffee from the mug into a paper cup, and laughs as she puts a plastic lid on it. "Oh, Lindy! You're so suspicious! And you know, if I was murdered, I couldn't come to the phone because I'd be dead!" Another giggle. "But yeah, you know where to find him. That Wealth Management place. And I wrote his home number on the note I left for you. See you!" And with that, she's out the door.

I go to the window to watch her cross the yard, get in her Fiero, and drive away. I don't know why she trusts someone she didn't know before spending half an hour with him at a bar. Or why she would drive two hundred miles just because he beckoned, BTO tickets or not.

Sunday. I've been expecting Kristy's return since early afternoon. K.C. has told me about a hundred times not to worry. We're at the island eating supper, and I'm just about to suggest that we go looking for her to make sure she's not in the ditch somewhere, reminding him how bad the Fiero is in snow, when we hear a vehicle drive in. When a car door slams, K.C. unnecessarily says, "That must be her now."

In a moment the door opens and Kristy comes in. "Hi, guys," she sings out as she closes the door behind her, "any of that left? I'm starving!"

"Sure," I reply. And then I can't stop myself from asking, "How come you're so late?"

"Well, we got up late." She kicks off her boots and sloughs her jacket onto the back of a stool. "Then we went for brunch at that pub, Big Al's. The food is crappy. Dunno why Donny likes it so much. He says they're getting a new cook. About time in my book. Then Donny insisted on giving me a tour of the area so he could point out all the places his company has financed, or has mortgages on. Why he's so proud of that, I have no idea. It's not like it's actually his company. I didn't get away until nearly four. He wanted me to stay another night so I could take in one of their meetings, which is tonight. So sorry I missed it! Yeah, right!" She gets a bowl and helps herself to chili and a piece of cornbread before joining us at the island. "Anyway," she continues, giving me an intense look, "after their party last night, I seen enough."

"How was the concert?" K.C. asks.

"Great! They did some of the old Guess Who songs. And when they did American Woman the place went wild 'cause of course everyone had to scream out the words and people were dancing in the aisles. And the noise! Our seats were the pits, could hardly see the stage. Donny cheaped out on the tickets. Some big shot!"

She spreads butter on her cornbread and eats a bite before continuing: "And the men! Donny's friends! The way they treat their wives! We females got shuffled off into a corner so the men could talk about important man stuff. All the women could talk about was recipes. Kids. Quilting, for chrissakes! Least it got a little interesting when they started tut-tutting about poor Alfred, whose wife ran off. The bitch! 'Course they didn't use that word. I said something like I didn't think he'd be alone for long, not with a bulge like he's got in his jeans. The gasps! I thought they might of swallowed their tongues. As if none of *them* ever noticed! Maybe Pillerton's where they got the idea for Stepford Wives. I wonder how Alfred's wife ever got the balls to dump the asshole." She takes a mouthful of chili, chews, swallows and says, "Mmm. This is so good. We should offer chili alongside the soup du jour in the Bistro. Wouldn't have to make cornbread to go with it. It would go great with that bread we already serve with the soup."

"Salt rising. Barney's recipe," I comment, more to have something to say than because it adds anything K.C. or Kristy didn't already know. If I was worried she might move to Pillerton and get religion, my fears evaporate. Plus, she said *we*, not *you*. She sees a future for herself at Wacasko-Wâti. I'll put her on the payroll tomorrow.

That look told me she has something she wants to talk about, but it'll have to wait until K.C. is elsewhere. I get up and start clearing the kitchen, humming the Charlie's Angels theme song.

It's not until Monday morning that Kristy and I have a chance for a private conversation. Well, we tried later Sunday night, but K.C. wouldn't go to bed without me. Once, she whispered, "Would you believe Butch—" just before K.C. came along and asked what the whispering was all about. And he accuses me of being a stickybeak!

Next morning, he hovered around until after Kristy went to the Bistro. If you do night feed, you don't have to do morning feed, but I had hoped he might have other things to do so he would be out earlier. No such luck. He sat there, had more coffee and read the farm equipment section of Car and Truck Trader with so much interest you'd think we could afford to lay out cash for more equipment right now. He was on his third or fourth cup when I went to my office.

I'm still at my desk when Kristy comes up from the Bistro with a couple of mugs of coffee, sets them down on my desk and pulls the kitchen chair out of the corner to sit on.

"How many hours did you put in this morning?" I ask.

"Two, I guess. Don't mark it down. I'm working for my board and keep."

"Nope! You're officially on the payroll," I insist. "Minimum wage plus tips to start. And we pay your Medicare."

"Well, that's great, Lindy! Might be temporary, though, you know."

"I know."

"I mean, not that I'm going to leave, but if it's okay with me working for you, if you're really offering me a job because you need someone, I'll have to find somewhere else to live. Can't be sponging off you forever."

"We do need you! And there's no rush for you to move out."

"Great. Thanks."

"You're welcome." I lean back and swivel my chair as I sip coffee, waiting for her to tell me what she couldn't last night, but she puts her mug down and gets up.

"Hafta pee," she says. "Be right back."

The first thing she says when she returns is, "By the way, you asked me to let you know when Trina came in?"

"Yeah?" Maybe it's underhanded to make Kristy my snitch, but I think Red is covering for Trina.

"She came in just before I came up here."

I shake my head. That girl! She's on salary, but she's late so often she rarely puts in a full day. I'm going to put her on hourly and have her punch the clock. I've been wanting to do it for a while now, but have been putting it off, dreading Red's response.

"So, Katawasis Girl/friend," Kristy says, breaking into my thoughts, "what do you think I wanted to talk to you about that I didn't want K.C. to hear?"

"Other than I think it involves Butch somehow, no clue," I admit. "I'm intrigued you mentioned Butch. I thought you meant Donny."

"Nope. I meant Butch. Remember when you and I drove from Pillerton to Regina and there's that industrial area about halfway between?"

"I do."

"Well, Donny's bragging tour took us through there. Mostly empty warehouses, and nice ones, too. I was thinking, all this warehouse space so close to where Butch's company is located? Why would he rent space at Wacasko-Wâti? And guess what? They do have a warehouse there."

"Wow! Really?"

"Yeah, the sign on the building says Johnston Distributing, and that drew my attention because isn't that who brings our take-out boxes and cups and stuff?"

"Yeah."

"But in the warehouse right next door, I mean, at the loading dock, there was one of those panel vans like the ones that always come here. The one with the logo about some electrical supply, which of course we know it's nothing electrical they're bringing here. And the driver, I um, I think I recognized him. I think he's been here, like working for Butch.

"He's been here?"

"Yeah. Good looking guy. You've noticed him, too."

"They're kind of a tough looking bunch, but I think I know who you're talking about."

"You think? For chrissakes, Lindy, just admit it. There's that one really good looking guy. The one with no beard. I seen you gawking at him. You wouldn't kick him out of bed for eating crackers any more than I would."

"Well, in other times I suppose."

"I wish he'd hang around more. Seems like his crew just shows up, unloads, and leaves right away. You'd think they could come in for a coffee break so we could get to know them."

"Tell me you're not really thinking of hooking up with another bad boy?"

Kristy's reply is a shrug and a giggle.

Obviously she'd be open to it. I just hope it doesn't come to that! Seems she has enough other irons in the fire with Donny and Butch, not to mention her husband. Nothing I can do about it. Best change the direction of this conversation. "So, anyway," I say, "maybe that's their warehouse. No sign on the building, though?"

"Nope. But the really surprising thing was, if you leave that industrial park out the back, like heading east instead of back onto the main highway, there's a junk yard. Well, I guess you'd call it auto wreckers. Bunch of motorcycles in front of the shack. And guess who came out the door just as we were driving by?"

"Dammit, Kristy!"

"Butch! Butch came out the front door."

"Butch?"

"Butch! In the flesh. And right behind him, a woman. They went to one of the motorcycles, which must of been his, although I never seen him with one, have you?"

"No."

"Anyhow, before he climbed on, they had a nice smoochy grab ass. And then she went back inside."

"Oh my god," I gasp.

"Don't think Butch saw me."

"Unless he kisses everyone like that, she was more than a friend. No innocent explanation for that. Poor Trina."

"You're not surprised, though, are you? Not after me and him—"

"No. And I wouldn't be surprised if he has, er, something going on with other girls. He could easily start something with either of those girls we met at Cow Town. And one of them did say something about him having a motorcycle. I wonder why he's never ridden it here."

"Too far? Maybe doesn't like driving it on gravel roads? Whatever. Doesn't mean he's hiding anything," Kristy opines. "But obviously we can't just come right out and ask him about it. We don't care if he does, do we?"

"I guess not."

"I was wondering if he's got a girl at every tack shop."

"Could be. A reminder to steer clear? I mean, you steer clear, because he doesn't like me so I'm not in any danger," I say.

"And you're happy about that!" She looks dead serious. "I wonder if I should meet him somewhere else like he suggested."

"Why on earth would you do that?"

"A few reasons. First, he's a dirty dog and Trina is blind to it. That might be the only way she'd break up with him. She'd hate me."

"She might, but Red would be happy."

"So that's good."

"Yeah. So. What's the other thing?"

"Well—and this is the big thing—you know those crates you were so curious about?"

"Yeah?"

"I've been wondering. Why do those saddles smell so bad? I mean, dog shit? Really? Even if that's true, they don't smell like dog shit. They smell a little like leather, but more a sort of oily smell. And they're so heavy two guys can barely lift them? Why? There's only three or four saddles in there. It's not like they were packed solid right to the top. And why in wooden crates? Everything else up there is in cardboard boxes."

"That's what made me wonder about them."

"Plus, if they have another warehouse, this one out here in the boonies makes even less sense. So. Remember when I asked you what you thought would be in the crates? And you tossed out what seemed like a stupid idea, that it could be guns?"

"I didn't think it was a stupid idea—"

"I know you didn't, but I did. But now I'm wondering, what if it's not so stupid? What if they're using this place *because* it's off the beaten track? If you think about it, it makes it perfect for stuff they don't want anyone to know about. Guns have a chemical smell. Especially when they're new."

"You know what guns smell like?"

"Kyle had a gun, remember? Only one when you met him, but when we first got together, he had a few. He was ex-military and he liked them. I spent many a Saturday at gun shops with him."

"Oh yeah. I forgot that about him." A mental image of her second husband, the one she was with when I first met her in Katawasis Lake, pops into my head. Kyle, the handsome hardbody who attacked me and is responsible for Henry's limp, now in jail for murder. I shiver at the memory.

"Anyways," Kristy continues, breaking into my thoughts, "Donny had a rifle he just got, and he was so proud of it he hadda get it out to show to me."

"What does he need a rifle for?"

"Oh, I don't know. To compensate for his tiny dick?"

"Tiny dick? Not another one?"

"I don't actually know, I'm just guessing. I told you I hadn't made up my mind about sleeping with him."

"And you decided not to?"

"Don't look at me like that! It happens, you know. After the shitty seats at the concert and expecting me to stay in a crappy room in the back of the Prairie Equity whatzit office that doesn't even have a shower, on top of crappy food at Big Al's, and treating me shitty like his buddies treat their wives? He didn't really think he'd get laid, did he? If he did, he's an idiot."

I shrug and shake my head. "So, if he ups his game, you'll see him again?"

"No. I think I seen as much of Pillerton as I can stand."

"Like you said. So, about the gun?"

"Oh, yeah. He got me to hold it like as if I was gonna shoot something. I think it was so he'd have an excuse to dry hump my ass because he didn't want me to actually shoot it. He said he hasn't tried it himself yet, and anyway, it's way too much for a girl, shoots real fast and he hadn't even cleaned it yet. But the smell! I realized I'd smelled it before. Kyle called it Cosmoline. They use it so the guns don't rust."

"Oh my god."

"And that rifle that shoots fast? He called it an AR something. According to him, it's a legal hunting rifle, but modified to be fully automatic, and he has a special magazine for it. He made me promise not to tell anyone about any of it. 'Course I promised. But I asked myself, why not?"

"I think maybe being modified so it's fully automatic makes it illegal," I suggest.

"That's what I figured, too. So I put on my best I-know-nuthin' I'm-a-dummy act. I bet it's guns like that they're hiding in the saddle crates. I think we should call your friend Dwight and tell him the guns he's looking for are right up there in your loft, just like you figured."

I think about it for a minute, then press my lips together and shake my head. "As much as I love the idea, Kristy, we can't go and tell him we know they're in there because you smelled them."

She draws a deep breath, exhales slowly, and with a shrug, says, "I guess not."

"No. He couldn't possibly move on info like that. He'd be nice about it but he'd explain no judge in the world would give him a search warrant because a couple of women smelled guns in a barn, even if they were Charlie's Angels and not just Katawasis Girls."

"You're right. We need to get a better look," she concludes. "Can you tell by looking at them if they've been, um, made illegal?"

"I don't know if anyone can, but for sure I can't. Maybe we just need to connect Donny to Butch and go at it that way."

"How do we do that?"

"I don't know. When you saw Butch, Donny didn't react? Like as if he knew him? Peep the horn or anything?"

"No."

I draw a breath and sigh. "Well, if they don't know each other, then I guess we have to find out how Donny came by an illegal rifle. I don't know how we do that. Donny or Butch, one or the other might tell you, but I'm pretty sure Dwight would want something more solid than just pillow talk. We'll have to think on it."

"Yeah." She looks past me and out the window. "Oh! Speak of the devil, there's Dwight!"

I swivel my chair to look out and see his cruiser pull up to the Bistro.

"We won't say anything about guns, right, Kristy?"

"Right." She's already on her feet and heading out the door. I grab a jacket and follow.

When we're all settled around a table, Stu says, "So! You got news, buddy? Something on Lindy's earrings, maybe?"

"I got news," Dwight replies. "I can only stay long enough to grab a quick bun and a coffee, but wanted to let you know two of the bodies have been identified."

"Really!?! Two?" Stu says.

"Yeah," Dwight confirms. "Surprising, isn't it? Didn't think we had a chance of identifying any of them."

"So, who were they and were they from around here?" I ask.

Dwight takes an extra long time stirring his coffee, gives me an odd look, then says, "Well, kind of. The male is from Swift Current. Went missing in 1971. It was a big deal at the time, him being on city council. Also a prominent realtor. Turns out he was a member of the not-church group that used to meet here."

"Really? So, the not-church guys suddenly began cooperating?"

"No, not at all. Thought they might after Major Crime paid them a visit, but all that happened was that they got their lawyer involved. That's enough to pique everyone's interest, so they're looking at them harder now. But the guy in the dirt? The dentist's name is on the missing persons report and what do you know? The guy still had records. So it's a positive ID The wife remarried but we tracked her down. She and her husband back then both attended meetings here, and he was pretty high up in the hierarchy. An Elder. Then they ran into some sort of disagreement, and he quit just before he disappeared. Members looked at the not-church back then, of course, but ran out all the leads and with no body, they figured the guy just split. There were rumors about a girlfriend and funds missing from the realty business. The case went cold. Anyhow, the current thinking is that he was murdered here. Probably hung. Have you noticed any rafters up in the loft there that have nooses on them?" He barks a laugh; it sounds forced and no one laughs with him. He puts a good chunk of bun in his mouth and washes it down with a long drink of coffee before continuing, "That explains why he was buried so far from the other two bodies—his murderers didn't know the correct burial location! Ha!"

"Oh, jeez," Red says, "ain't you just full of jokes today."

"By the way, would you believe cutting off that finger is part of becoming an Elder? What a fucked up not-church! Pardon my French," he says, and gives Red a grin and a wink. I guess he thinks Red has never heard the word before but Kristy and I have. Then he looks at me and seems perplexed for a second before adding, "Sorry, Lindy."

I've been told many times I should never play poker because my face always gives me away. I don't think that's true because I'm a pretty good liar, but Dwight saw something and concluded I was shocked or offended by his swearing. In fact, if I looked shocked, it's because I'm remembering my ex Jake and his missing finger, and his friends with their missing fingers. I know they were in a religious cult that was behind trying to steal Wacasko-Wâti as well as rustling and murder. And I wonder if Butch really amputated his finger on the hay elevator. Should I tell Dwight? But I have no evidence.

He's still studying me for a moment before shifting uneasily in his chair and getting up to refill his mug. When he sits back down, he makes eye contact with me and says, "There's more, Lindy. Sorry to say, those earrings are a match to the pendant. It looks like the small female was your grandmother."

Chapter 15

I haven't accepted as fact that it's my grandmother's bones that were under my feet all this time, but I've gone along with making arrangements for burial in the St. John's churchyard. Turns out old Mr. Barth is the guy who looks after it. When we met with him this time, instead of giving us the bum's rush, he couldn't have been nicer. Maybe it helped that we were paying for an interment service and offered a donation to the maintenance fund when he complained no one cares about the graveyard anymore, and the church doesn't have funds for proper upkeep. We secured a plot, and he will arrange for the grave to be dug once the remains are released. He may even come up with some graveside mourners.

It'll be interesting to see what the pastor and the other good folks of Maple Creek think of what will be Red's contribution. Stu tried to convince her that since Mabel wasn't Cree, maybe she didn't warrant a Cree ceremony. Or at most, we should have our own private ceremony, and have the generic Lutheran graveside service. Maybe the Round Dance should take place where she rested all these years? Red agreed the Round Dance didn't have to happen, but she won't be talked out of the graveside singing and praying. She's insistent on Trina and other members of her family joining us. She's going to place sweet grass and the pendant in the coffin. I would like to have the pendant, but when I suggested she could be buried with the brooch instead, she gave me a hard look and in a sharp tone, told me she was wearing it when she died and it should stay with her. I didn't suggest it again.

Apparently we are to have three days of feasting and praying when we have the bones. Everyone seems sold on the feasting, if nothing else. I'm not sold on any of it, but try to accept it in the spirit it's intended, which is to help me accept the fact it's her, and to help everyone heal. Closure, as everyone says nowadays. I don't know who needs closure, since none of us ever met her and I'm the only person who even gave her a thought all this time, but Red has planted her feet, and we all know better than to argue. I guess it's nice she's doing this for me.

The question is, and this is the argument I face every time I say they might not be my grandmother's remains: if not hers, then whose? Who else would have her pendant? I don't have an answer so I've quit voicing my doubts.

I push the whole funeral thing out of my mind by focusing my thoughts on the guns. I've got to sneak into the loft and check out those crates. I don't want to involve Kristy in case things go sideways, but she refuses to be left out. I figure we can be in and out in under ten minutes. Of course nothing can happen until Stu and K.C. can be depended on to be away for a few hours and we need Butch and his guys to be elsewhere as well.

The opportunity arrives on Saturday. K.C. and Stu left early, headed to an auction in Lethbridge. It's not unusual for the two of them to go together. Today there are quite a few Thoroughbreds going through, and K.C. has been talking about getting me a barrel horse, so he's not going to miss this. Result? Lethbridge is easily four hours of travel time each way, so they'll be gone for a full day. I'm glad they're going, but I'm a little worried about road conditions. The sky is solidly overcast and dark. There may be more snow on the way, but when I mention that, both men brush off my concerns.

Butch is seldom around on weekends, and this time, Trina is going with him. She's been bragging about how he's taking her to meet his family ad nauseum. I wished she'd shut up about it. That is, until we learned K.C. and Stu would also be away. Then we needed to be doubly sure Butch wouldn't be around. Kristy asked him to meet her at the Best Western in Swift Current. He said he would reschedule something to make it happen, meaning he would ditch Trina. No surprise there! Kristy nixed that idea, but had to agree to meet him at some future date. Something will come up to make that impossible, of course.

Butch and Trina should've left last night, but Butch got into the Friday night poker game down in the tack room with K.C., Stu and Russ and a couple of guys from Farmer Ben's. It went late, so he slept over. They finally left half an hour ago. If he'd procrastinated any longer I may have had to sic the dogs on Trina just to stop her grumbling.

With Trina gone, Kristy is needed in the Bistro, but she's still entitled to a half hour lunch break. That's more than enough for what we plan. She went up to the house, then out the back and around the equipment shed so no one in the Bistro could see her crossing the yard. Red is busy in the kitchen and the boys have gone out with the horses, so she can't send one of them to fetch me. We're good to go.

Now Kristy and I are at the door leading to the loft steps. She has a cat's paw as well as the bigger pry bar. I have the hammer and my key, but we're stymied. My key is for the lock in the doorknob, not for the padlock that wasn't on the door the last time I noticed. I flick the padlock and hiss, "When did he put this here? And why?"

"I have no idea when, but why is because he's got something he really wants to hide and he knows you have a key for the other lock."

I give her a look and shake my head. She often states the obvious, but then, I did ask.

Kristy asks, "Is there another way in?"

"Yeah, there's a big door on the back of the loft just like the one on the front but you'd have to climb up the wall like a lizard to get to it." I blow out a long breath. In case she's considering it, I add, "So that's a no."

"What do we do now? Wait until he goes away and forgets to lock it?"

"No. We might never get another chance. I'll have to go get my lock pick tools and see if I can unlock it." I hand her the hammer and trot up to the house, dig the tools out of the junk drawer and return to the barn.

"Remember when Jim gave me this?" I hold out the little leather case. "I haven't tried picking any locks since Katawasis and I was never very good at it. Jim could probably unlock this sucker with a paperclip in a couple of seconds, but I'm not sure I'll be able to do it at all."

She stands beside me to watch. I open the case, take out a couple of tools and hand the case to her, then grip the padlock, insert the tension wrench, and slide the rake in. I feel a couple of pins move, but not enough to release the lock. I give up on the rake and give it to Kristy.

"Hand me the one that looks like a crochet hook, please."

"Which one? There's a few that look like hooks." She holds the case open so I can see for myself.

I choose one. More jiggling and more frustration. "Might not get this unlocked before K.C. and Stu are back," I grumble. I check my watch. I've already been at this for more than five minutes. "Our ten minute plan is not going to be do-able."

"If ever there was a time for Jim to show up." Kristy giggles.

"Is he? Going to show up, I mean?"

"Yeah. Sometime. Not sure when."

"At least you're talking."

"We'll see where that goes."

I replace the hook and try the rake again. Conjuring Jim does the trick. With a click, the lock releases. "Eureka!" I pull the padlock off, release the hasp and open the door. I hang the lock back on the hasp and in we go, closing the door behind us.

It's such a gray day there's only dim daylight from the window on the first landing, and farther in it's too dark to see much other than vague shadows. I'm tempted to turn on the lights, but since no one is supposed to be here, that's not a good idea. Not that there's anyone around to notice or care, but better plans than ours have been foiled by small details.

"It's so frickin' dark," Kristy observes. "How are you going to be able to see well enough to pry—"

"I'm not," I reply. "There's no one out back to notice if I open the big door a crack. Just enough to give us a little more light."

We proceed cautiously. Once we reach the counter, we go behind it to the nearest bank of shelving and follow that. The wooden crates are stacked two high at the end. I go past the last crate and bump into Butch's cot before finding the door. There's a chain and padlock on it. "Look at this. More beefed up security. He's been a busy guy," I say.

"Definitely hiding something," Kristy says.

"I'd say so. Damn! Why didn't I bring a flashlight?"

"Do you have one?"

"Yeah, of course. Up at the house. It would be faster to go get that than for me to fool around trying to pick this damn thing." I make my way back to where Kristy stands next to the crates.

"I can see better now," she says.

"Me, too. But not well enough to see what's in the crate once I pry a couple boards off. How about you go get the flashlight while I start working the pry bar in? If there's guns in here, they'll be under the saddles. Maybe under a false bottom. Don't need to pull more than two or three boards to get a look."

"Yeah, they'd be at the bottom, because I couldn't see nothing looking in the top," Kristy agrees. "So, where's your flashlight?"

"In the laundry room, on the shelf above the sink."

"Okay. Be right back," she says, hands me what she's holding and heads back toward the stairs.

I put the lock pick set in my pocket and lay the bigger bar on the floor, but I've barely started trying to work the cat's paw behind the board when Kristy hisses, *"Lindy! He's back!"*

"What!?!" I hurry back toward the stairwell. Kristy is at the window on the landing; I trot down the steps to stand beside her to look out. Trina is almost at the door to Red's trailer and Butch's truck is heading our way.

"Oh *shit*," I moan.

Kristy says, "I'll take care of this!" She scurries down the steps from the landing with me on her tail, but when she opens the door and steps out, she closes it quietly behind her, leaving me on the wrong side of the door.

"Oh, baby, you came back!" Kristy sings out. "Change your mind about going away with me?"

If she hadn't shut the door on me, the two of us would've been standing in the open doorway when Butch came into the alleyway. As it is, if Butch notices that unlocked hasp, he'll think either someone broke in and come blasting in to find out who, or he'll assume he forgot to lock it, in which case he will correct his mistake and I'll be locked in. Unless Kristy can lead him away somehow, I'm in the soup. I press close to the door to hear as much as possible.

"I forgot something," he says. "Something important. Mmmm. You."

They're quiet for a minute or more and then there's a sort of thump as the door I have my ear against jiggles. I think she must have backed up to it, or he pushed her back against it. I can only imagine what they're doing from the murmuring and smacking slobbery-kissing sounds.

"Hey, baby," Kristy says, and giggles. "Slow down."

"Let's go up," Butch says. "I'm ready."

"So I see. I am too. But we don't need to go up there, baby. K.C.'s gone and Lindy's gonna be away for a while. We have the house to ourselves. If we hurry, we can shower together after. Or even better, before *and* after!" She's speaking loudly enough for me to hear, which of course means anyone near-by could also hear.

I hear a shushing sound—Butch warning her to be quiet. She laughs about ten times louder than her usual giggle. Then her tone changes. "Something wrong?"

"Hey, what are you doing in here, anyway?" he asks.

I suppress a groan. This is a bad time for him to suddenly start thinking with his big head. I'm not sure what Kristy does to remind him of his little head, but she reverts to her sugary tone and replies, "Looking for you, of course."

"But you knew I was gone. My truck—"

"Sure, I know you left, but I thought you came back. I seen a red truck go by on the road and sometimes you come in the back gate and park behind the barn, so I came out to check. Why are we even talking about this? Are you coming with me or not?"

No answer. I hold my breath. Finally he says, "You, er, you go first. I'll wait until the coast is clear, and follow."

"Oh yeah, we don't want anyone to see us. I know that," Kristy says. "Don't worry. We'll go around behind the equipment shed. I'm ready too, baby! You can't get me all hot and bothered and then make me wait! I want you now. Come with me or I'll use the massage shower and you can go deal with *this* yourself."

I'm pretty sure I know what, exactly, she did with *this* when he utters a series of groaning *oh gods*. Then it's all quiet outside the door. Safe to exhale. I tiptoe back up to the landing and peer out the window in time to see them disappear around the corner of the shed, then make my escape, closing the door and replacing the lock on the hasp.

I start to go up to the house, then realize there's something better than simply interrupting them. This is an opportunity. To think that when we were talking about putting a phone in the tack room, I grumbled about the extra cost!

I call Red's house. Trina answers.

"Trina? I want to talk to you about your hours," I tell her. "Come to my office, please."

Trina discovering the love of her life in flagrante delicto with Kristy doesn't have the effect I thought it would. Of course they hadn't actually gotten around to doing much. It would've had more punch if they were in bed, but then I would owe Kristy big time.

"He didn't do nothing," Trina wails. "It was all *her*! He came here to talk to Lindy and Lindy wasn't here so she grabbed him and started taking his clothes off! She's been after him since day one! Sticking her boobs in his face! She even went up to the loft and tried to seduce him! Yeah, he told me about that, too!" She turns her tear-streaked face to give Kristy and me a murderous glare. "*She* made him do it!"

"That's a lie," Kristy says. "He's lying to you. You don't think I could get his pants off without his help, do you?"

"Everything was fine until you showed up and then right away you try to take my b-b-boyfriend," Trina sobs.

Red glares across the table at me as if she believes Trina. I have to admit her wronged girlfriend act is impressive, but is Red falling for it? Since she's never liked Butch, this is surprising. Is she wondering if I called Trina to my office to make sure she discovered Kristy and Butch together? But if she's figured that out, I would have thought she'd be thanking me.

"Why did you want to see Trina, Lindy?" Red asks. She's looking at me through narrowed eyes, so it's safe to assume she suspects I'm involved.

"She said she wanted to talk to me about my hours," Trina squawks.

"What about her hours?" Red demands.

I turn to Kristy and say, "Would you mind stepping out for a few minutes?"

"Not at all," she replies. "They'll be needing me in the Bistro, anyhow. I'll see you down there."

Once the door is closed behind her, I say, "Red, I've been meaning to talk to you about this for a while now. Trina is going to have to start punching the clock. From now on she'll be on an hourly rate, minimum wage and six months' probation like everyone else."

"What? Why?" Trina demands. "I'm not everyone else! You and Mom don't punch in and I bet you don't work for minimum wage."

I could tell her that being the owner/boss means we're the last ones getting paid, so minimum wage for the hours we put in looks pretty appealing. Instead, I say, "Being on salary, you have to log forty hours a week. That would be eight to five with a half hour for lunch and two fifteen-minute coffee breaks, five days a week. Or split shifts adding up to forty hours. Which you never do, without even factoring in all your smoke breaks."

"You don't run the Bistro, I do, Lindy," Red reminds me.

"Come on, Red," I coax. I don't want to remind her that while she runs the Bistro, I sign the checks. "You know I'm right."

Before Red can reply, Trina says, "If you think I'm working for minimum wage, you're dreaming. I'll go with Butch and get a job in Regina."

An awkward silence falls over my kitchen. I don't know how Red has taken this because her frown is replaced with a neutral expression. This might be a good time for me to mention the woman Kristy saw Butch with, but Trina wouldn't believe me anyway. I'm a small enough person to think she deserves to learn the hard way. Besides, I wouldn't want to say anything that might change her mind about leaving. So I keep my mouth shut.

"I mean it," Trina adds.

"Okay then, Trina," Red says, "but yer welcome to come and visit whenever you want."

"Mom!"

"I see Butch's truck is still down at the barn. It ain't too late fer you to go with him today," Red says. "Let Lindy know where to send your last check."

Trina bursts into angry sobs, jumps to her feet and races out the door, slamming it behind her, leaving Red and me looking at each other. After a moment, she says, "I know yer right, Lindy. Somehow she got the idea she was entitled. This needed doin'. I'm sorry I didn't take care of it myself."

"Oh. Well. I'm sorry if it's ruined, you know, your relationship with Trina."

"She'll come around. Or if she doesn't, at least I got to know her. I wonder what she'd be like ..." Red sighs without completing her thought, gets up and takes her mug to the dishwasher, then heads to the door. "Kids today! They sure don't know how to work. She just damn well better come back for Myrtle's funeral, is all I can say." The door closes behind her.

I'm still unsure why it's so important to Red that Trina attend the funeral. Maybe there has to be a reasonable turnout for the spirit to be laid to rest? If my grandmother had been Cree, the whole tribe would show up. We white people just aren't that spiritual, I guess. I know I'm not. I really don't care if there are gravesite mourners or not. She's my grandmother and no one else is related to her, so if I'm there that's all that matters, in my view.

I'll do up Trina's severance check so she can take it with her. I go to my desk and issue the check, adding in the vacation pay she has coming and a little bonus that she doesn't have coming. Even if she notices the note explaining the bonus on the stub, I doubt she'll thank me.

Trina's pay envelope in hand, I go to wait outside the Bistro near Butch's truck so I can intercept her. In a few minutes she comes out of Red's trailer with a duffle bag in each hand, and heads my way.

"Here's your check," I tell her, and hold out the envelope. "Let us have your new address so I'll know where to send your income tax T4."

She tosses the duffle bags in the truck, then snatches the pay envelope out of my hand and snaps, "Give it to Butch." She gets in the passenger seat to wait for the man in question without another glance my way.

Kristy comes out of the Bistro with a coffee mug in each hand, and gives one to me.

"So, Katawasis Girl," I say, "nice work, if I didn't mention it before."

"Thanks. You could've sent her a little earlier, though."

"Don't blame me. She does nothing in a hurry."

"Don't I know it!"

"So. About the massaging shower head—"

"You really want the details? That's not like you."

"No, you're right. But next time you're in the shower for twenty minutes, keep in mind I know what you're doing."

Kristy giggles and says, "You ought to try it."

"Maybe next time K.C.'s away."

Butch's truck rumbles to life. We watch as the shiny red Silverado crosses the yard and stops at the road. Trina and Butch are facing each other and Butch is punctuating whatever he's saying by jabbing his finger at her face. Then they drive off.

"You see that?" Kristy asks. "Not even out of the yard before they have a fight."

"Didn't look like he was sucking up."

"Nope."

"He'll find a way to make her believe it's her fault."

"Yeah, no doubt he'll convince her he struggled real hard and although he outweighs me by a good fifty pounds, he couldn't stop me from getting his pants off." Kristy clicks her tongue and shakes her head. "If she thinks he'll change, she's in for a rude surprise! I wonder how he's going to explain Trina to that other woman."

"And I wonder if he'll think that pry bar I left up there by that crate is his."

K.C. and Stu don't get home until late, bringing with them four Thoroughbreds. "We gotta go back again tomorrow to get the other six," K.C. tells us.

"Six more? You bought ten horses?" I draw a sharp breath. A stream of recriminations floods my brain. I bite my lower lip to lock them in. I was hoping we'd be cutting our rescue numbers down, and instead, well, this.

Despite the fact it's full dark and very cold, we're at the corral, watching the four new horses come out of the trailer. Stu says, "Ay-yuh. I'll follow him with the two-horse tomorrow. Seems like a bunch of folks ain't got much hay this year and have to dump good horses. Them we're lookin' at have Jockey Club papers and even some race wins in their history. Mostly sound or will be, nuthin' with anything horrible going on that we could see. Most we got fer meat price."

"Great. You know the purchase price of any horse is the cheapest part of owning one. So we feed 'em all winter and then what? Hire a couple more wranglers to get them saleable?"

"Me and Johnny can do it," Charlie says. The two of them already argued over who gets the tall black horse. "We worked with off-the-track horses before, remember?"

"Don't worry, babe," K.C. says. "We got the four of us. That's plenty. And they'll go on to have a life."

"They've been rode and handled lots so it ain't like they ain't broke," Stu assures us. He loops an arm around Red and says, "I'm hungry enough to eat a horse. I know it's late, but any chance you could rustle up some bacon and eggs fer yer man, darlin'?"

"You keep dragging more hungry mouths to feed back here, and you may have to eat a horse." Red sighs. "Come on, you big galoot. I'll fix somethin' fer you."

K.C. turns to the boys and says, "Okay, fellas, how be you take care of night chores while us old farts get into our jammies."

The boys agree. Us old farts head up to our respective houses. Kristy is in the living room watching TV but joins us in the kitchen. I start frying bacon and eggs while she stands by the toaster to make sure it pops up before it starts the toast on fire.

"You guys need a better toaster," she says. "Between the two of you, this was the best one you had?"

"I know," I reply. "Isn't that always the way?" We exchange a look that says, do we tell K.C. about the Butch/Trina/Kristy debacle now or later? Do we have to tell him at all? But of course we do, both because Trina won't be around and because Butch might, just might, say something to him. So when he's seated at the island with a full plate of bacon, eggs, toast and beans in front of him, I take the stool next to him, and Kristy sits on the stool on the opposite side.

"So, K.C.," I begin, "we have something to tell you."

Between the two of us, we tell him what we did. He's astonished enough to stop eating a couple of times.

He shakes his head but says nothing until he's finished his meal to the point of buttering a slice of bread and using it to mop his plate. Then he looks at me and says, "It just isn't safe for me to go away for a day. Lindy, how many times have we talked about—"

"I know! I promised not to stick my beak in. But this wasn't a full beak stick. It was just reconnaissance."

"Pfffttt! Reconnaissance? And yet somehow, Trina's gone?"

"That's a good thing," I assure him. "Even Red thinks so."

"Okay. If Red thinks so, I guess I'm okay with it. Regardless of the very sketchy circumstances." He puts his knife and fork on his plate and pushes it away. "I can't wait to hear Butch's take on it. When's he back?"

"Don't know. He doesn't keep me posted on his comings and goings. Besides, he won't tell you everything. He doesn't know why Kristy rushed him off, after all. If he mentions it at all, he'll make a joke out of it. And Kristy—"

"You think he'll know I set him up? And be mad at me?" Kristy asks.

"He's not going to hurt you, if that's what you're worried about. You don't seriously care if he's mad at you, are you?" I reply. "He'll more likely want to pick up where you left off."

"Gaaahhh!" Kristy gasps. "That's bad enough. Twice we been interrupted. What if I'm not that lucky next time?"

K.C. looks perplexed, and asks, "I know you'll think this is a stupid question, but what's wrong with him?"

Kristy and I exchange a look, then she replies, "He's creepy, that's all. For one, he speaks to me as if I'm a dummy. Then there's the creepy looks. The accidentally brushing my ass when he passes."

I say, "You're a man, you wouldn't get it. He's so full of himself he must think he's god's gift to woman."

"He's a ladies' man, I'll grant you that," K.C. says in a tone that leaves no doubt it isn't a compliment.

I add, "He might be on his best behavior for a while. So we'll have time to think of something to make him back off."

"That's all fine and good," K.C. says, "as long as he doesn't know what you two were up to."

"How would he know?"

"What's he going to think when he finds that pry bar, Lindy?"

"I, er, um...well, he'd never think Kristy somehow cheated his padlock and left it there."

"No, but he might just think he forgot to set the padlock, remember you have a key for the other lock, wonder what Kristy was doing and where you were. And suspect she was in such a big hurry to get him out of the barn before he went up to his office because you were up there snooping around."

"No one's that smart," I opine.

"Does Kristy ever go into the barn without you?"

Kristy and I say no in concert.

"And you've both been so interested in those crates. Now a pry bar shows up right beside them? So it's not a big leap. If he's got something to hide, he'll be more suspicious than someone who doesn't. And he put that extra lock on the door for a reason." He drums his fingers on the counter, then says, "Tell you what. Next time he's here, I'll go up with him. If he sees it and thinks it's his, no problem. But if he wonders about it, I'll say something like, oh that's where I left that thing. And I'll ask to see the saddles in that crate."

"Why would he show you and not me?"

"He popped the top up and let Kristy have a look, right?"

"Well, that's another story."

"The conversation you had with him that day didn't go so well either, as I recall."

"So it's just me he has issues with?"

"Maybe," K.C. allows. "It's like he said, the two of you have a personality conflict. He'd probably like you fine if you weren't so, um, *unaffected* by his charms. Don't get me wrong. I'm glad about that. But maybe you don't have to make it so obvious."

"Charms my ass! Kristy doesn't like him either, remember?"

"Well, he hasn't quite figured that out."

"Are you going to tell him Kristy smelled guns?"

"Hell, no!" He grins and chuckles. "Remember I told you if you got a barrel horse, your saddle likely wouldn't fit it? Well, we got Thoroughbreds now. Their withers are too high and narrow for our saddles. We need at least a couple new ones."

"But if there's guns in there, they'll be under a false bottom. You won't be able to see them just looking in from the top."

"We'll haul everything out."

"Er, so, you're not mad at me?"

"Lindy, with you it's always damn the torpedoes, full steam ahead. You'll never change. You know I can't stay mad at you." He gets up and comes to stand behind me, places his hands on my shoulders and plants a kiss on the top of my head. "Most of the time, I love that about you. I just hope you and Kristy together again doesn't mean you get into twice as much trouble."

"No more than Russ is a bad influence on you guys. The poker games are always his idea, right? And he fleeces everyone every time, right?"

"Well, as a rule, Stu leaves before Russ can clean him out. But otherwise, that's pretty much true," K.C. says, and sighs. "I just need to be more like Stu and do like Kenny Rogers says and learn when to fold 'em and walk away while I still got lunch money and my dignity. But him getting me into a poker game doesn't put me in physical danger. If you're right about the guns, you don't want to piss those people off. They're dangerous."

"We know," I assure him.

"Well, knowing you, even knowing they might be killers isn't enough to get you to back off. You can't blame me for being worried, can you?"

"I, um, no. You're sweet to worry."

"Sweet? I worry and your first thought is that it's sweet? Jeez, Lindy." He gives my shoulders a squeeze, then says, "I'm going to have a nice hot shower to get the chill out of my bones and get to bed. Got another early morning and long day tomorrow. Don't stay up too late." He heads down the hall. In minutes, we hear the bathroom door close and water running.

"Wow," Kristy says, "he's going to help us."

"Yeah. He helped me in Katawasis, too. He grumbles, but I think he likes sleuthing as much as I do. Once he gets into it, anyway."

"He doesn't know about Katawasis Girls, though, does he?"

"No. And maybe it's better if we keep it that way. You know. So he doesn't worry."

Chapter 16

K.C. arranged for Butch to show him the Indian saddles, so we're on our way up to the loft at the appointed time. I didn't want to go, and K.C. knows it. He thinks I avoid Butch because of his I'm-The-Greatest attitude and perpetual smirk, both correct. On top of that and what I can't tell him is that every time I look at him I get a mental image of a gherkin in his pants. But he insisted, claiming Butch would think it odd if I wasn't there since the saddle is for me. I told K.C. I'd rather wait until I can afford a saddle that doesn't stink.

"Okay, then," K.C. said, "we'll just tell him one is for a woman. If you don't come with me, I'll have to take Red or Kristy. You know Red would flat out refuse. Kristy, well, let's just say, you're it. You're the one with the suspicions. You can't jam out! What kind of a spy would even think of jamming out?"

So, he shamed me into it and here we are. K.C. has one end of the saddle stand and I have the other. When we emerge at the top of the stairs and put the stand down, K.C. calls out, "Hey, Butch! We're here!"

Butch comes out from behind the shelves, prybar in hand. I have a moment of panic when I think he's going to demand to know how that bar got here, but apparently he doesn't realize it's not his. "Hey, I opened the crate. Come on back."

We follow him to where the crate stands open. It's on top of another crate, so all we can do is peer in over the edge.

"Butch, we gotta take the saddles out so Lindy can try them," K.C. says. "Help me lift this down." Between the two of them, they shift the top crate and half lift, half drop it to the floor. "Damn!" K.C. exclaims. "I forgot how heavy these damn things are. Surprised we didn't get a hernia when we brought them in. Here. Let's have a look." He hauls a couple of the saddles out, sets them over the edge of the crate and says, "Jee-sus, these things stink."

"That's 'cause in India, they use dog shit to tan the leather," Butch says.

"It's not shit I'm smelling."

"Well, that's what I was told. You ever smelled anything that came from India before? It's just what stuff from India smells like," Butch says. "It'll go away once you start using the saddle."

"But what if it doesn't?" I ask.

"It will," Butch insists, louder this time.

I don't think he really has the necessary salesperson skills, treating a potential customer like that, but I have to admit, he doesn't always smirk. When he looks at me, it's more of a glare. If he was a bear or dog, I wouldn't make eye contact. But he's only a human, not much bigger than me, and although I doubt I could beat him at arm wrestling, I lock eyes with him and press on. "How do you know?"

"I know because that's what other, er, that's what the tack shops have told me."

"But they don't use the saddles."

"Maybe not them. But their customers do. Their customers tell them."

"Really? They've sold some? I thought these were the first imports."

K.C. cuts my line of questioning off by moving between Butch and me. He lays a hand on the saddle in front of me, gives me a discreet shove with his hip and asks, "You like this one?"

I give him a frown, then reply, "I know it's not a popular colour, but I like the black one." After all the talk about them being so cheap that they'd only be sold by the crate, I was expecting them to look worse than they do.

"Okay, that'll be the first one on the stand, then," K.C. says. "Help me get the stand, Butch?"

The two men go to where we left the stand at the top of the stairs and return with it. The saddle is placed on it and I climb aboard.

"Seat's way too big," K.C. says. "Got a measuring tape?"

I climb off; Butch goes in search of a tape measure and on his return, hands it to K.C., who measures from the pommel across the seat to the cantle. "Nineteen inches! Hell, I don't even know anyone who would need that big of a seat," K.C. says. "Fifteen or sixteen inches is more common. There have to be smaller ones."

The saddles in the first crate are all different, odd sizes, and some have defects such as obvious colour variations and fenders that are too long or short. Apparently quality control isn't a high priority. We select one that has a seat just a hair under fifteen inches, looks decent, feels okay when I sit in it, and we agree to buy it.

"You have English saddles too, right, Butch?" K.C. asks. "We figure we might as well pick up at least one before they're all gone."

"Really? What do you need an English saddle for?"

"So, with those Thoroughbreds, we'll likely get some ladies looking for hunters or jumpers coming to try 'em. We'll need an English saddle for them. So they'll be comfortable. More what they're used to. You'll make us a good deal on two saddles, right?"

"Yeah, of course. But goddamn, are horse people really that fussy?"

"Well, I wouldn't call that fussy, but horse people *can* be a real pain in the ass," K.C. agrees, and give me a pointed look. He barks a laugh. "You ain't seen nothing yet. When my ex and I had the tack shop, one time we had the latest style of ladies' shirts. One style had eyelet yokes. Nice little frill trim. We had 'em in six colours. A woman came in, tried on a bunch of different styles and settled on that one. Then she said, 'I love this shirt but don't you have it in puce?' Ended up not buying anything and leaving us with a bunch of messed up shirts. Hell, I didn't even know what colour puce was. Still don't, for that matter!" He laughs again.

"Women," Butch says, and chuckles along with him.

Butch goes to the front counter and returns with a clipboard of documents. He flips through them, then reads, "Crate 11A. Jump saddles. I guess that's what we're looking for."

"Good start, anyway," K.C. agrees. "What's in this one, though?" He indicates the crate that was under the one we opened, with the number 12B stenciled on it.

Butch runs a finger down the spreadsheet until he locates the number, and replies, "It says all purpose, whatever that is. Anyhow, that crate is really cheap. Bottom of the line. You don't want something that cheap. Let's see. 8A has the more expensive ones."

"All purpose would be better than a jump saddle. Cheaper sounds good, too," K.C. says. "Who knows how much we're even going to use it? Let's at least take a look. Where'd you put the pry bar?"

"Nope, I can't let you even look at something that crappy."

"How bad can they be?" K.C. presses on. He spots the prybar leaning against the shelves and gets it. He's starting to pry the lid open when Butch grabs the pry bar and wrestles it out of his hands.

"I'll let you have one of the better ones at the same price." His nostrils flare, and if I didn't clamp my teeth together I might have told K.C. to check out Butch's face if he still wants to know what colour puce is. Then Butch relaxes, smirks and says, "Friends and family deal, after all. You guys clear that saddle off the stand while I get 8A open."

"Sure," K.C. agrees. "But let's move this out of the way first." With an effort, he pushes the open crate to one side. "Damn, this thing's still so heavy," he says. "What's in it that it's still so heavy? All I see is cardboard on the bottom."

"They tell me there's hardware under that," Butch explains.

"Hardware? What hardware?"

"Um, for the saddles. You need that too? Go ahead and pull some out."

K.C. gives me a look, then leans over into the crate, pulls out a sheet of corrugated cardboard, and then some plastic bags with bits in them. He hands them to me, then leans in again and pulls out a couple more bags. These contain stirrups for English saddles. "Well, no wonder," he says, and opens a bag. "Whew! That's where that smell is coming from. I guess these are treated with some kind of oil so they don't rust."

I draw a deep breath. Yes, it's some kind of oil. Cosmoline to be exact.

K.C. says, "You know, Butch, we're going to have to unpack all these crates. You can't be giving this hardware away with the saddles! For starters, these stirrups are for the English saddles. Why would they even be in with the westerns?"

"What do you mean?" Butch stops prying at the crate. "I never thought about it. I just figured it was all part of the package deal."

"Could be, I guess," K.C. says, and shrugs. "I have an idea for you, though. Why not put all the saddles out with the others? When folks come to look at the horses, maybe they come up here and buy a saddle from you while they're at it? Give them a deal, twenty-five percent under retail maybe, still more than wholesale so there's something in it for you, too. And we'll get all the hardware out so if someone buys a headstall, they can buy a bit to go with it. And of course stirrups to go with their English saddle."

"I could set up a retail sales area here."

"Exactly. And the tack shops are only ordering saddles so they won't even know you offloaded the hardware. It would be a sweet bit of extra income for you."

Butch's face works as he thinks it over. I'd bet money he's thinking about the extra cash in his pocket and that his uncle doesn't have to know about it. Then he says, "Sounds good, but there'd be nobody here to man it half the time."

"That's just a detail to be worked out," K.C. says. "We could help out there. Lindy and Kristy both have time when they're not busy doing Wacasko-Wâti stuff, which is most of the time. They could open the store if customers show up when you aren't here. Right, Lindy?"

"Umm—"

"So that's solved," K.C. says, catches my glare, and winks.

There's so much I want to say but can't. I think *my* face is turning puce. I mutter, "Carry on, then." By now both men have tuned me out. As I'm escaping down the stairs, I hear them discussing possibilities for Butch's new enterprise, with Butch enthusiastically planning how much one-on-one training time Kristy will need. From the excitement in his voice it's obvious he hasn't become a one-woman man just because Trina is living with him. At least my name isn't mentioned again.

Now Butch will be around more than ever? I'll give him a wide berth, but Kristy will be thrown in his lap. Damn you, K.C.! You know how we feel about that guy!

I know I should be happy no one is running guns out of the loft, but at times like this I could give K.C. a good kick. In the ass or the shins, doesn't matter which. This time, maybe even in the nuts.

He's laughing so hard that when he goes to his recliner, he nearly collapses into it. He manages to sputter, "Goddammit, Lindy, I don't know why you always have to antagonize him, but it sure is funny! If looks could kill! You should've seen your face!"

"You wait until you see your face after I get done pounding on it!" I hiss. Of course I'm not really going to kick him or even hit him. It's just something I do in my mind. "You know I was hoping to get out of the lease at the end of the term and you not only encourage him but do your damn best to make expanding his operation feasible?"

"You actually said me and Lindy do nuthin' most of the time?!? And you *volunteered me* to work for him, too?" Kristy asks. The look she's giving him makes me think she might like to join me in pounding him.

"Okay, girls, how about you go get me a beer and a couple pieces of pepperoni, and I'll bring you up to speed on what happened after Lindy left."

Kristy says, "I'll get it."

"Okay, thanks," I respond. I turn to K.C. and say, "Do you really think we want to hear all the gory details of his new retail space?"

"I think you will," K.C. says. "Pull my boots off, will you?"

"Who was your slave last year?" I snap, but I'm intrigued enough and let's face it, I like him enough, that I get up from the couch and go pull his boots off.

Kristy returns with his beer and pepperoni, and when we're both settled on the couch again, K.C. says, "As it turned out, it might be a very good thing to keep an eye on what's going on up there." He takes a long draft of beer, belches, and sits back with a smug expression on his face.

"What? Why?" I ask.

"See! I knew you'd be interested," he replies. "So, remember that crate? The one that was under the first one we opened and he got his panties in a bunch when I wanted to pry it open?"

"I do," I say.

"Well, I suggested that since I had the time right then, we might as well start unpacking the crates so we could figure out what sort of store fixtures he'll need to organize the retail area. We unpacked the two that were open and a third one, all three were stacked on other crates, all okay. But when I went to start on that one, a bottom crate, he said he'd take care of the rest. Got really worked up about it, then grinned that shit-eating grin of his and said he had to take off so we were done for the day."

"And you think—"

"I think if you want to hide contraband guns, having a few decoy crates that are just as heavy and also smell of Cosmoline is probably a good plan. I think the ones with the guns are on the bottom, because who's going to bother taking one of those heavy crates down to access one under it when they all look the same?"

Kristy says, "Huh!"

I'm stunned.

Kristy says, "So, K.C.? You're not in love with the smarmy bastard anymore?"

"In love? Where'd you get that idea?" He lets us think about that while he takes a good, long swig of beer. "Anyway, let's just say it might be a good idea to keep an eye on the goings-on up there. I think there might be more than one reason he wants those trucks to come in at night and unload into the back door. Let's arrange a meet with Dwight."

Detectives At Large may be back to a full complement of three, but we can no longer call ourselves Katawasis Girls.

Chapter 17

A few days later the electrical supply cube van pulls up to the back of the barn. Butch isn't around, so K.C. goes up to offer his help. They send him away.

Our meeting with Dwight takes place over a mid-afternoon coffee break, such a normal occurrence no one would question it. The only other customers are seated at the windows on the far side of the floor, so we're free to speak. We bring Dwight into the picture re: gun runners renting the loft.

"Hmmm," Dwight says as he peels off a section of his cinnamon bun and spreads butter on it. "So, K.C., you're on board with this too, I take it?"

"I definitely think it's worth a look."

"I agree," Dwight says, and stuffs pastry in his mouth.

I'm pleased, but also irritated. Before I can stop myself, I say, "Well, that's nice, Dwight. If a man validates my suspicions it's *worth a look*?"

From the looks I'm getting from K.C., Red and Stu, I'm guessing that was a little harsh. At least Kristy is nodding instead of glaring at me.

Dwight isn't glaring either. He smiles and says, "Stand down, Lindy. I know better than to ignore your suspicions. I have something else to tell you guys. Remember Major Crimes became interested in that company in Pillerton when we learned of their connection to the not-church?"

When we all nod and mumble agreement, he continues; "So, while they were keeping an eye on them they noticed something funny. Those Al Capone tunnels we talked about before are on the same street and were getting a lot of midnight traffic considering they're supposed to be boarded up. They convinced a judge to give them a warrant, and found the blocked entrance is easy to unblock. In other words, it's a fooler."

"They had guns in there?" K.C. asks.

"If they did, they were gone by the time we got there. But there's definitely been more than just four-legged rats in there, and recently. There were empty cardboard boxes. Tags indicate they're from India. And a number of wooden crates, new looking. Looks like the cardboard boxes came through an import company and whatever was in them got repacked into wood crates before being shipped out. All speculation, unfortunately."

"It could be those repackaged crates are coming here," I conclude.

"Could be. That's why what K.C. mentioned is—"

Kristy interrupts, "Hey, Lindy! 'Member I told you I seen—"

I make eye contact with her and give my head what I hope is an imperceptible shake. It's enough to stop her from completing her thought, which I'm sure would be that we might know where that import company's warehouse is.

"Seen what?" Dwight asks.

"I, er, rats. I seen rats. Down in the feed room. I was wondering if they might be coming in with those crates. You know Russ sleeps in the tack room an awful lot and you know rats will chew your face when you're asleep."

Everyone looks at her. I imagine they're wondering what rats have to do with guns. For me, I'm impressed with how quickly she thought up that lie. She may soon give me a run for my money in that department.

"They'd only get one bite, 'less Russ was passed out drunk," Red says. "Would serve him right."

"Well, we had rats before they started bringing crates in. But you're right, maybe there's more now," I say. I don't point out that we rat-proofed the tack room when we did the big renovation on it because I know she's not really worried about anyone's face being chewed. "So, Dwight, will you be able to get a search warrant for the loft?"

"Not with what we have now."

"Maybe they could follow one of the trucks leaving the Al Capone Tunnels and see if it comes here?"

"It's still going to be thin. We got skunked on that tunnel search, so we'd really have a problem if nothing turned up here, either. I wouldn't want to be the guy that had to explain another fishing expedition to the brass, especially if you're right and the not-church is connected. You can bet they'd get their big money lawyers involved again."

"But if they did that, it would prove they're guilty," I say.

"There's no law against your tenant being connected to a money management firm. In fact it makes sense."

"So we need to find the guns so we can find the guns."

"That's right. The ol' Catch 22."

"So the good guys have to play by the rules, and the bad guys do whatever they want."

"Welcome to my world," Dwight agrees, and gets to his feet. "Well, folks, thanks for everything. I better make tracks. I curl in a couple hours."

Thoughts of guns, Pillerton and our tenant may be gone from Dwight's head, but they're rampant in mine.

Kristy and I are in the laundry room. The noise from the washer and dryer means we can talk without being overheard. K.C., who's in the living room watching TV, sometimes has very big ears.

"Why didn't you want me to tell them about seeing the van at that warehouse? And Butch at the junkyard?" Kristy asks. "I thought it was important."

"It is important," I agree. "But if you told them, what's the first thing they'd do?"

"What?"

"They'd want to know what you were doing there, first off. I guess that would be okay, although at this point we don't want them to know we were, um—"

"Snooping?"

"I'd rather call it reconnaissance."

"Reconnaissance."

"And then Dwight would say he'll pass it along and they'll look into it, and he'd forbid us to do anything else. Like we might spook them. Or it's too dangerous. And we should leave it to the cops because that's their job after all. And then although K.C. acts like he's with us, he'd pile on too."

"Well, it might be dangerous," Kristy says. She takes her laundry out and heaps it on top of the dryer, then puts the next load in the washer. "Maybe we should leave it to them."

"Can I throw my underwears in with yours so I don't have to wash them with the jeans?" I ask as I'm already digging through my hamper.

"You would wash your panties with jeans? I'm glad I didn't let you do my laundry, even though I won that bet."

I take that as a yes, pull out all the granny panties I can find and stuff them into the washer with Kristy's cute little bikini panties. "Anyway, it might be dangerous. Probably is dangerous. But they take too long and we're not stupid. We'll have a plan."

"What plan?"

"Well, okay, so I don't have one yet. But if you could find out from Butch when he'll be here next, that would be a good start. You have his Regina phone number?'

"No."

"Oh. Crap. That means we'll have to wait until the next time he's here. We know he's pretty well always here when a shipment comes in. So once we have his schedule, we could go to Pillerton a day ahead of a shipment, and watch. And maybe we go to that Johnston Distributing warehouse and pick up some Styrofoam cups and stuff. For the Bistro. So we have a legitimate reason for being there."

"But they deliver."

"Yeah, they deliver. But they charge us for it. We could say we decided to save the bucks and, um, because we had to go to Regina anyway. Haven't figured out what for, though."

"Well, you wouldn't think of it because you're not a shopper, but why couldn't we say we were going there to shop? That's what we did before, after all."

"Sure. But Red might want to come with us. She likes Cow Town. Besides, that wouldn't take us to Pillerton."

"No." She busies herself folding t-shirts, then turns to me and says, "What if I had another date with Donny? I could arrange to meet him somewhere for supper or at least drinks. I might even suggest Big Al's. You would have to come with me. I'm not going to be the only one choking down the crap food."

"Yeah. Mayonnaise thinned with pickle juice does not Caesar salad dressing make," I say, "but I can choke it down. That's a good idea, because we might be able to get more information out of him. But he'd want to, umm, you know—"

"I'd have you as an excuse! We'd share a room. So no hanky-panky."

"You're a genius."

Kristy has reconnected with Donny and the two of them have agreed to meet when she's next in Regina. All we need now is to find out from Butch what his schedule is. If Kristy is feeling the same as I am, she's better at hiding her angst. She's just going along as usual, serving everyone cheerfully, bussing tables, doing whatever needs doing. What I'm feeling is not angst as much as anticipation, apprehension and worry. I guess that's the definition of angst.

It's been weeks since Butch was here. I was so certain he'd show up today that I've been on pins and needles since morning. Nothing. It's getting late and daylight is fading. I've paced from the living room, through the kitchen, into my office and back again numerous times, waiting and hoping to see Butch's truck drive in. I've given up on him coming today when a strange SUV drives in and parks at the barn door. A couple of men get out and head inside. In a minute, the loft lights are on.

I see K.C. coming along the side of the barn. He rounds the corner, stops when he sees the strange SUV, then heads inside. I'm so curious about who those guys are, what they're doing here and where Butch is that I'm about to go down to find out, when K.C. re-appears in the barn doorway and heads my way. Now my curiosity is in overdrive. I go to the kitchen to meet him.

"What's up?" I ask.

"Well, you don't have to worry about Butch expanding his operation to include retail," K.C. says, and shakes his head. "The reason he hasn't been around? He's dead."

Chapter 18

When Butch was killed, Trina went back to her adoptive parents. I hoped she'd stay there or at least stay in Regina, but apparently a couple of weeks of them was more than she could take, she didn't find a better-than-minimum-wage job in Regina, and she's back. Her relationship with Butch was brief, but from her wailing and sighing you'd think they'd been together for decades and she hadn't caught him with his pants down just minutes before they moved in together. Of course that last bit was Kristy's fault, in Trina's mind anyway. I don't know about everyone else, but I'm tired of hearing her moan that she doesn't know what she's going to do now. How about whatever you did when you didn't know him? Of course that's just me being hardhearted, so I zip my lip.

That he was murdered does make his death worse. Any sudden death is shocking, but murdered? I'm guessing we're all wondering how terrified he must have been. I wouldn't wish that on anyone. Trina is taking it harder than seems reasonable though, and I guess she needs time to grieve, but that doesn't mean staying in bed until noon and then spending the rest of the day on the couch in pyjamas. Red assures her it's better to keep busy, and that means getting to work. She won't start back until next week, and then she'll be on the clock just like everyone else.

Kristy is moving out. A ranch about halfway from here to Maple Creek put a note up on the bulletin board at the feed store that their bunkhouse was for rent. Kristy jumped at it.

Red has been suggesting Trina should find her own place too. When Trina argues that she doesn't have a vehicle so she has to live with Red if she's going to work here, Red said, "Well, high time you bought yerself a car then. I'll co-sign a loan fer you."

In other words, my good friend take-no-shit Red is back.

In the Bistro at break time this morning, Russ offers both Kristy and Tri-na a room at his place. "I got three bedrooms," he says, "only use one myself. You ain't seen it. Come and have a look. It's a nice new house. Two biffies, even one they call a *on sweet*. First time I ever heard a shitter bein' called sweet."

"Thanks, Russ," Kristy says, "but I got my own place."

"That drafty old shack? Fine fer cowboys but a fancy little gal like you? You ain't gonna like it, plus I'll make you girls a good deal," he insists. "Won't hardly cost you nuthin', just chip in fer groceries and electricity, not much, if you do a little housework and maybe cook the odd meal. I'd be real happy to have someone living there. Fer security, you know, bein' as I'm away on the road so much. Comin' into the time of year most rodeos are in the south so I'll be gone a lot. You'd have the whole house to yerselves half the time."

"It's good of you to offer, Russ, but I'm too old to rent a room. Like I said, I want my own place."

"It ain't far but it's still gonna be a commute, Kristy. What're you gonna do when the roads're bad? You know that jazzy li'l car of yers ain't good in snow."

"Then I guess I stay home until the roads are cleared. We might be closed on snow days anyhow," Kristy says. "Or maybe it's time for me to sell the Fiero and get a truck and a cowboy hat so I look like everyone else when I ride around the countryside."

"You ain't never gonna look like everyone else, girl," Russ says.

"She just wants more privacy so she can seduce someone else's husband," Trina says.

"Pfftt!" Kristy snorts.

Before I can point out that Butch wasn't her husband and in fact was barely even a boyfriend, Trina continues, "I'd be happy to live at Russ' place. What choice do I have, since Kristy snapped up the only rental around and doesn't want a roommate?"

It's surprising Trina would consider rooming with Kristy because I doubt she'll ever forgive her for that Butch incident. With the tension between them, forget living together. I don't know how long even just working together is going to last. Trina must've wanted Kristy to say no when she floated the idea of them being roommates, I suppose because it's one more bullet in her ammo for future arguments. Kristy lets the comment pass, just gets up and goes to the coffee bar to refill her mug.

Trina glares at Kristy's back, then turns to Russ and says, "Tell you what, Russ. I'll make you a deal. Give me the bedroom that has the ensuite and if you let me use your truck, I'll do all the cooking and cleaning and even grocery shopping, and we got a deal."

"When do you wanna move in?"

"How about this morning?" She gives him a brilliant smile. He smiles back. They quickly finish their coffee and head out of the Bistro, Trina on her way to pack, and Russ tagging along with a smug expression.

"Dunno about that," Red says as we watch them go into Red's trailer, "what with him always playin' so fast and loose with the ladies."

"Hell's bells, darlin'," Stu says, "that don't mean nuthin', that's just Russ bein' Russ. You know he always was that way. 'Sides, he knows she's our kid. He won't do nuthin', knowin' what a lickin' he'd take, first from me and then from you."

But going by the look on his face I'm not so sure Russ realizes Trina is hands off, and Trina looked a little too self-satisfied when she left. Thinking of his frequent risqué comments and how grabby Russ is, especially when he's been drinking, I share Red's misgivings but say nothing. If she doesn't fend off his advances it can only mean she welcomes them, and since they're adults and single, it is entirely their own business.

It doesn't take a brain surgeon to figure out the motivation of a woman cozying up to a man more than twenty years her senior who has a nice new house, a fancy truck, a thriving business and no kids to split the inheritance with. But that's just me, suspicious to a fault.

I make a mental note to be careful with Trina. I have a feeling Wacasko-Wâti is headed for some drama, and not the Hallmark kind.

As for Prairie Outfitters, activity around the loft seems to be carrying on as if nothing has changed, except sometimes the crew rolls up on motorcycles. If anything, their business seems to have increased, but they no longer need K.C.'s services, which is good, because the arena build is moving forward. Between the trades working on the arena and Prairie Outfitters guys in the loft, the Bistro is busy. We haven't had to lay anyone off yet. We even had a little cash transaction on the side, because after offloading crates, they've frequently filled the truck with hay. Apparently Gary, the big guy with the long gray beard, needs it for his wife's horses. The way he approaches and loves on our horses makes him likeable despite how rough he looks.

In fact, the guys all look kind of rough, but at least they have no problem running the elevators. They're always friendly and polite. I agree with Kristy: the tall, well-built clean shaven one who introduced himself as Max, is easy to look at. They never make noise after nine p.m. and are nice to me, so in many ways, they're an improvement over Butch.

One good thing about Trina being back is that when Kristy and I need to go to Pillerton, there's still enough staff at the Bistro we won't be missed. When we figure out the date for that, I'll just write up everyone's shifts to accommodate it. I haven't told K.C. about this plan, but over supper, I wonder out loud if the guns are still coming and going.

K.C. says, "Whatever they had going on, I'd say it hasn't changed. Why would it?"

"Well, Butch said his uncle was the boss of the tack business. You think his uncle could be a biker? He'd have to be sixty."

"Not necessarily. I have an aunt that's only four years older than me. Besides, bikers get old too. Plus, since we never met him, we don't know he's old. Or a biker. Butch wasn't a biker, after all."

"I guess," I agree. "But there's something else I've been thinking about. Is it just a coincidence that Butch was murdered right after that discussion about selling off the hardware? What if he never told the big cheese about that, and the big cheese found out and took exception to offloading the, er, camouflage, um, what would you call it? Ballast? Plus they might consider it to be skimming."

"He barely had time to get started on that side business and anyway, there wouldn't be enough money in that to get him killed," K.C. says. He frowns and shakes his head.

"Maybe not, but they might not have wanted those crates messed with. Remember how resistant he was to opening them? And then suddenly there's a bunch of crates that are way lighter than the others. That's going to raise red flags if, say, the cops get suspicious about a shipment and check out a truck? And what if skimming wasn't all he was doing?"

"Well, he did something that earned him a bullet to the back of the head, that's for sure. Let it be a lesson to you, Lindy. I know those guys are all friendly and polite when they come in the Bistro like you say, but what you see might not be all that you get."

"I know," I insist. "Besides. Dwight's task force is looking at that whole operation pretty hard now." I'm not sidelined that easily, but I won't mention it. I hope he doesn't make me promise to stay out of it, because I don't want to lie to him.

"Even Dwight thinks she could be right," Kristy says. "She's been right before."

"Yeah!" I say. And to add weight to the argument, I add: "I may not always be right, but I'm never wrong."

Without Butch to tell us when he's expecting a shipment, waiting in Pillerton for a truck to leave the Al Capone Tunnels and then following it in hopes it might be headed for Wacasko-Wâti is a non-starter. There is no way Kristy and I can surveil the place night after night. If it was closer, say in Maple Creek, it would be difficult enough, but being two and a half hours away, it's impossible. We scrap the idea and go back to advancing the Kristy/Donny relationship.

Originally the point of Kristy buddying up to Donny was to confirm the not-church's connection to Butch. Butch is dead, but he wasn't the top of the food chain. Maybe we can find a link between Donny and Butch's uncle, or even better, the uncle's boss. But how?

"I think you have to ask him to get you a gun," I say. We're in my office. Kristy is on her break, and just brought me an extra large Columbian Dark Roast. "Not a big gun. Just a little pistol you can carry in your purse."

"Sure, that wouldn't be suspicious," Kristy says. "Phone him up wanting a date after giving him the shove off, and right away I ask him where I can get a gun?"

"Why would that be suspicious? Say you're sorry, your ex was giving you grief but now you're over it. And you're worried about your ex, and also sometimes guys follow you when you leave work, so you need personal protection. Or ... Hey! Now that you moved, maybe you're worried about living alone out there."

"He's not stupid. He'd take me to a gun shop."

"Yeah, where you would have to show your license."

"How do you get a license?"

"I dunno. I think you have to take a course. Maybe belong to a gun club."

"So why wouldn't he just tell me to get a license?"

"I guess he might. Maybe say it would take too long and you need it right away. Or maybe you wouldn't pass a criminal background check?"

"Really? I've been in trouble with the law?"

"You could casually mention your ex, the one that's in jail for murder. Make it sound like you could've been involved somehow but beat the wrap. I dunno. We have to talk it over some more."

"Why don't you do it? *Two* of your exes are in jail for murder."

"Well, they weren't husbands and in fact one was barely even a boyfriend. You're the one with the connection to Donny, though. I guess you could say the gun is for me."

"Like I'm asking for a friend?"

"Well, okay, if you put it like that, it sounds fake. Maybe we both need a gun? I don't know what Donny's background is, but if he knows anything about ranchers, he'd know every ranch has at least a twenty-two. Dad had a couple rifles with scopes. I gave the Winchester thirty ought six to Felix and Stu has the Remington. I still have the twenty-two, but I can't pack that around with me. I need something smaller."

"Okay so now you *need* a gun. What's wrong with bear spray? It saved you and Henry in Katawasis."

"Yeah, dunno how well it works against bears but it's effective against two-legged vermin, that's true. I still have a can in my truck."

"I left mine in Calgary! Maybe I should get some more. I'd feel safer in the bunkhouse with a can of that by the door."

"That's a good idea. You might as well have the one out of my truck. Just replace it next time you're in town. But about our story for Donny. We need a plausible reason to actually be scared enough to need a gun, and quick," I say. "How about this: I take cash deposits to the bank, right? Often it's after hours. Easy peasey to grab me and take the deposit wallet. The punks hanging around Fast Eddie's are capable of that. Jake's kid used to hang around there and now that I think about it, I wouldn't be surprised if he hangs out there again now that he's out on parole. Maybe he blames me for his jail time. His and his father's. He might want to get back at me. I need a gun now, a nice little number I can put in the back of my jeans like in the movies. I can't walk around with a rifle and I can't wait for the whole licensing thing, plus maybe I'd be denied anyway owing to my history with those same criminals."

Kristy chews her lower lip, then sniffs and shakes her head. "I wish you hadn't started thinking about it. Because now I'm starting to worry that you actually do need a gun."

"I wish I hadn't thought of that, too," I agree. A shiver courses through me. I give myself a mental shake and say, "It does make for a good argument, though. Go ahead and contact Donny, would you?"

Chapter 19

I decide to tell Red about our planned trip to Regina. Fortunately she's even less of a shopper than I am and doesn't want to come along, but since we're going to be in Regina anyway, she suggests I pick up my grandmother's remains. It's more a demand than a request. She gives me her smudging things and a quick lesson on how to do it. I have watched her do it enough I don't need a lesson, and also, there's no way I'm going to do it anyway, but I listen carefully because she wouldn't be satisfied otherwise.

Of course it takes planning. I can't just show up and expect them to hand me the remains. I need to know how to arrange it, and the only one I know who can point me in the right direction is Dwight. I call him.

Turns out Dwight was just about to call me.

If that was all I was going to Regina for, I can save myself the trip. The remains aren't my grandmother's.

Dwight is in civvies tonight because we closed the Bistro early and we're having a little get together for Stu's birthday. Dwight's in an extra good mood because he's got a new girlfriend, Theresa. He's acting all proud as he introduces her to everyone and explains they met thanks to a fluke of scheduling at the curling rink. It seems like he's pretty serious about her. She's wearing a pendant with the RCMP crest on it, and tells everyone Dwight gave it to her. *Well, duh!* She seems nice enough, if a little clingy. I get it that Dwight's the only one she knows here and maybe she feels uncomfortable, but couldn't she'd go for a bathroom break so I can have a minute alone with Dwight? I've been watching for an opportunity, but the woman must have a cast iron bladder. Even though it proves I was right when I said the bones weren't my grandmother's, I need to know how, exactly, they determined they weren't before I accept it as fact. But no, she just hangs on him. In her defence, he seems to like it.

"The ladies room is just down that back hallway," I tell her, and point the way. "I mean, if you need, er—"

"Thanks," she says, but doesn't budge.

Finally I can't wait any longer, and ask, "So, Dwight, if that necklace really was my grandmother's, how did a bored housewife in Bismarck, North Dakota end up with it?"

There was no obvious lead in to that question, so I can't blame Theresa for looking at me as if I have two heads. And maybe Dwight doesn't tell her about cases. He gives me a frown. "The necklace was given to her," he replies.

"Well, sure, but who gave it to her?" I ask, although I know the obvious answer: my father. I'm ready with two arguments against that conclusion; one there could be other pendants just like that one (that's kind of a stretch); and two, anyone who stayed here had access to my father's trailer and could have taken it.

Dwight pulls Theresa's arm out from around his hips, gives her a smile and says, "Honey, would you go and get me another Bud?"

"Oh, okay," Theresa says.

I think a light went on in her head.

She smiles at me and says, "I'll be right back."

So I guess I was wrong about that light. Unless she ignored it like I ignored the one that went off in my head when he didn't tell her to give us a minute when I asked about the necklace, which he would have done if he wanted to talk about it.

"Lindy," Dwight says, "you had a right to know the remains aren't your grandmother's, obviously, but more than that—well, I can't talk about an ongoing investigation."

"Ongoing?"

"Of course. Like I told you, the file will never be closed until the case is solved. But this new info has opened up new leads."

"More leads because of identifying a victim as a woman from Bismarck," I say. "But can't you tell me how you know for sure—"

"This is what's public record: she disappeared in 1960. Her daughter remembers her mom's boyfriend giving her a pendant. When she saw the photo in the paper. Maybe TV. Whatever. She dug out a photo of her mom wearing the necklace. The photo has been released to the media in hopes it will generate more tips, so you should see that popping up in the news. But she wasn't ID'd from the photo. There are dental records."

"So. It's a definite ID."

"It is."

"So, the guy who gave her the necklace. Is he in that photo?"

"He is, or at least there's a man with her. But his face is turned away. Unless you can identify him from his ear, it doesn't help us."

"Like he didn't want to be photographed," I conclude.

"Or, it could be nothing more devious than that he just happened to look the other way when the photo was snapped."

"Well, ears are pretty distinctive."

"Could be, and maybe we could match the ear in that photo to a person, if we had a suspect."

"You don't have a suspect?" I hope his next sentence won't be *not a live one.*

He takes a deep breath and looks off to his right. "Here comes Theresa."

"But—"

"Lindy, please!"

I smile and rub his forearm. "I'm sorry. I just don't ..."

"I understand, Lindy. You're thinking of your father. We may never prove who the boyfriend was or that he was the killer. But like I said, it's an active investigation and the work goes on. Okay?"

"Okay," I agree, and take a deep breath. "So. About the guns—"

"Lindy, for chrissakes, stand down." He sounds irritated, but there's that grin tugging at the corners of his mouth, letting me know he's not really mad at me. Maybe just mildly irritated. He adds, "At least for now. And take my word for it, we'll follow the evidence, no matter where it leads. Or to whom." He gives me a pointed look. Theresa resumes her position, fastened to his hip by either a powerful electromagnet or a tractor beam, and hands him the beer. Dwight may not be really mad, but the set of his jaw warns me the conversation is over.

As we're getting into bed, I tell K.C. everything Dwight told me. Which was nothing much and a whole lot at the same time.

"He said they will follow the evidence no matter where it leads, or to whom," I say. "Emphasis on the *to whom*. And that look he gave me! I think he might be preparing me for, um, like, what if her boyfriend was my Dad? I hate to admit it, but that's the first conclusion I would come to."

"It would be something they looked into, I'm sure. Maybe they've already ruled him out. How would he know a woman in Bismarck, anyway?"

"Through rodeo, I imagine. Bismarck's not all that far from here. You could drive it in a day so it's not a stretch to think he'd go to their rodeo. I think if he was ruled out, Dwight would've said so."

"I guess," he allows. "But he was a die hard poker player. He lost a lot of land that used to be part of this ranch. And didn't he win that trailer Red and Stu live in?"

"Yeah. I'd say winning that trailer doesn't make up for all the land, though. What's your point?"

"My point is, he was a pretty serious gambler. Could you see him digging out that old necklace if he was out of cash and wanted to stay in the game?"

I give him a shove back against the pillows. He flails around like a turtle that's been turned on its back. I straddle him, capture his wrists and pin them one on each side of his head as I lean down and smother his face in kisses. "Of course! Of course! Depending who won it, that pendant could've gotten anywhere. You're a genius."

He breaks out of my grasp, takes me by the hips and flips me off of him and onto my back, and then he's on top of me. "I hate to rain on your parade, but I'd say since it wound up back here where it started, the killer is still going to be someone connected to this place."

He's right, of course. It was bad enough thinking my grandfather was a serial killer. Now it's more likely my father? I feel my euphoria evaporate as I deflate like a hot air balloon with the burner turned off. "So I should prepare myself for the bad news?"

"Nope. Just put it out of your mind, and take the win: your grandmother ran off with the Watkins man and lived a long, happy life selling liniment."

"Sure! I wonder if she might still be alive! But—"

"Really?" He nuzzles my neck. "You want to talk about serious stuff after climbing all over me like that?"

I get his point.

Chapter 20

The first time Kristy and I walked into Big Al's together, everyone in the place stopped what they were doing and gawked. This time is no different, other than the place is nearly full and Donny is in the big banquette in the corner instead of at the bar. When he sees us, a look of surprise crosses his face. Shock would be more accurate. He wasn't expecting me and doesn't look happy about it. After a moment's hesitation, he stands and draws Kristy into a hug.

"Hey, baby," he says, and gives her a quick kiss. "Good to see you! So glad you made it." He herds her onto the bench and slides in beside her. I sit across from them.

"Well, yeah. Lindy had to come pick up our, um cups and stuff, so I thought, what the hell? I'm due a couple days off. Maybe we could make a weekend of it. So I called you."

"Sure, good. I'm glad you did," he says. "Have you guys eaten?"

"Nope. We thought we'd get a bite here," I reply. He looks across the table as if startled to hear a voice coming from that part of the bench.

"Well, you're in for a treat. We, that is, Big Al's, has a new cook and a new menu." He waves at the waitress and calls out, "We need menus, Marge!"

"Wow, actual menus," I say. Maybe that was a little snide. When Donny frowns at me, I give him my warmest, most charming smile.

"Yeah, because now there's too much to write on the blackboard. My company gave this place a big infusion of capital, so there's been a number of improvements, including hiring better waitresses. Now they're all as gorgeous as Marge," he says, referring to the red head who has just appeared at the table armed with menus. "Thank you, gorgeous."

"Sweet talker," Marge says. She asks, "Can I get you a drink to start?"

We each order a drink and then study the menus. Between asking Donny his opinion of the various selections, we give him the broad strokes of what's been going on in our lives. We're careful not to talk about anything gun-runner, Butch-related, or specific enough for him to figure out where we live and possibly show up there sometime. Kristy tells him she's moved into her own place. "It's still on a ranch. It's cool, like as if I have my own house on an acreage. Cows come right up to the house practically. Can't even see the ranch house, just the back of the barn. Nice view for a city girl, eh?" She giggles.

"Why'd you move? I thought you were already living on a ranch."

"Well, yeah, I was, but that was just a room in Lindy's house. That was cramping my style!" She giggles again. "Least having my own place, nice and private, no one will know about any overnight guests I might have."

Donny looks at her as if she's warm apple crisp with ice cream melting on it. A look I've often noticed men have when they're talking to Kristy. I wonder if he needs a napkin on his lap. "Sounds perfect," he says.

"Would be, other than I've had an unwelcome guest. Local trucker. Spent some time with him one night at the pub and then he followed me home so of course now he knows where I live."

"Did he, um, threaten you?"

"Jeez, Donny, just coming to my place out there, where I'm all alone, and not leaving when I told him to—that was scary enough. He didn't have to do nothing more."

"Maybe you need to get a dog," he suggests.

"I was thinking more about getting a gun and learning how to shoot," Kristy says. She looks at me and with a smile and a little nod, I convey congratulations on skillfully getting to the point so early in the conversation. "I'd have to get you to show me how to use it!"

"But if you shoot him, you might go to jail, whereas if the dog bites him in the ass? The worst he can do is sue you."

Well, that didn't go where I hoped. "She isn't home enough to have a dog," I say.

"Tell you what," Donny says, "I got a pair of men's work boots I don't need. I'll give 'em to you. You put 'em on the porch next to the door. No jerk off is going to bug you if he thinks there's a big tough laborer guy living there."

"Oh, um, gee thanks, Donny," Kristy says. "That sounds like a good idea."

"Sure. And maybe get a heavy chain and a big dog food bowl to put out there next to the boots. No one's gonna bother you. Except the guys you want to bother you."

He's looking at Kristy with such intensity I worry he might suggest the two of them go to get those big work boots of his right now. Marge breaks it up by coming to ask if we're ready to order. I know I am.

Friends of Donny's come in just as our table is being cleared. When Donny invites them to join us but doesn't budge, I take the hint, scootch over so I'm right beside Kristy, and the two newcomers slide on in. Suddenly the corner banquette doesn't seem so big.

Introductions are made. Rick, Marty and Donny were stars of the high school football team, and although they've been out of high school for years, that's what we talk about. The glory days like in Bruce Springsteen's song.

The Rick friend is right beside me. Any closer and he'd be in my lap. Funny, but he's so cute I don't mind. I ask him, "So you guys live in Pillerton, too?"

"Not right in town. Marty's place is south. My family farm is west of here. We're lowly farmers, not big money guys like Donny."

Kristy says, "But I bet you both have nice trucks!" She nudges me with her elbow. When I met Kristy, I declared myself done with men and relationships, unless a hot cowboy with a nice truck came along. It was kind of a joke, but after some disastrous relationships, starting another one seemed like too much trouble. Katawasis Lake isn't prime cowboy country, so it was unlikely any candidates would present themselves. And then I met K.C.

Rick takes the comment at face value. "My truck is just a typical farm work truck. Runs good but not pretty to look at. You want to see a pretty truck? Donny's got a new Chevy." He takes a long swig of beer, then looks across the table to make eye contact with Donny. "Never figured having a nice truck would be a turn on for the ladies. I guess you did, though, right, Donny?"

"Yeah, he did," Marty contributes. "I wondered why a city slicker like Donny would want a pickup. Now I get it. Think maybe I should trade mine in." He gives Kristy and me a charming smile.

The chit chat goes on and on. I'm not bored, exactly. Who would be, with three handsome men in attendance? But I want to steer the conversation away from trucks or the impossible catches in the end zone in the dying minutes of the biggest game of the year, back to how we're living in fear and need guns. "So, Rick, you're a farmer? Not a rancher? Got no livestock?"

"I have a couple horses my sister and I ride once in a while, and a milk cow that hasn't freshened in years. I just raise hay and canola," Rick says. "Marty's a rancher. He has cattle. What about you?"

"We have cattle. Quite a few horses too. My uncle buys them out of the kill pen and we sell them again once they're fit and going good under saddle. Or if they're too old or crocked to be riding horses, they go where they can live out their lives as lawn ornaments. There's actually a demand for those, what with city people moving onto acreages everywhere."

"Hmm. Sounds crazy to me, but who's to tell anyone what to waste their money on? Just remember, next time you need to buy hay, I'm your guy," Rick says.

"Kind of a long way to go for hay," I say. "Marty, have you had any problems with cougars? We had a newborn calf taken by one a few weeks ago. The Conservation Officer said he thought the cougar came up out of the Badlands."

"I'm surprised it would come where there's people around."

"No. It was my fault. The late calvers were out in the pasture closest to the badlands, farthest from everything, because there was still a lot of grazing there. No use bringing them in, where we have to feed them, I figured. But they're in the near pasture now, busy eating us out of house and home. I still worry, though. What if that cat learned how easy it is to grab a newborn and followed the cows to the home pasture?"

"Aren't the Conservation guys going to shoot it?" Rick asks.

"No, they don't want to. They're a threatened species."

"Pffft! Thanks a lot! Just let it keep taking calves?" Marty says.

"I know. It's not just that. I worry about riding out. What if I come face to face with it? If my horse spooked and I fell off, I'd be his supper."

Kristy looks perplexed. How many times have I told her Chica is bombproof? I only just got her riding my horse by assuring her that if she spooks, which is almost never, it's just a little scoot and nothing more. I think she's remembering that now. I give her an intense look, and breathe a sign of relief when she says, "Yeah, I'm scared, too. Lindy's house is in a pretty busy yard. Big barn. Corrals. Another house. People around all the time. I live by myself. Not even near another house."

"Cougars are shy. Unless you leave your garbage outside, nothing to attract them, you won't even see them," Rick tells her.

"It's not the cougars I'm worried about," she says. "It's coyotes. The two-legged kind. Some pretty sketchy guys have been following me when I leave work lately. I told the cops about it, but they don't do nothing. Supposed to call them when it happens."

"Yeah, well, don't bother calling. By the time they got there, you'll be raped anyhow," I say. "Or worse."

"Don't you have a rifle?" Rick asks. "Couple warning shots might be all that's needed to keep them out of your yard.

Thanks for the suggestion, Rick! I jump right on that. "She doesn't have a gun, but I've got an old single shot Cooey and a scabbard for the saddle. I figure by the time I get the gun out, I'm done for. And if my horse has headed south, it's gone with her anyway. I could loan it to you to keep at your place, Kristy."

"Is it a big gun?"

"Not really. Pretty small and light."

161

"Do you have to hold it with both hands, like hold it up to your shoulder?"

"Yeah, it's a rifle, but—"

"Nope, don't want a big gun like that. A little pistol. Something small enough to grab in a hurry," Kristy says. "Small enough to keep in my purse."

"I get it. I like the idea of a six-shooter like they had in the Old West. So it stays with me if my horse doesn't."

"You don't want nothing that big and heavy," Donny says. "Better to get yourself a nice little Sig Sauer or Glock. You can have that in a holster. Small, neat little gun. Get yourself one of those."

"Well, yeah, that sounds good, but..." I say, make eye contact with him then look away and take a swig of wine.

"But what?"

"Well, um, there's the criminal background check. So..." I let that comment hang.

"Usually doesn't take long to get one."

"Usually."

"Oh," Rick says after a moment. "So, get your friend to buy one for you when she's getting one for herself," Rick suggests.

"Oh, um, about that," Kristy says, "it's that pesky criminal background check."

"Both of you? What could you possibly have done?" Donny wants to know.

"Well, it wasn't me, you know," Kristy tells him, "it was my ex. He's in jail for murder. Which he did, no doubt about that. All I did was ditch the gun for him but I never knew nothing about the murder. I mean, not until after." Man, she really is getting good at lying.

"Didn't you wonder why he wanted you to get rid of the gun?" Donny asks. Damn! He's turning out to be smarter than he looks.

"He told me it was so he wouldn't have to register it," Kristy says. "I thought it was stupid to throw something like that away so I thought I'd pawn it. My mistake." She giggles.

"So when you found out the truth, you turned him in?"

"Hell no! If he went to jail I'd have to live on waitress wages! Now I got to anyway."

"Crown Counsel was just lookin' for brownie points. They charged her, thought it would be a slam dunk. Her lawyer was too good for them." I shrug and shake my head. "People bitch about lawyers and technicalities, but a lawyer like that one is worth whatever you have to pay 'em."

"Why do cops waste their time on stuff like that anyways?" Kristy asks. "The murderers or bank robbers makes sense, but someone just selling a gun?"

"This whole background check thing does no damn good anyhow," I say. "I bet you know guys who couldn't pass it, and yet they have guns. Mmmy right?" I hold up my empty glass, smile what I hope is an innocent smile and ask, "'Nuther drink?"

I don't miss the look that passes between them. I hope they're thinking about procuring guns for us, since we obviously have a jaundiced view of the law and are unlikely to turn them in. My tongue is starting to feel a little thick. I make a mental note to slow down on the wine or the dumb drunk act won't be an act.

Donny waves the waitress over and orders another round. I notice a couple of guys in cowboy hats on the stage at the far end of the room fiddling around with the equipment there. I nudge Kristy and point. "Oh! There's a band," I say.

"Wahoo!" Kristy hoots.

"I told you I had a surprise for you," Donny says, and puts his arm around Kristy to draw her close. They kiss a sloppy, lip-smacking kiss.

I wonder how I'm able to keep my Caesar salad down watching that, and focus on the task at hand. We've planted the seeds for them to help us get guns. We can't be the ones to bring up the idea again. If Donny doesn't think of it, hopefully one of his friends will. Otherwise, we'll have to suggest meeting them for breakfast tomorrow. After Rick suggested firing a few pot shots to keep stalkers away and Kristy said she wanted a small gun, I didn't think they'd be so slow to come up with the obvious solution.

Rick may not be quick at connecting the dots, but he asks me to dance and proves he's plenty quick on his feet. We two step and sit drinking and two step some more. Finally, after a string of fast numbers, the music slows. I tell him, "I need a break." I start back to the table but he catches my hand and pulls me back toward him, into his arms. I inhale the intoxicating scent of him as we slowly move together on the darkened dance floor.

He pulls me closer than I'd want K.C. to witness, and I'm way more conscious of his body, his hard muscles, the natural grace of his movements, than I should be given I'm in a committed relationship. I excuse my response by telling myself it's only an involuntary physical attraction. And just because I'm on a diet doesn't mean I can't look at the menu. And so on. And now he's nuzzling my hair. I experience a rush of desire. No! I stiffen and pull away slightly, recognizing guilt when I'm in the clutches of it.

At that moment, a commotion at the entrance draws my attention. I push out of Rick's embrace and spin away. As I plow through the other dancers, I grab Kristy's arm and tear her away from Donny.

She squawks, "Jesus, Lindy! What—?"

"Grab your coat. We gotta get outta here!"

I tow her back to our seats. I grab my coat and purse but Kristy's moving so slowly I hiss, "Hurry up!"

She looks at me with a mixture of annoyance and curiosity, but seems to be frozen in place. I exhale loudly, grab her things, then clamp onto her upper arm and start pushing her toward the exit door at the far end of the pub.

Rick and Donny materialize beside us. Rick says, "Lindy? What the hell?"

"We, uh, lost track of the time. Late for, er, another meeting. Thanks, guys!" I say.

Kristy finally moves her feet so I don't have to drag her out the door, but as soon as we hit the sidewalk, she digs in. "What the hell, Lindy! What other meeting? What's got into you?"

I point down the street.

We're in jammies in our hotel room, having a cup of chamomile tea before turning in.

"What are chances they don't know each other?" Kristy asks, for probably the tenth time.

"Slim to none, I'd say."

"Yeah, that's what I thought." She drains her cup, gets up and puts it on the desk next to the coffeemaker. "So now what? Is the fact they we seen them in the same bar enough? It isn't, is it?"

"No. But we couldn't stay there and ask them if they knew those bikers, could we? And we can't let Max and the rest of his crew know we're sniffing around. What possible reason would we have to know Donny? If we spook them, they go farther underground and there goes however many hours the cops have put into their investigation. Dwight would never speak to me again. And for nothing, because Donny knowing them—"

"—does no good," she finishes my sentence for me. "We have to get Donny to sell us guns."

"Or at least have him put us together with whoever he bought that illegal rifle from. He's going to have to tell us who that is. If it's those bikers, I'm not sure what we do."

"Abort the mission?"

"I'm afraid so. But we're not there yet. You can still call Donny in the morning and act all sorry we had to dash off, and offer to buy him breakfast to make up for it."

"I guess."

"Ready for bed?" I ask.

"I am," Kristy replies.

We brush our teeth and take turns on the toilet, then come back to bed and climb in under the covers. I turn off the bedside lamp. Soon I hear rhythmic snuffling from the other bed and envy Kristy's ability to fall asleep so fast. In the twilight zone of pre-sleep, I fantasize a scenario where Kristy and I meet some very rough characters, more bikers maybe, in a back alley. They open their trunk to show us their wares. Everything's going fine. Then one of us says something that spooks them. There's a scuffle and in the blink of an eye, we're in the trunk with the guns, on our way to the Badlands to be executed.

I realize how enormously stupid this idea is. There is no question Max has seen Dwight at Wacasko-Wâti, even after hours. He must know we have a friendly connection. Maybe Max didn't see us at the pub tonight, but did they talk to Donny and friends after we left? Did they mention the two of us bolting like we did? Did he tell them our names? What are chances of there being two other Lindy and Kristy combos?

Max would ask Donny how he knows us. Would Max believe a female would drive three hours for a date with Donny? He's not much in the looks or personality department and you don't have to know Kristy for long to realize she doesn't have to go far for a date. Sure, the first meeting was accidental, but it might not look that way to them. And we're looking to buy guns? Supposing neither of us could pass a criminal background check, that can't be true of everyone at Wacasko-Wâti. Anyone could go to the hardware store right in Maple Creek and buy whatever we wanted.

If I hadn't spotted the bikers before they got right into the bar! A second later and we'd have been done for. Things always seem worse in the middle of the night but I'm pretty sure that even in the morning, my brilliant plan is going to stink. I don't know why it took me so long to admit it to myself. Why does Kristy go along with my hare-brained ideas?

Dwight's right, we need to leave this to the cops.

Chapter 21

The whole trip was a wash. Well, not completely. We went to Cow Town. Kristy bought a nice pair of boots, which she needs since she's riding now, and I got K.C. a new show shirt to put away for Christmas. Other than that, we've got nothing to show for it.

"Ain't you got the Johnston order?" Red asks.

"No, because, um, we, er, it wasn't open when we went," I explain.

"That's what you went there for? Styrofoam cups? Didn't it cost more for gas in the truck than what they charge to deliver?" K.C. clicks his tongue, shakes his head and blows out a breath.

It's obvious to everyone that I'm not his favorite person at the moment. I was wrong. I do have something to show for that trip. I've managed to get K.C. mad at me. Really mad, for the first time since we've been together. The shirt that was supposed to be his Christmas present didn't mellow him out and now I'm going to have to shop for another gift besides.

I thought I could tell him everything but there's just no way to make *we went to get evidence on gun runners* sound any less ridiculous than it is. He knows I'm holding something back. I wilt under his glare but say nothing. He finally quits staring at me when Red says, "You wanna keep that gal home, yer gonna hafta chain her to the porch right alongside of Henry."

Just then Kristy comes up beside K.C., carafe of coffee in hand. She asks, "You're chaining Henry up?"

K.C. gets up from the table and takes his dirty dishes to the dish pit. When he comes back he stops behind me, leans in close to my ear and says so quietly I'm the only one who can hear, "Did you even give a thought to whether I might like to go with you?" Then he straightens up and says, "We'll talk later. Unless you're planning to sneak off somewhere again." I watch him walk away.

Well, that sounds ominous. I don't like the way Red is looking at me either. Kristy had been buzzing around offering customers coffee top ups to save them a trip to the coffee bar. This is something she wanted to try, for a better customer experience, she said. No need for extra staff, any of us can grab a carafe and circulate any time we have a few minutes with nothing else to do. Just now she came along mid-conversation so it's no wonder she looks perplexed. She should count herself lucky she wasn't on the hot seat like I was. Then again, she's not the one who deserves it.

"Why do you want to chain Henry up?" she persists. "He didn't bite someone again, did he?"

"No. Nobody wants to chain Henry up," I say.

Stu shakes his head but says nothing, just sits there nursing his coffee, his brow furrowed in confusion.

I hear jake brakes outside and welcome the excuse to escape. "I better go see who that is," I say, and leave. I locate the rig I heard at the back of the barn. A couple of the biker guys are getting the elevator in place. I say hello and I'm about to leave them to it when Russ drives in and parks next to the trailer. After exchanging a hello, I ask, "What are you doing coming in the back gate and parking back here? Aren't you going in for coffee?"

"Nope, no time today. Just seen these guys come in and figgered I'd swing by and invite them to my poker game Friday night."

"How is it your poker game if it's in our tack room?"

"Could move it to my place, I guess."

"Do that," I say. K.C. might not like me chasing Russ away, but I'm already on his shit list, so piling this on won't make a difference. Maybe he'll save some money and stay home if he actually has to go somewhere, and not just wander out the door and across the yard to the barn to get in the game. Besides, Russ never asked if it was all right for him to have his game here and I don't like a bunch of strangers smoking and drinking and making a mess of the place, plus bothering everyone with their comings and goings. My ranch. My rules. I smile, say, "See ya," and walk away.

It's chilly at the Larsen/Garland house and not just because the weather has taken a turn. K.C. didn't care about me nixing the poker game, but he hasn't quite forgiven me for my jaunt to Regina/Pillerton. It's not that I can't go anywhere without telling him, it's just that sneaking away was, well, sneaky. I knew that, of course, but what I didn't know was that it would hurt his feelings. I apologized and promised the next trip would be just him and me. Dinner out. Maybe a movie. Night in a hotel, one with a pool and hot tub, definitely one with nice sheets on a bed someone else will have to make. We kissed and made up. Sort of. He's speaking to me again, but there's still a hesitancy to our conversations. Saying we've got a ways to go is an understatement.

On top of K.C.'s cold shoulder, winter has set in. Today there's blowing snow and drifts deep enough to bury a car. Schools are closed and we're way down the list for our road to be plowed, so we aren't expecting customers and won't open today. Fine with me because I can use the uninterrupted computer time. The miserable thing is a time-saver; it prints checks that fit perfectly in window envelopes so I don't have to type all that anymore, but I'm not proficient yet and still have to refer to the manual often.

I'm muddling along when, in the good old unbeatable rancher spirit, half a dozen hardy souls arrive on snowmobiles. They're part of the group of local seniors who can be found in the Bistro most weekday mornings enjoying coffee, a pastry and a chinwag.

I know Red is in the kitchen working on wholesale pie orders when they arrive and will let them in, but she'll need some help. I leave the obstinate computer and go down to pitch in. The carafe of coffee Red made for herself and any of our guys that might wander in is enough for everyone's first cup. We get the Bunn Airpots on the go for when they need seconds, and a batch of muffins in the oven. No time to make fresh cinnamon buns, but they can have one of yesterday's leftovers for free, and we'll even warm them up. Stu brings in a load of stove lengths and gets a fire going in the fireplace.

It was a slow start, maybe, but everyone seems pretty happy. I add to the festive atmosphere by turning on the radio that's already spewing Christmas music even though we've barely had time to take down the Halloween decorations. Red doesn't need my help now that they're all settled in, but when a second group of snowmobilers shows up, explaining they were summoned by the first group and ask about today's lunch specials, suddenly we're short-staffed.

Earlier, I called Kristy and Trina and told them not to come in. Now I see that was a mistake. Kristy will be housebound until her landlord plows the driveway, but Trina can get Russ to bring her over, so I call her. Russ answers, I explain my dilemma, and he agrees to bring her. He has a tractor, a three-quarter ton four by four and a snowmobile. He could get here if it was Armageddon, and he's been bringing Trina and staying for coffee most mornings anyway.

I'm assigned to make a pot of chili. Stu opts not to start the barbeque but gets a couple of chickens ready to go in the oven instead. Red has just started the soup and salt rising bread when another snowmobile pulls up. Russ. Rather than Trina, it's Kristy who's on behind him. I greet them just inside the door. "Good morning, you guys. Wasn't expecting you, Kristy."

"Well don't look too close! A toque? Definitely gonna be a bad hair day. And a rush job of putting on my makeup? Didn't think I'd be coming in today," Kristy says, and giggles as she stamps her feet and brushes snow off her pantleg before stepping off the mat.

"I didn't think you would be, either. What happened?"

"Russ called to say Trina was under the weather and offered to pick me up. My first snowmobile ride!"

"Lucky you."

"Yeah! Too bad it's so damn cold, and I don't exactly have snowmobile-riding clothes! I'll just put my stuff away and then grab a carafe and go see how those folks are doing." She pulls off her parka as she heads into the kitchen.

"I'll be back to git you later," Russ tells her as she walks away.

"Hey, Russ, thanks for going to get her," I say, "but why not Trina?"

"She's still in bed. Poor gal was tuckered right out."

I almost ask why, but I bite my tongue when I see his expression. He's smirking. All she did yesterday was hover around doing the minimum, as usual. Slower than molasses except when on her way out for a smoke break. And with the storm coming, we closed early. Whatever it was that tuckered Trina out, it had nothing to do with working here, and I'm pretty sure Russ wouldn't be wearing that look on his face if she was tired from doing housework. Was Stu naïve when he said Russ wouldn't start anything with Trina?

"Anyhow," Russ continues, "you gotta get used to her not bein' here."

"Oh? Why's that?"

"Well, she missed me so bad on my last trip, she's comin' with me this time. We're headin' out in a couple days. I got bulls booked on the U.S. tour and she ain't been further south than Minot. Goin' all the way to Abilene this trip."

"She's..."

"She said to tell you she quits. What she actually said was, take your shitty minimum wage job and shove it, but yer an old friend so I wouldn't hurt yer feelin's sayin' it that way." He chuckles, gives my shoulder a rub and says, "I'll grab a coffee and see what the white heads are up in arms about this morning. Warm up a cinnamon bun fer me, would ya?"

Trina's going with Russ? She never goes near the stock around here, not even the horses, and would be even more useless as a swamper on a bull hauler than she is as a kitchen worker. I'm gobsmacked. I stand frozen in place as I watch him go to join the seniors at their table. It's only when he looks my way and grins that I give myself a mental shake and go into the kitchen. Red's busy and doesn't look up. I decide against giving her the news until I get my head around it.

By the time I've got the warm cinnamon bun and a couple of butter pats on a plate, Russ is head to head with Alva Betteridge. Alva is giggling like a school girl. He's flirting with her even though she's a good twenty-five years older than he is. That'll make Alva's day. If either of them notices me or the cinnamon bun, they give no sign.

I glance into the kitchen to see if Red's still busy. She is. I decide against telling her the news. Maybe Trina should be the one to tell her. I call out that I'm going to my office, and leave. I can't help running mental movies of Trina up in the passenger seat of the Kenworth, hanging around the corrals at the rodeo grounds, generally getting in the way or whining about how bad it smells or her feet are getting muddy, and (even though I try to avoid this one), rolling around in the sleeper with Russ, as I feed the sheets of checks into the printer. I print one to be sure everything lines up. It doesn't. I open the cover, confirm both sets of tractor pins line up with holes, then realize there's a little bulge in the middle of the paper. I don't have the tractors quite far enough apart. I adjust it and am just about to run another test when the phone rings. I curse under my breath. The last thing I need with this damn printer being so uncooperative is an interruption. Half a dozen rings, and the answering machine picks up.

"Lindy? It's Dwight. Give me a call when you get a chance, please."

I grab the handset. "Dwight! I'm here."

"Oh great," he says. "Hope I didn't interrupt anything."

"Nope. Nothing important, anyway. I'm just fighting with the printer to get the checks lined up so I can do payroll and pay some bills. I'm about to tear my hair out. Your call is a welcome break." It's lying to a cop, but I guess it's forgivable as it's partly true, and is what you'd call a white lie, at that. "You've got a question for me?"

"Uh, yeah. Anyone else in the room with you?"

"That's your question? Don't you want to know if my fridge is running, too?"

We share a chuckle, and then I say, "No. I'm alone. No one's stupid enough to come in here when I'm swearing at the computer. Why?"

"Well, just something I've been working on. I could ask Stu, but I, er, well, I don't want to put Stu in an uncomfortable spot."

"Stu?" I draw a breath and sink to my chair. What could Dwight want to know that would make Stu uncomfortable?

"It's a question about the rough stock contracting business," Dwight continues, "specifically, Mr. Benson's business."

"Okay, but why me?"

"You do his books. You have financial records, particularly payment records? Like, who's paid him?"

"Of course."

"I figured. So, how far back?"

"Seven years, for sure, like Canada Revenue requires. I haven't been doing his books that long, but he gave me boxes of the old files he never bothered to burn. I think it was everything paperwork-related that he threw in boxes when he moved. I took out what I needed. He said he didn't want any of it back, no reason for me to keep it, so I had the kids burn everything." I look for my coffee mug, find it half full of cold coffee, and drain it.

"So, got any idea how long he's been in the business?"

"I'd guess since the Sixties, maybe early Seventies. He started his business before I met my dad, which was 1976. He's always says he quit riding to actually make money off rodeo without risking his neck. Stu says he quit because he was no damn good at it."

"So could the Rocking R have been in business in the Fifties?"

"Maybe. Well, no. He only got the Rocking R brand when he partnered with us and we started the bull business. Before that it was Jackpot Cattle Company. Like Jackpot Rodeo School in Rocky Mountain House? He claims he was part owner of that back in the day."

"I see. Hmmm." I hear paper rustling at his end of the line, like he's flipping pages in a file. Then he asks, "So. Do you think your father went everywhere Russ did?"

"I don't know. All I know is, I didn't meet Russ the summer I followed the rodeo, and if Dad talked about him, I don't remember it."

"About your dad. Did he leave any mementos of the rodeos he went to? Old photos maybe? Maybe if you got me a list of the rodeos Russ supplied stock to over the years, we could figure it out from there."

He wants to know where Russ was as a means of tracing my father's whereabouts. My stomach churns, and not because of the cold coffee I just poured into it. "Why do you need to know where they were back then?" It's a stupid question and one I know the answer to.

"You know—"

"I know. You're not going to tell me. It's an ongoing investigation," I say, and blow out a breath. "I'd have to get that from his tax files. I can't tell you anything about his taxes unless I have Russ's permission. Or a judge tells me to. Meanwhile, though, if you really want to chew this bone, get your team to start phoning rodeos and find out if they have dealings with Rocking R. Or Jackpot. Maybe there's someone still around that remembers from way back."

"Of course, Lindy, but do you have any idea how many rodeos there are?"

"I do, actually. Thousands, I'd guess."

"Yeah. Thousands." I hear a long, loud exhale; then he promises, "I'll tell you everything, eventually. For now, thanks. I'll let you get back to work."

The line goes dead, leaving me listening to the dial tone, wondering if that coffee is going to stay down. There's only one reason Dwight is wondering what rodeos Dad went to all those years ago. Maybe Red was right when she said he could've been the murderer. I don't think there's such a things as a murderer gene, but even if there is, I tell myself it doesn't matter. I'm not like him. But Trina and Russ and pondering whether the loft tenants are gun runners are two subjects Dwight's call have pushed to the back of my mind.

No use fighting with the computer as frazzled as I am. A coffee break is in order. I pick up the bundle of mail that I haven't looked at yet and go to the kitchen to make a fresh pot of coffee, sorting through the envelopes while I wait. One from the bank isn't like the usual statement. I open it and find the check from Prairie Outfitters for this month's loft rent marked NSF.

With cash flow a chronic problem and at the beginning of our seasonal downturn, the rent check bouncing couldn't come at a worse time. I heave a sigh and collapse onto the nearest stool. I sure hope this counts as the third thing.

Chapter 22

I put the box on Dwight's desk and take a chair across from him. "He didn't have a lot. Comes with living out of a camper for decades, I guess. He had a good saddle, the one he won in Tulsa in 1969. That's the one I use now. Stu says there were others, some with more silver, but what happened to them, he doesn't know. Sold, or lost in poker games, I guess. He must've forgotten about these or they'd be gone, too. If you're trying to nail down his movements, these will prove where he was over the years, on a few dates anyhow."

When I thought to check the boxes gathering dust under the loft stairs in the barn for the mementos Dwight asked about and found this box under a pile of moldering saddle pads, I agonized over turning it in. What if it's the evidence they need to connect my Dad to the disappearance of that woman from Bismarck? In the end, here I am, giving the box to Dwight despite my misgivings because it's the right thing to do and as K.C. pointed out, it's even possible it will exonerate him.

Dwight pulls the box onto his blotter, pokes through it and pulls out a big silver buckle. "Wow," he says. "There must be dozens of these. He must've been really good."

"Not as a boyfriend or as a father, but as a rodeo cowboy? Yeah. A champion many times over."

"Look at this! NPRA, whatever that is. 1967 Saddle Bronc Champion."

"I think that was close to the end of his glory days. He was making a comeback when I met him in the summer of '76. He was killed in a plane crash on his way to a rodeo a few months later."

"Ahh, yes. I remember that. That was when Stu and Red moved onto the ranch."

"Well, once the government finally agreed that I was his only living relative and allowed me to inherit it, anyway. Stu moved in to look after the place, along with Dad's horse and, um, a couple other rodeo horses. When Red joined him, she cleaned out the trailer, moved a bunch of boxes to the barn, and gave me that jewelry box. You know. The one with the silver earrings in. I didn't build my house until six or seven years later."

"Well, it's a good thing she didn't put that jewelry box with the stuff in the barn, or who knows when it would've been found. Without it, we'd never have ID'd the female victims."

"Victims? Plural?"

"Yeah. I was just briefed this morning. It'll be on the news later today. All three have been ID'd now, the latest was an Alberta girl. Just twenty-two when she disappeared in 1976."

"Okay. So, two murders, sixteen years and how many thousand miles apart? Is there a connection to the other woman?"

"A loose connection. The woman from Bismarck was dating a cowboy. So we looked at missing persons who were connected to cowboys. And where do you find cowboys other than at the bar? At horse shows, horse sales, and most of all, at rodeos. This young woman was a barrel racer."

A tremor courses through my insides. I was following the rodeo in Alberta in the summer of '76. Is it possible I knew her? I study my hands and try to absorb this new information. When I look up, Dwight is studying me, eyes narrowed.

He says, "Something strike a nerve, there, Lindy?"

"No, I—" I draw a sharp breath, shake my head and not for the first time, wish I had a better poker face. I get to my feet. "I'll let you get back to work. I'd like to have Dad's buckles back when you're done with them."

"Of course."

I start for the door and I'm almost out when I turn back and say, "About a killer stalking women at rodeos, you know, cowboys are more gentlemanly than that. Tipping their hats, protecting women, you know. Chivalrous. There's lots going on around rodeos. It's not just rodeo people there. Big crowds. Usually a fair and of course there's a bunch of roustabouts working the rides. Now, those are some rough guys. Probably lots of them have criminal records. It wouldn't necessarily be a cowboy."

"Cowboys are people same as everyone else. But the crowds and fair workers, that's true," he agrees. When I don't say more, he says, "Would fair workers know about your ranch, though? If you know something, you have to tell me, Lindy."

"Um, of course," I promise, and hurry out of the detachment. Once in my truck, I fold my arms on the steering wheel and rest my forehead on them. Memories—snapshots of the first rodeo other than the Calgary Stampede that I ever went to—flood my brain, all strung together like the music videos on MTV. High Prairie, Alberta, July, 1976. I met my true love, Nick. His friends Melon and Gorgeous and Wiggles, and of course Red and Stu. And that Saturday, after years of wanting to meet my father, I finally did. He said everything I hoped for. How he'd wanted to be a part of my life but my mother wouldn't allow it. How sad he was to have missed all my birthdays. Christmases. Holidays. The next day, he walked away without a goodbye or even a thought for the daughter that just the day before he claimed to care so much about. Snuggled up next to him was a woman not half his age. A barrel racer.

I know I should've told Dwight. I will tell him. Just not right now.

Aside from trying to remember the name of that barrel racer I met once all those years ago in hopes it's not the murder victim before I tell Dwight about it, I've been harboring the Russ and Trina secret for days now. Well, not completely harboring. I told K.C. about both dilemmas. He said I need to tell Dwight immediately whether I can remember the barrel racer's name or not, but he agreed Trina should be the one to tell Red that she's hooked up with Russ.

I phone Dwight and tell him about my father and the young barrel racer. I say I don't know if I ever knew her name but if it comes to me he'll be the first to know. I'm certain the date was mid-to-late July, 1976, at the High Prairie Rodeo. I ask him if that's the last time anyone saw her. He says he's not sure.

No sign yet of Trina. Not even a phone call. It niggles at the back of my mind every time Red and I are alone together. They're leaving tomorrow, so Trina must not be going to tell Red. In that case, I'll find the right time, and tell her.

Kristy has left for the day, and Red, Barney, Marci, and I are busy cleaning up, when someone starts banging insistently on the glass door. I go to see who it is, and find Trina and Russ there. I turn the thumb lock to open the door and let them in.

"What's up? We're busy on close right now." Unable to muster a smile, I turn away and head back into the kitchen.

"Hey, Lindy," Trina says as she follows me, "have to do real work since there's no more rent checks coming in?"

"More like because I'm short one kitchen worker," I reply. "Aren't you heading out tomorrow?"

"What?" Red says. "You goin' somewhere?"

"That's what I came to talk to you about," Trina replies.

Red is wiping down the counters. Without looking up or pausing, she says, "Dunno if there's coffee left but grab a Coke and I'll join you when we're done here."

"You can finish that later. We haven't got all night."

Red frowns, puts the rag in the sink, and heads for the entrance. "I'll take over," I tell her as she passes me.

"No!" Trina cries, "this concerns you, too, Lindy."

"How?" I ask.

"You'll see."

Do I really need to be there when Red kills Russ? "I'll join you when I'm done," I say. My curiosity is aroused but I don't respond well to being told instead of asked. Besides, I'm more than a little peeved that they couldn't have shown up earlier. I turn my back.

"You're part of this, Lindy." It's Russ' voice this time. I turn to see him hovering beside Trina. "But we'll git a drink and wait 'til yer done. It's okay, Teeny. We got time." He takes an unsmiling Trina's arm and propels her out.

Teeny? That's cute, considering she's as tall as I am, which means she's also as tall as Russ. I procrastinate by doing an extra thorough job of cleaning, even using a knife to scrape the crud out from under the lip of the sink, then take my time getting a glass of wine and joining them. Stu and K.C. have come in, so we move to a bigger table. Once everyone's settled, Trina says, "So, me and Russ are together now, and we're going to be away for a few months."

"Yer together? Goddammit, Russ!" Stu exclaims. "She's young enough to be yer daughter fer chrissakes. What the hell's wrong with you?"

"Well, she ain't my daughter, she ain't yers, and Red can't run her life neither." He squares his shoulders, puffs out his chest, and with a lift of his chin adds, "I'm a catch and she was smart enough to see it."

"I do what I want," Trina says. "I got bigger news than that, and that's not what we came to talk to you about, anyway."

"No? What could be bigger'n that?" Red asks.

"So, you know Russ has been around since way back in the day, right?" Trina replies. She looks at me and utters what I'd call a cackle. "He knows who my father was. Lindy, I'm your sister."

Everyone mumbles something but I can't make out what. It's as if there's a buzzing in my ears and everyone is far away. I feel as if all the oxygen has been sucked out of the room. I gasp. The only way for her to be my sister would be if my father was the pervert who had sex with thirteen-year-old Red.

"Whaddaya mean?" Stu asks.

"You know what it means," Russ replies.

At last I mumble, "That's not possible. It just isn't possible, is it, Red?"

All eyes are on Red, who looks as if she'd like to be anywhere else. She presses her lips together and I think if she wasn't so strong, she'd be crying. But she says nothing, and that speaks volumes. Now I know why she refused to name him. And why she was so adamant Trina attend what we thought was going to be my—our—grandmother's funeral.

"It ain't just possible, it's a fact," Russ chimes in. "I might never of figured it out. Then Trina said her birth mother's name was Beulah. Not a common name. Something niggled at me and finally I remembered a skinny kid with that name, all those years ago. We all knew you were jail bait, *Beulah*. Didn't matter in them days. I seen you with Gobbler more'n once. He's it, ain't he? We'll git a paternity test if yer gonna make a stink about it."

"How can you get a paternity test?" I ask. "Wouldn't it require some of my father's blood or something?"

"We use your blood, Lindy," Trina says. "It'll prove I'm related to you. Only one way that's possible."

I'm flooded with conflicting emotions, the one front and center at the moment being annoyance she presumes I'll give them a blood sample. Do I want confirmation she's my sister?

"You ain't gonna need to do that," Red says quietly.

"Good! That's settled, then," Russ says. "Which is why we wanted to talk to you before we left so you can git yer shit together."

"What do you mean?" Red asks. "You want me to have his name added to your birth record?"

"Surely that's not important after all this time," I say.

"It's important," Russ says, "because it means she's entitled to half of Wacasko-Wâti."

Chapter 23

"So there goes what was left of any respect I had for my father, and I lose half the ranch besides? That whole thing about bad things coming in threes is a joke. It's more like they come in *herds*," I grouse, and drain my fourth or fifth glass of wine. I already have a raging headache and I know tomorrow morning is going to be unpleasant, but I fill my glass again anyway. "Did you hear her brag about how schmart she was to snag a millionaire? Russ? A millionaire? She's not even trying to pretend she isn't after his money, and boy, is she in for a surprise. And her joke 'bout how she's gonna love living in this house?"

"I'm not so sure she was joking," K.C. says, "about the house, anyway."

I continue as if he hasn't spoken: "And how snotty she was when she said Russ can have his poker games in the tack room whether I like it or not and I can't stop him because she's an equal owner now and she says he can? I don't know why he wants to, anyhow. But goddammit! I curse the day you brought her here."

"I didn't know—" K.C. starts.

"I know you didn't, sweetie. I'm not blaming you. It was the right thing to do," I assure him, and sigh. "No one could've predicted this. But I really doubt I'll be able to stop myself from killing her if she insists on being anything but a silent partner. I don't know how we're going to get out of this."

"Well, for starters, we need a lawyer. Not sure if that's Jesse, but he can recommend someone if he thinks it's outside his area of expertise. At the very least, I'm damn sure she can't come along now and take half of what you've built. From what you've told me, there wasn't much here when you inherited this place other than a barn with a leaky roof, and an old trailer."

"A few corrals and a couple old sheds, too, but that's it. I wonder if she'll still want half if she had to take half the debt, too. And minimum wage for a forty hour work week? Forget that! How about eighty hours and no wage at all." I make short work of my wine and refill the glass again, this time emptying the bottle. I don't know why, but I'm surprised it's empty. I drank a liter of wine in under an hour? I'm going to have bedspin and a conversation with Ralph, for sure, but at this point I care so little I may even open a second bottle.

"All she sees is assets, babe. She doesn't have a hot clue about business. One thing puzzles me, though," K.C. says.

"Just one thing?"

"Well, more than one, I suppose, but this stuck out for me and I'm not sure I heard it right. I had just come in and you were all in the kitchen. I thought she said something about you having to do real work since you had no rent income?"

"Yeah. I guess I heard something about that. Sort of went in one ear and out the other, though because my only thought was that I have to help because she's not working."

"So, what's bothering me is, how did she know the assholes broke the lease? Who have you told, besides me, Red, and Stu?"

"Oh." I pick through my brain, trying to remember if I talked about it when anyone else was around. Charlie or Johnny maybe? But if they overheard me, even if it tweaked something in their teenaged rodeo-crazy Nintendo-addled brains, they couldn't have said anything to Trina or Russ because those two haven't been here when the kids were home. "I don't think so, but I'll have to think about it sometime when I'm not drunk. Is it important?"

"I don't know. It puzzled me, is all," he says, and drains his beer. "I wonder if she still has ties to them? Did she keep in touch somehow, after Butch was killed?"

"Why would she?"

"Maybe so she could be a spy? If they're smuggling guns like we thought, she could give them a head's up if we were on to them? Like, any plans we might have or if we're talking to the cops."

"We're talking to the cops all the time. They're in for coffee all the time."

"Dwight's really the only one we sit down with, though. And he's pretty involved in that task force. Maybe they wanted someone on the inside who can hover around eavesdropping when Dwight comes in."

"She's real good at hovering around, but she doesn't seem smart enough."

"Don't have to be smart to be devious. Maybe it was a mistake for Red to let her back in so easily."

"Felt sorry for her, plus she thought she'd learned her lesson. Besides. What else could she do?"

"Nothing, I guess. Anyhow, what's done is done. She probably wants money, so maybe we pay her off."

"Pay her off? With what?"

"I don't know. Another mortgage? We'll figure it out. Come on, babe," he says as he gets to his feet and takes my hand to tug me off my stool, "let's get some sleep. Maybe we'll have the answer in the morning."

As bad as things are, there's one bright spot: K.C. said "we" instead of "you".

Jesse Bird isn't tall and he's a little chubby, but he's handsome, well spoken and impressive nonetheless. His office, however, is unimpressive, located in what used to be a Red & White store before it was squeezed out of business by the Safeway supermarket. The wood floors still bear scars where the checkout and banks of shelves used to be. He says he likes the location and doesn't mind the old building smell. He'll renovate, including refinishing the floors, when he can afford it. He's Cree, and does so much pro bono work for people from the Rez he may never be able to afford it, but when I pointed that out he just shrugged and said, "I was never any good at hunting. They keep me in venison."

Today, Red, Stu, K.C. and I are in chairs clustered around the battered World War II army surplus desk near the middle of the old store sales area. At the desk near the door is Jesse's wife with headphones in her ears, busy transcribing dictation. From the stacks of files on desks, chairs and file cabinets, it appears they have plenty of work. Hopefully he'll get paid in something other than venison for at least some of it.

"So," Jesse says, "as I told you, I don't do wills or inheritances, but after our call this morning, I looked into intestacy rules. You were wondering how long children of someone who died intestate have to make a claim on the estate? Six months."

"Oh great! We're well past that!" I say.

"Well, yes. But she could petition the Court for an extension. I found case law where an extension of six years was granted."

"Six years? We're still okay, then," I conclude. "It's been nearly eight years."

"That six year extension didn't change the law, but Trina's lawyer could refer to it as a precedent to support her case. If they could extend it by six years, it's easy to justify an eight year extension. Her challenge could be granted." Jesse shakes his head. "Look. I'd like to help, but I wouldn't be doing you a favor if I took this on. I wrote down a couple of suggestions for firms who specialize in this type of thing. One in Swift Current, a couple in Regina." He hands me a sheet of yellow foolscap.

"What if we just paid her off without going through all that lawyer and court stuff?" K.C. asks.

"That would be one solution," Jesse says. "But whatever you do, don't give her any money without having her sign a quitclaim. The whole thing should be negotiated through lawyers. I'd be happy to take care of that for you."

The cowbell over the door jangles as a couple of cowboys come in. "Have a seat, guys," Jesse calls out. "I'll be with you in a minute."

"Go ahead, Jesse," I say as I get to my feet. "I think we're done. I'll let you know if we decide to go with a payout. Thanks for your time. You know where to send the bill."

"No bill necessary," he says, and stands. "A bottle of wine and we're good. I go past your place all the time. I'll drop in and pick it up."

"You can't pay yer mortgage with wine," Red says.

He laughs and says, "No, but I'll sure have friends. At least until the wine's gone."

"Well, we'll make it a case," I say, and reach to shake his hand. When we've all said our goodbyes, we head out the door onto the sidewalk. The wind has picked up and has a sharp, icy edge to it. I zip my jacket as far up as it will go, and shiver.

"How about lunch at the Jasper?" K.C. asks.

"Would be nice. I hardly git off the ranch. But I don't think so," Red says. "I don't like this wind. Think we need to hightail it home."

We all agree there could be another blizzard on the way, so we head for the truck. We're on our way out of town when a couple of RCMP cruisers pass us heading north and turn onto Fourth Avenue.

"Seems like they're in a hurry. Wonder where they're going," I say. "Nothing out that way but the old folks home."

"Maybe there's a new donut shop we don't know about," K.C. suggests.

"Or maybe it's just regular folks had a robbery," Red says. "So, about what Jesse said. The payout K.C. suggested. How can we do that? Ain't our credit maxed out?"

"Pretty much, or at least it soon will be, what with the seasonal slow-down," I confirm. "I don't know. Maybe we could set up a payment plan or something."

"I still have most of the money for the arena build. We could use that."

"K.C.!" I exclaim. "If you spend that, how will the indoor ever get finished?"

"Maybe it was a foolish dream anyhow," he says, and sighs.

I wish I was sitting in the front so I could take his hand. The money he's offering came from selling Windsong Stables when we left Katawasis Lake, and it's all he has in the world aside from his truck and trailer. He needs the indoor arena to grow his training and coaching business. I can't let him give up his dream! I reach over the seat and give his shoulder a squeeze. "We'll talk about it, sweetie. There must be something else we can do. The ball is in her court, as the saying goes. It's not up to us to give her legal advice and we're sure as *hell* not going to give her what she wants without a fight."

"So, here's what I thought. Remember when Russ wanted both Trina and Kristy to move in with him?"

"Yeah?" K.C. replies. He has one of the rescue Thoroughbreds in the crossties in the middle of the alleyway, getting ready to trim her hooves. He glances at me with my mug of rapidly cooling coffee, and returns his attention to the mare, giving her a scratch on the withers as he tells her, "You're a good girl. You're an old hand at this, aren't you."

"So I was thinking," I say, and move so I'm on the same side of the horse that he's on, "he said it would be good to have someone on the property. For security, he said. Because he's away often, sometimes for weeks at a time. Remember he said he'd be away so much it would be like they had the whole house to themselves?"

"Sure, I guess he said something like that." He bends over, picks up the mare's near front foot and starts paring the sole and frog. "Why?"

"Well, I was wondering. Since Trina's gone with him, does he have someone coming in to make sure everything's okay? You know, to make sure the furnace hasn't packed it in or a pipe leaked or anything."

"You want to volunteer?"

"Well, I want to go there. Don't know if he needs to know about it, though."

K.C. releases the mare's foot and stands up straight so he can give me his *you can't be serious* look. I'm sure he's got plenty to say and the reason he's not speaking is that he's sorting out which argument to lead with.

Before he can start, I continue: "You know how cold it's been. He's got oil heat and you know sometimes when it's this cold, you have to add kerosene to the tank or it, um, freezes."

"It doesn't freeze. It just gets waxy and stops flowing."

"End result's the same," I insist. "Furnace quits and pipes in the house freeze. We need to go check. It's the neighborly thing to do."

"Neighborly, my ass. I'm learning why Red calls you a stickybeak. Goddammit, Lindy, what are you up to?"

"Um..."

"Never mind." He huffs out a loud breath. "He's got Jonesy coming to feed every day. How do you know he's not taking care of the house, too?"

Jonesy's ranch is some distance east of here. Stu has known him forever but he's not really in our circle of friends. I only met him when he rode with us patrolling the Community Pastures for cattle rustlers a handful of years ago. "Jonesy?" I say.

"Jonesy," K.C. confirms.

"Why Jonesy? Why ask someone who has to travel so far when we're practically right across the road and the boys work for him enough they know exactly what to do? And not only that, Stu's a partner in that business. Why wouldn't he look after the cattle when Russ is gone?"

"Who knows why Russ does anything? Maybe he thought it was too much to expect of the boys, what with school and so on, and Stu's getting on. Maybe it would be too much for him, what with the snow. What do you think you'll find if you snoop through his house, anyway?"

"Well, um..." Before I can give him my standard answer, which is *I'll know it when I find it*, the alleyway door slides open partway to admit Stu. He closes the door and walks toward us.

"Hey, Stu. Speak of the devil. What's up?" K.C. asks. "Thought you had a big project in the wine room today."

"Felix has a handle on it. Pretty soon he'll know more'n me and won't need me in there no more. And whaddaya mean, speak of the devil? Why were you talkin' 'bout me?" he asks.

"We were just wondering why Russ didn't ask you, or us, to feed while he's away," K.C. tells him.

"Oh, well, he said Jonesy needs the work, and it's a write off so no use me doin' it," Stu explains. "The kids got work here too, plus Christmas exams comin' up." Stu admits.

"Okay. Makes sense, I guess," I say. "So. Did you come out to give K.C. a hand?"

"If he needs it, sure. But mostly I just have some bad news."

"Oh, great," I say, and sigh. "On a scale of one to ten, with ten being the worst, how bad?"

"Dunno yet."

"Well," K.C. says; he slides the knife into the loop on his chaps and reaches up to scratch the mare's neck while he gives Stu his full attention. "Go on, then."

187

"Yeah. So. You know our semen orders are way down. I bin callin' around, tryin' to nail down orders fer next spring."

"It makes sense," I say. "Being pro-active and all."

"Yeah. Well, some of our customers, folks we shipped to ever since we started this business, ain't ordered. When I asked 'em why, they said it's just finances or downturn in demand fer their bulls or they got their own bull. Stuff that sounded reasonable. Then one breeder told me he thinks he never got Domino's semen, he got somethin' else instead."

"What would make him think that?" K.C. asks.

"He got a calf that looks like a Hereford outta a full Brahman cow. Ain't no Hereford in Domino."

"But there is in some of his sons," K.C. completes the thought. "What do you think happened? Mix-up with ampules?"

"That could happen," I agree. "If he's going to make a fuss about it, send him a couple freebies."

"Ain't gonna be that simple. He's been talkin' to some of the other guys and they all had suspicions. He found out a whole mess of 'em got the wrong semen. They don't think it was an accident. They're right."

"You mean you've deliberately been shipping another bull's semen instead of Domino's? And *you knew*, Stu?" I can hardly believe it. Stu, the most honest, salt-of-the-earth guy you could ever want to meet, in on a fraud like that?

"I just found out about it myself in the summer." He sighs. "Russ admitted what he done. I never said nuthin' 'cause I figgered I put a stop to it then and never did nothin' more about it. But then I walked into the breedin' shed when Russ and his buddies were collecting from one of the yearlings. Nice young bull. Spittin' image of Domino even though he's outta a half Hereford cow. I asked him what the hell they were doin'. This bull is going to be a bucker, not a stud. At least not unless he turns out to be a good bucker. He said he knew that, this was fer a friend, a favor, it's not gonna be froze, just fresh cooled, he's puttin' it on the bus to Red Deer. No chance of it gittin' mixed up with Domino's. Talked his way outta it, like always. But it dawned on me—that's why he nixed Domino's breedin' soundness exam. The first one, he was pretty close to sub-fertile. Not unusual fer a older bull. But he'd fer sure be sub-fertile now. Not great even if it's yer own bull and yer pasture-breedin' but if yer sellin' fer big bucks you gotta have better quality semen than that."

K.C. is frowning and I think he's as flummoxed as I am. I say, "Well, we better stop it now."

"Might not have to do nuthin' to stop it 'cause with the rep we got now, it'll die on its own. Damn!" he exclaims. "Russ always rode a little close to the line, but I never thought he could look me right in the eye and lie his face off. I shoulda known better then to partner with him. Couldn't be a worst god-damn time fer this."

"Maybe it's not a total loss," I tell him. "Maybe just focus on breeding for meat until one of his sons gets established. Let's not be too quick to write the business off."

Stu leans back against the wall, studying the floor. After a moment, he says, "Okay! I guess we could git ourselves a couple good beef bulls. Angus? Charolais? Or keep one of our young purebred Herefords. But I'll tell you what. I'm gonna turf all the semen we got stored before that asshole gets back. I'd be a damn fool to trust that it's what it's supposed to be."

"I'll go with you!" I offer. I turn away from K.C. so I don't have to see his frown, and say, "How about now?"

Chapter 24

While Stu is busy in the lab pulling everything out of the liquid nitrogen canisters, I take the opportunity to go through the adjoining breeding shed and into the barn. Just to have a look, I explain.

"To snoop, you mean," K.C. says.

Except for half a dozen stalls on the left side of the alleyway that have hay in them, the barn is empty. That is, there are no animals or bedding in any of the stalls. It looks as if there haven't been animals in them for quite some time. Nothing to see here, I think. Good time to check out the house. I don't have my lock pick set with me, but it's possible there's still a key on the doorframe. I'm heading toward the far end of the alleyway thinking I'll go and check, when K.C. calls out, "Where are you going, Lindy?"

I turn to see him entering the far end of the alleyway. "I, er ..."

"Yeah, I know what you're up to. I really wish you'd forget snooping in his house," he says, "and I mean forever. But for today, Stu's done so we're leaving."

I sigh, but turn back. Then I'm struck by a thought. "This is odd," I say.

"What's odd?" K.C. asks.

"Well, why stack the hay like this? Instead of two bales high, why not three or four? Then it would all easily fit in one or two stalls."

"A lot easier to stack this way, and they aren't using the barn anyway. Looks like alfalfa. Those bales are probably a hundred pounds. Who wants to lift them any higher than you have to?"

"I guess. No reason to, when you've got the room. But another thing. Why these small square bales? The cattle and horses are all outside at the round bale feeders."

"If it's really bugging you, Stu would know. Ask him."

"I'll do that," I agree, and we both head back to the lab, where Stu is waiting for us.

"All done?" I ask.

"Ay-yuh," he replies. "I'll leave the deep clean fer when we start collectin' again. Goddammit anyway." He huffs out a breath. "So. Where'd you guys go?"

"Just took a look in your barn. What's all that alfalfa for, anyway? Don't see livestock eating anything but the round bales out in the paddocks."

"That's something Russ wanted and you know what he's like when he gits set on somethin'. Up till now we always fed our own hay. The round bales. He said he was going to keep the horses in the barn overnight and it would be fer them. So far that ain't happened. No one wants to clean stalls and what's the point with him gone and not ridin', and none of my horses here?"

"No point, I guess. So if you don't need it here, maybe we can buy some," K.C. says. "I'd like some for our Thoroughbreds."

"Hell's bells, buy some? Just take it. I'm the damn fool who paid fer it," Stu says.

I remember Stu writing checks when there wasn't enough money in the Rocking R account. "That's right, it's always you writing checks. But he repays you, right?"

"Not so far."

"You mean the guy who brags he's a millionaire doesn't repay you?"

"Nope. Never does. Throws money around like there ain't gonna be no tomorrow, but he's always skint when I ask him. Matter of fact, payin' Rockin' R bills is keepin' me in the poor house." He clicks his tongue and shakes his head. "Now this b.s. with the semen and him hookin' up with Trina and tryin' to git half of Wacasko-Wâti! Time I put the brakes on this partnership. Startin' with takin' my hay home so at least our horses can eat it. Long as we're here, let's git a load on the truck."

"You sure about this?" K.C. asks.

"I am," Stu confirms. "In fact I been thinkin' 'bout it fer a while now. Lindy, you back the truck up to the door and K.C. and me'll git loadin'."

I drive the truck to the alleyway door and K.C. directs me back in as far as the first stall door. I get out and climb into the box in time for K.C. to heft the first bale in. He was right. These bales are ridiculously heavy. It's all I can do to slide the damn thing, forget lifting it. "Goddamn! Who makes bales this heavy?"

"These ain't meant fer ladies," Stu says. "Or ole fat men fer that matter."

"You just pull the bales out of the stall, Stu, and I'll take them from there. And don't worry about it, babe," K.C. says. "Just get the first layer slid in place if you can, and then stay out of the way."

As much as I hate being dismissed, he's right. So, I get the bottom layer of bales situated and hop down off the truck to watch as the two men load bale after bale onto the truck. We have about half a load. K.C. has just put a bale on the truck and Stu has gone into the stall to pull the next bale down, when he exclaims, "What the hell?!?" He backs out of the stall and points.

K.C. goes to see what Stu is pointing at, and not to be left out, I go too. After a moment, I say, "Forget loading more. We need to call Dwight."

What we're discussing is so sensitive we can't risk being overheard, so instead of meeting at the Bistro as usual, we're at my house. There are five of us and only four stools at the island in the kitchen, so the men sit and I stand leaning back against the sink. Red comes up from the Bistro with a tray of still-warm cinnamon buns, sets them on the island, and gets plates for everyone as I pull the buns apart to put one on each plate. Then she joins me at the counter.

Sitting next to Dwight is a muscular twenty-something man in well-worn farmhand clothes introduced as Constable Rivers. "Just call me Boyd," he says.

"In case you're not aware," Dwight says, "this is nothing to fool around with. These folks mean business."

"I thought you'd seize the guns, though," I say.

"We thought about it. Then we figured we'd put electronic tags on them and wait to see who showed up to move them."

"And follow them. So you can get the big guys," I conclude.

"Right," Dwight agrees. "That's where your new employee comes in."

"When I joined the RCMP I thought my days of sleeping in a barn were over," Boyd says. He's referring to the cot we set up in the lab, which is where he'll be living for a while. Besides the little combination TV/VCR from my Katawasis Lake days, there's a microwave and of course a fridge as well as a bathroom with a toilet and sink. He'll have to come here to shower. He'll likely be coming to the Bistro for supper anyway.

"Your parents made you sleep in the barn?"

"Not my parents. It was when I was working on a custom harvesting crew. Not every farm had room in the house," he explains, and grins.

"Oh, I see. Well, I'm sorry there's no cable TV. Hope you like to read."

"I do. Plus that little TV plays videos, so I'm good."

"Any issues with Jonesy?" K.C. asks.

"No. He said it was strange you'd take someone on at this time of year, but he was friendly enough," Boyd says. "I told him our story, that I worked for K.C. in Katawasis Lake. Lost my job when Windsong shut down and never found anything since, so I came here thinking K.C. might hire me again. Got no place to live, so the room in the barn at the Rocking R suits me fine until I find something more permanent. Meanwhile, I'm on site twenty-four seven, which is good security. He looked at me kinda funny there."

"Most folks around here don't even lock their doors," Red says.

"Guess that's true at home, too. Now that I've seen enough B and E's, I wonder why not. Anyhow, I asked him if I could help, and he got me on the tractor delivering hay out to the pastures."

"Good thing you can drive a tractor," I say.

"He caught this case because he's a farm boy," Dwight says. "He didn't get those biceps at a gym. We just hope no one from Katawasis Lake shows up and starts asking awkward questions."

"All he needs to know is that Katawasis is the Cree word for beautiful, Katawasis Lake Lodge is ridiculously expensive and Tall Timbers is a great pub," I say.

My phone rings and I answer it. It's Kristy. "Hey, what's up?" I ask.

"Jesse Bird is here. He wants to talk to you," Kristy responds.

"I guess he came for his case of wine," I say. "I'm a little busy right now. Let him pick out whatever he wants."

"I told him you were in a meeting but he says it'll only take a minute and he really wants to speak to you."

"Okay. I'll be down in a minute." What next? More bad news? I don't know how much more I can take. I turn and tell the others that I have to go.

"I think we're finished up here anyway," Dwight says, "or we will be when we finish our coffee."

"Okay! See you next time, then." I head out the door, grabbing my jacket off the hook in the porch and pulling on my snow boots before stepping outside. Surprisingly, there are half a dozen cars parked at the Bistro, unusual for a Tuesday. Folks must be taking advantage of the sunshine and newly-plowed roads to get out of the house. I cross the yard and go in the patio door. Jesse is at the staff table with Kristy standing over him, carafe in hand.

"Hey, guys," I say as I slide onto a chair, "Jesse. What's up? Don't know if I can take more bad news."

"What? No. It's great news," he says. "Have you been to see one of those high-priced lawyers I referred you to?"

"No. At their rates, I'm not in a hurry. Plus I'm procrastinating. Figured I'd wait until I see what Trina's next move is and get a lawyer involved then. Is that a bad idea?"

"No. I'm glad you did that. Because after our meeting last week, I've been thinking about what you said, that Trina didn't know who her father was until recently. I assumed that was because her parents were estranged or maybe her mother never told him she was pregnant or maybe she didn't know for sure. Then I wondered if it was a mistake for me to assume that she lived with her mother all this time and maybe she was given up for adoption. Do you know?"

"Yeah, she was adopted. She came here looking for her birth parents. I'm surprised you didn't know that Red's her mother. I thought you were on the Rez enough you'd've heard it. But Red wouldn't name her father. I didn't understand why, just assumed she didn't know. That assumption was my mistake. Turns out Russ—our partner in the Rockin' R—knew who Red had been with back in the day."

"So why didn't she name him?"

"She, er, didn't want me—or both of us now, I guess—to think badly of him being as he was a pedophile, after all. Or maybe she thought I'd blame her for my mother and him splitting up."

"Oh." Jesse thinks for a moment, then says, "Okay, then."

"Why? Is it important?"

"Well, not that Red's her birth mother. But it sure is important she was adopted, because then she inherits from her adoptive parents and can't inher-it from her birth parents."

I draw in such a huge breath I think everyone in the place probably heard me gasp. "Oh my god! Jesse! You have no idea what a relief that is! I could kiss you! Thank you, thank you, thank you!" I leap to my feet, grab his hand and give it a vigorous shake. "I have to go tell the others."

I'm heading for the door at speed when I see another vehicle drive up and park. I wonder if I've lost track of the days and it's actually Saturday, when it wouldn't be unusual to have this many people in for lunch. The driver gets out. I stop short just inside the door.

I turn on my heel and go back to the kitchen and announce, "Kristy, there's someone's here to see you."

Everyone's digested the news that we don't have to worry about Trina's claim anymore, and I'm back in the Bistro just generally wiping this and that. Not that I want to be here. I tried to work on the books but my brain is too fraz-zled by all that's going on. I just needed something mindless to do that also kept my hands busy.

"I was expecting him," Kristy tells me for about the fifth time as she comes up beside me. It sounds like an apology.

"It's okay, Kristy."

"I just don't want you to think I was, you know, being secretive about it. I told you we've talked on the phone a couple times. I wasn't sure he'd come, Lindy," she replies, and clicks her tongue. "When I say I expected him, it's not that I invited him."

"Is he, er, um, going to be a problem for you?"

"No. In fact it's the opposite." She takes a deep breath and picks at the chipping polish on her thumbnail. "I think maybe leaving him was a mistake."

"Oh! Well, that's great, Kristy!" I don't have to feign delight. I've always liked Jim and honestly, if Kristy hadn't gotten to him first, I would have been happy to hook up with him. Of course that was before K.C. and I got together. "You've patched things up, then?"

"Pretty much," she replies. "He doesn't have to be back at work until Monday so he'll be staying with me until then. Ask me Sunday night if I still think leaving him was a mistake."

"You need some time off?" I ask, hoping against hope she doesn't because that'll leave us short two people and would mean I'll be working in the Bistro more than I'd like.

"Just this afternoon? Then tomorrow and Thursday as usual."

"What's he going to do out here in the middle of nowhere Friday and the weekend, then?"

"He's mentioned he'd like to meet Dwight, and of course now there's Boyd. And he can shadow K.C. maybe."

"K.C. might put him to work."

"He'd be good with that, I think. He likes the horses."

"And maybe he can go hang out with Boyd. Share RCMP stories or just be bored stiff together. Or they can talk about how they met in Katawasis Lake." I chuckle. Kristy giggles. "Actually, when I think about it, it's not a bad idea."

"I'll suggest it." She picks up a carafe of coffee and heads out onto the floor with it.

Damn! We may be heading into our slow season, but there's still the Christmas and New Year's parties we have booked. If Kristy and Jim get back together, no question she'll leave Wacasko-Wâti, and we'll be without our best server.

I must be a bad person to be thinking of myself instead of being happy for Kristy and Jim.

Chapter 25

I had almost forgotten about the cop cars speeding past us as we were on our way out of town after our meeting with Jesse a few weeks ago, when I saw today's edition of the Maple Creek News. It's not often someone is arrested in connection with a decades old cold case, let alone three of them.

"I doubt he'll ever see the inside of a courtroom," Jim says. He and K.C. have just come back from town, where they had coffee with Dwight. "He got away with it for so long and might never have been caught, if he hadn't hit his caregiver over the head with a frying pan and then run out into the street in his underwear screaming that he killed him. He kept saying the guy's name, that he had it coming, and shouldn't have come back. Minutes later, he wondered why paramedics were with his caregiver, who was obviously still alive, and had no idea who the cops were talking about."

"He had a caregiver?" I ask.

"Yeah, because of his dementia. You met him, Lindy," K.C. says. "It's that guy at that senior's residence. Apparently he thought his caregiver was a man he killed decades ago. He was dead. That's what he meant when he said he shouldn't have come back."

Jim says, "According to some of the other residents, for quite a while he's been talking a lot of gibberish, glorifying his role in horrific acts. Now they're charging him with three murders and they're not so sure he wasn't telling the truth about other, um, insane stuff."

"What insane stuff is that?" Boyd asks.

"Well, there's the amputation ritual for elders. Elders being given blow jobs as part of the Communion Ritual, to be finished up with mass, um, *fornicating*—he used a different word starting with F—he called it the Mingling. What he talked about the most, though, was the rape of girls as young as eight," Jim replies. "Some kind of bizarre purification ritual. Nobody believed it so no one reported it to anyone, just laughed about it behind his back."

"They might believe it now," Kristy says.

"They sure will," K.C. says. "Funny thing is, he copped to so many obscene acts, even admitted a murder, but denies knowing about the two females."

"Selective memory, maybe," Jim suggests. "He'll probably admit it before long."

I shake my head as I try to process it all. "Well, this proves what I've said all along. My father was not the killer," I say. I look around the table with what is likely a smug grin. In fact, I had serious doubts myself at times. "Those stories have to be cult rituals. Have they connected that guy to the not-church?"

"They're trying," Jim says. "Looks like the big wigs in Pillerton will stonewall them again."

"But Dwight said they figured the C.O.D. of the male victim was hanging," I point out. "They thought it was probably done right in our loft. If he's not connected to the cult that had meetings here, I don't see how he could be the killer. Did he say he hung the guy here?"

"No. Now they think they might have been wrong about that," K.C. says.

"How would he even know about this place otherwise?"

"Well, he was a farmer, so even though he didn't rodeo he might've known your father and grandfather."

"He was a farmer? He could bury the bodies out in his own back forty, and no one would ever find them. Why would he decide, hey, that manure pile on the Larsen ranch would sure be a good place to dispose of bodies?"

"I wondered about that too," K.C. says. "Only thing I can think of is, he wanted them to be found so he could frame one of the Larsens."

"Why would he do that? I mean, frame a Larsen?"

"Now that, I got no answer for," K.C. admits.

"Anyhow, it's obvious he didn't do it alone," Jim contributes. "Other members of that cult or not-church as you call it, had to be involved. But unless the current Elders cooperate and give up the names of others who attended meetings here, the case has hit a dead end. Even knowing they're looking at them for the gun running on top of three murders, the Pillerton cops aren't much help. Dwight thinks they're a little too buddy-buddy with the not-church Elders and the bikers, too. Strange town."

I couldn't agree more, but I'm not about to say so. I look at Kristy, who's biting her lower lip and not saying anything either. She spent a lot more time there than I did—even attended that cult party with Donny—but she just takes Jim's hand and says nothing.

We all fall silent and after a moment, Boyd gets up. "Well, I have to get back," he explains. "Never know when the bastards will show up."

"I'll go with you," Jim says, gives Kristy's hand a squeeze and gets to his feet. He looks down at her and asks, "When are you off?"

"Eight," she replies, and stands. "My break's over too." They share a sloppy kiss. Strangely enough, their lip-smacking, which I normally find as annoying as fingernails on a blackboard, doesn't irritate me. She scoots off into the kitchen and Jim follows Boyd out the door. They pass Red, who is on her way in.

"What are you doing back here?" I ask. "Can't you even give yourself an afternoon off? Haven't you got a Louis L'Amour book you haven't read yet? Go back to your house. Grab a glass of wine, put your feet up and read for a while. I'll bring supper up and tell you all the news then."

"Naw, it's not about our supper." She sighs and sits in the chair just vacated by Boyd. "It's about Trina."

"Trina? What about Trina?" K.C. asks.

"She phoned. Collect. From Austin."

"Oh, they're in Texas," I comment, stating the obvious. "What's going on? Is she wondering about her claim on the ranch?"

"No. Well, maybe. But right now, she needs me to send her some money."

"Seriously? What for?

"Bail."

"Bail? She's been arrested? What for? And what happened to Mr. Millionaire Benson?"

"She ain't been arrested. He has."

"She says it was nuthin' serious, just speedin'," Red says.

"Don't suppose she tried her, um, her other parents?" I ask.

"They told her she made her bed and she should sleep in it," Red replies. I think that's what Red should have done, but a warning look from K.C. and I zip my lip.

Red, Stu, the boys, K.C. and I are at the table in Red's kitchen, having just polished off the chicken from the Bistro, and mashed potatoes and creamed carrots Red made to complete the meal.

"You don't get arrested for speeding," K.C. says.

"Not here, but in Texas?" Stu says. "Sure, they give you a ticket which you gotta sign. If he wouldn't sign or if he argued with the trooper, he'd git arrested. Knowing Benson, I imagine that's what happened."

"Well, he didn't stay in jail, anyhow," I say. "He was out as soon as Western Union delivered your money transfer. Right, Red?"

"Right. and Trina's moanin' about how unfair it was and so on," Red tell us. "Knowin' Russ, Stu's right, it was that smart mouth of his got him arrested. Let that be a lesson fer you boys." She gives Charlie and Johnny a pointed look before adding, "Doubt I'll git my money back."

"What I don't get is, why he didn't post his own bail?" I say.

"He had checks but no cash," Red explains. "Hadn't been to a bank. Offered to sign one over to them or give them a personal check, but they wouldn't take it. According to Trina."

"Trust him to come up with some lame excuse. He never ponies up fer nuthin'," Stu says.

"Well, whatever. It ain't slowed 'em down," Red says. "They're workin' their way back up north."

"So he's going to no show his court appearance and forfeit the bail money, knowing they won't come after him for a speeding ticket," I conclude.

"Ay-yuh, like I said before, Russ always rides close to the line," Stu says.

"Wait'll they're back in Canada. I know our cops are going to want to talk to him about the guns in his barn."

"Lookin' at his itinerary, he'll be back next week fer a couple days, then off agin till Christmas," Stu says.

"Tell Dwight when he's expected," I say. "I can't wait to hear him try to talk his way outta this one."

Chapter 26

On my list of things I've looked forward to eagerly that ended up disappointing, what happened when Russ came home and was taken in for questioning is at the top.

The Bistro is closed and the last customer has gone. Red, K.C. and I are at the table nearest the fireplace. It's peaceful in the after hours and neither of our houses has a fireplace, so we often get together at the end of the work day in front of the fire. At least when it's too cold to be on the patio. Now, we're wondering why Stu is so late getting home from town and while we wait, we throw around ideas as to what story Russ told the cops. We agree he would have come up with something good. He is Russ, after all.

"Whatever he came up with, it was good enough he was granted bail," I say.

"That must've burned his ass, havin' to pay his bail outta his own pocket," Red says. "Went pretty quick, I thought. Didn't see neither him nor Trina, it was that quick."

"They might have been too ashamed," K.C. suggests.

"I thought I'd hear from them even if they wanted to avoid a face to face," I say. "Trina, at least. You know, to find out when she'll get title to Wacasko-Wâti."

"Apparently they're content to wait. But he couldn't wait for someone else to put up the money," K.C. points out. "They're already gone again."

"Had bulls to get to some rodeo somewhere, I suppose," I say. "Stu will know. Speaking of Stu, I thought he was just going to have a coffee with Dwight. He should be home by now. Unless they wound up going to the Legion."

"That's a possibility," Red agrees. "Wouldn't kill him to give a call if he's gonna do that."

"Maybe he forgot. Nothing to worry about."

"Well, if he doesn't show soon maybe I should take a drive around just to make sure he's not in the ditch somewhere," K.C. says.

The words are barely out of his mouth when headlights illuminate the yard. Red goes to the window to look out, and says, "Well, that's him now." She opens the door, calls out across the yard to let Stu know where we are, and returns to her seat.

When he doesn't come into the Bistro for a while, I say, "Wonder what's keeping that guy."

"Musta made a pit stop," Red says.

"Well, damn it! He knows we're all anxious to hear his news."

Just then he appears at the door. "Hey, Stu—" I say. I'm about to razz him for keeping us in suspense, but bite back the rest of the sentence. The man coming toward us is not the congenial, outgoing, gregarious person we expect. Gone is the bounce in his step and his customary grin. His shoulders are slumped and his face is gray.

"My god!" Red says, "what's the matter with you? Did you lose yer last friend in the world?"

He goes into the kitchen and gets a beer before coming to sit next to Red. He takes her hand and slouches as if his bones have gone soft, the picture of a thoroughly defeated man.

"Russ put the blame on me, darlin'," he says. He clears his throat and wipes his eyes on the back of his free hand.

"What? What do you mean? He put the blame on you? How could he?" I ask.

"Said the guns were here in our loft first. Then I wanted 'em gone 'cause Lindy got suspicious, so that's when they were moved over to the Rockin' R. Said he wanted no part of it but I'm the majority owner so he couldn't stop me. He even told them he wanted to report me but I threatened him. Something like he wouldn't know what hit him. I'd make up some story about an accident, like it was dark and I thought he was the cougar that's been botherin' the cattle. and we couldn't hide them crates with the big round bales, so I ordered baled hay. Told Dwight you'd confirm it."

"Confirm what?" I ask.

"That it's my hay. That I wrote the check fer the hay."

Of course. I cover my mouth with both hands.

Red scooches her chair closer so she can put her arms around him. "Come on, baby, you know Dwight ain't gonna believe that!"

He pulls her onto his lap and takes a deep breath before replying. "He don't want to. It'll come down to proof. His story... Shit! I might believe it! He told them about the fake Domino semen scam too. That's another thing I had goin' on and when he called me on it we had a big fight. Me and him had a bit of a set to at the Legion one day. 'Member I told you about that, darlin'?"

"I do," Red confirms, "but I don't recall what it was about."

"I don't neither. Nearest I remember, it was about him not payin' his share of somethin'. But we got a little loud. I bet money the waitress would remember that. Maybe some of the regulars would remember, too. So there's that, to prove we ain't been gittin' along. The guns and the semen is big money I didn't want to lose, so he believed me when I said I'd kill him."

"But Dwight didn't believe him," K.C. says, "or he would've arrested you."

"He's gonna talk to Lindy, you know, 'bout proof it's my hay. and I ain't supposed to go nowhere. I'm a person of interest. Shit, darlin'! I could go to jail for ten years."

We sit in shocked silence, trying to digest the news.

"Don't worry, Stu," I tell him at last, "we know you're innocent. We'll get a good lawyer. A really good one. They have nothing on you except Russ' word and they won't find your fingerprints on anything."

He's holding on to Red as if she might float away, and buries his face in her hair.

At last he mumbles, "What am I gonna do?"

Stu might not know what he's going to do, but I have to do something and I know where I'm going to start. I'm not worried about being caught because the RCMP have the guns and held a news conference showing off the seizure, so whoever really was involved won't come looking for them. Jonesy only comes around in the morning. Boyd has gone back to his real life. The coast is clear. It's only a little after seven but it gets dark early this time of year. Luckily there's a yard light and the rising moon is big and bright.

"What makes you think there'll be anything in his house that'll do Stu any good?" K.C. asks. He couldn't talk me out of going to snoop through Russ' house, so he is gamely tagging along.

"You know Russ is in pretty tight with those bikers. That's how Trina knew when that check for the loft rental bounced. The bikers told Russ and he told her. Likely thought it was funny. But the Rocking R—he's the occupier. He's a big man, no reason he couldn't have found a way to tell the cops about the guns. He could've done it anonymously, even. His story is full of holes! We know it. All we need to do is prove it."

"You really think there's going to be something incriminating in his house?"

"Yes. No. Maybe." I park at the end of the driveway; we get out and wade through the snow to the porch at the back door. I take off my glove to feel along the top of the door frame. The key is where I remember it. "I'm surprised he left this here. Don't need to pick the lock after all," I say, and open the door.

We stomp the snow off our boots and step inside.

"Give me a clue. What is it we're looking for?" K.C. asks. "Maybe a poster advertising illegal guns for sale?"

"Don't be a jerk," I respond.

"Well? What?"

"I don't know," I admit. "Maybe more guns the same as the ones in the crates? A paper trail? I really don't know."

We go through the back entryway and into the kitchen. There's clutter everywhere, dirty dishes in congealing water in the sink, pizza boxes piled up on the overflowing garbage can, and cases of empty beer bottles in an impressive stack in the corner behind the table. I open the fridge and quickly close it again. "Pee-yew!" I exclaim. "Damn! I think there's stuff in here that could come to life. This can't be from when they were here few days ago. Must be from the time before. Why leave food in the fridge when you're going to be away for an extended period like that?"

I check the freezer in case there are bundles of hundred dollar bills there. Nada. We wander through all the rooms, checking the closets and dresser drawers. The small bedroom facing the road is his home office. While I go through it, K.C. goes downstairs to check the furnace and pressure system for the well. Just because it's a good thing to do since we're here anyway.

I shuffle papers on the desk. A paper covered in Russ' scrawl is on top. It's the itinerary, which if accurate, shows they're on their way to Vegas. The desk drawers aren't locked, but there's nothing but junk in them. I spin through his Rolodex. No names I would recognize as being from Pillerton, and there's nothing on the cards other than what look to be legitimate clients for rough stock or semen. A box for a video camera on the shelf in the closet is a surprise, since I never saw him using it, but aside from that there's nothing interesting. If I said I was disappointed, it would be an understatement.

I go downstairs to join K.C. and find him standing at the closed door of the only framed-in room in the otherwise unfinished basement. He turns to me and says, "This door's locked. You get to show me your impressive lock picking skills after all."

My pulse quickens. Why lock this door? No one other than Trina would come down here. Why would he want to keep her out? I look at the lock and click my tongue. "Jeez, K.C., anyone could unlock this with a bobby pin. It's just a bathroom door lock. You know, the kind you just give a twist to lock? I learned how to cheat these when I was ten. Nobody with something serious to hide would be satisfied with a Mickey Mouse door lock like this."

Such feeble security makes me doubt there's anything worth hiding, but since we're here anyway, we might as well take a look. Lacking a bobby pin, I take out my pack of lock pick tools, select the smoothest rake and stick it in the hole in the knob. The lock releases. I push the door open, step into the room and flick the lights on. The floor is bare concrete. The walls and even the ceiling are black.

"I expected it to be bigger," K.C. says. "Crazy choice of paint color."

"Maybe Early Cave Man style is trendy this season," I suggest.

On one wall is a collection of framed photographs of bucking bulls. On another, a pull-down screen for slides or home movies. There's a TV and VCR on a stand. A small table has a movie projector on it. One recliner. Nothing else.

K.C. slowly examines the walls, tapping here and there, while I sink into the chair with a sigh. "A movie room? How does this need to be locked? And one chair? Does he watch old movies all by himself?"

"Weird," K.C. says.

"I'll say."

"No, not that he watches movies by himself. I mean this right here," he says, and taps the same spot again. He turns to me and asks, "Does that sound hollow to you?"

"You trying to find where the stud is so you can hang a picture? We might as well go."

"Not yet." He tugs the projection screen so it rolls up, then turns to me and asks, "Did you see any keys when you were going through his desk?"

"No. Why?"

"Well, what do you think?" He asks. His expression can only be described as smug. "Is this lock as easy to pick as the one on the door?"

I leap to my feet and go to see what he's pointing at. It's a small, inset lock, painted the same flat black as the walls, barely noticeable. Looking a little closer, we notice a seam in the wall, like two sheets of paneling butted together but not attached. A surge of adrenalin courses through me and I think I may actually be panting.

"No. Not that easy," I say, forcing calmness I don't feel. "It's like the lock on a file cabinet. Jim could pick it in seconds. It'll take me a while longer." I get out my kit and start working on it. "It's as goddamned miserable as I remember these things to be. If I can't pick it, I'll bump it."

I'm referring to unlocking it by forcing a specially-made key into the lock. Jim got one for me when I grumbled about my lack of skill with the picks. He cautioned me not to be caught with it, though, since these bump keys are not strictly legal, damage the lock and are considered a burglar tool.

And then he reminded me he gave me the lock pick set just for a bit of fun, like a puzzle, not to actually break into anything. Since the bump key requires no skill and would therefore be a rather stupid puzzle, I'm not sure how he rationalized giving that to me.

What do I care if the bump key damages the lock? If I have to bash the lock right out of there, I'll do it. Fortunately, I don't have to go crazy like that because the lock releases. I twist the tools and the door springs out far enough I can pull it open. In fact, it's two doors, one opening to the left and the other to the right. They conceal a shallow closet lined with shelves.

"What in the aitch?"

"Cowboy boots?" K.C. says.

"Cowboy boots," I confirm. Aside from a box of old VHS movies on the floor of the closet, that's all there is.

We empty the movie box and check the boots in hopes there might be something more interesting tucked inside. Nothing. There doesn't seem to be anything special about the boots, either. Some are high end leathers—ostrich, snake, crocodile—but others are run of the mill. Some remind me of my first pair, in other words, dude boots, but others look well worn. There's a range of sizes and colors. They're not organized in any way we can figure out. Small ones stand next to bigger ones. Black ones next to the beige. Some still have dried mud and horse manure on them. The only thing noteworthy is that there is only one of each.

"Mementos from the girlfriends Stu claims Russ has all over the place?" I suggest. "Some of these look expensive. Who would split a nice pair of boots to give one to a boyfriend?"

"A one-legged woman?" He chuckles. It is pretty funny. I chuckle too.

"Anyway," K.C. continues, "quite a few women did, because how else would he get them?"

"The Goodwill, maybe? Yard sales? Never figured Russ for a guy with a foot fetish. This really is weird,"

"You think a foot fetish is weird?"

"Yeah. Don't you?"

"Depends on the foot. You, babe, have particularly sexy feet." He grabs me and propels me back to the chair and once I've been dumped into it, grabs one of my feet as if to pull my snow boot off.

"What do you think you're doing? Stop it!"

"Did you see that little red boot?' he asks. "Cute as hell! Got me all hot and bothered. We got time for a quickie. It's kind of a turn on, knowing we'll be able to think about Russ lounging in the recliner we had sex on. Here. Lemme see those sexy li'l toes of yours."

I flail at him, pummeling him with my fists. "Not on your life! Let go of me, you damn pervert!"

He gives me a hurt look. We both burst out laughing.

Our exploration of Russ' place didn't turn up anything suspicious. A collection of ladies' boots is funny, but we can't even tell anyone. K.C. tried to convince me of that before we went, but I couldn't be deterred. If we found something really incriminating, I would tell Dwight, consequences of being accused of breaking and entering be damned. Now, we'll just keep mum.

"It'll be our secret," I say. "I'll take it to my grave."

He chuckles. "I doubt you'll be able to keep it to yourself even until the weekend," he says. "It's too juicy. A rough, tough guy who brags about having a girlfriend in every town, jerks off to girls cowboy boots?"

"Well, at least everyone'll get a kick out of it. And for us, it was a fun evening. Better than watching a rerun of Magnum P.I. Although Tom Selleck is pretty easy to look at."

"Maybe I should grow a moustache."

"No, don't. They're too Seventies."

"You might like it," he insists. "It'll tickle your fancy." He says that in a kind of sing-song and somehow manages to make a leer look cute. And a bit sexy.

"You can be a creep, you know?"

"You love it."

"Yeah, I do," I admit, and sigh. "Aside from entertaining us for an hour and giving us something to reminisce about when we're eighty, though, nothing in Russ's house helps Stu. On the plus side, if we ever feel a need to watch The Man From Snowy River or Cat Ballou, I know who we can borrow the video from."

"That would mean we'd have to admit we broke into his secret stash."

"No, not really. I'd just casually ask if he might happen to have it. Let his mind do cartwheels trying to figure out if I know his dirty little secret."

"You sure like to live dangerously," K.C. says, and mops up the remains of his hungry man size soup du jour with a second thick slice of bread. "Which likely means you'll do it."

I look out the window and see Dwight, in an unmarked car, pull in and park. He gets out, goes around to the trunk and lifts out a box. He comes inside and since there's only one other table occupied, has no trouble spotting us. He comes and sets the box down on the table. "Your dad's buckles, Lindy."

"Thanks," I reply. I can't help being a little picked that he would consider Stu a person of interest in the gun running. I imagine my current feelings toward him show on my face.

He seems to pick up on my thoughts and says, somewhat sheepishly, "Mind if I join you?"

"Of course not," K.C. says. "Take a seat."

I give myself a mental reminder that whatever's going on with Stu is not Dwight's fault, smile, and say, "Coffee and cinnamon bun?"

He pulls out a chair and slides onto it. "Just coffee today, thanks Lindy."

I get up and get it for him. Once I'm seated at the table again, Dwight says, "So, the buckles were useful. We were able to put together a picture of where he went and when. Not complete, but useful, like I said."

"What does it matter now that you've got that confession?" I ask.

"It matters a whole lot," Dwight replies, "because the woman from Bismarck was last seen at the state fair in Denver. Our guy was in jail when she went missing."

Minutes ago I was chuckling at the thought of Russ masturbating to his cowboy boot collection. Now my spirits take a nosedive. I mumble, "Tell me my father wasn't there."

"Wish I could. Your father won a buckle at that rodeo."

Chapter 27

Christmas Day is Sunday. We're closing early for Christmas Eve tomorrow and not opening again until after Boxing Day, so it'll be a nice break. Kristy is moving back to Calgary as I feared, but not until January, so she'll be here to work the parties.

"What a great friend you are, Kris," I tell her, "giving up a family Christmas to stay out here in no man's land where you're living in a shack and working in a glorified cabin."

"Glorified cabin? You're kidding, right? What you call a shack is a nice little cabin. And a lot of people would die for a house as nice as this place, if it had some carpet I guess. And a shower," she says. "Definitely a shower. Also the kitchen is way too big. But besides. You're more my family than my actual family."

On top of her help in the Bistro, her cheerful, upbeat demeanor is badly needed around here. In better times I'd be looking forward to the festivities eagerly, but with the specter of Stu going to jail and my father likely to be declared a murderer hanging over our heads, it's hard to get into the Christmas spirit.

Red put up a Christmas tree in her house, mostly because the boys wanted it, but the Bistro has all the decorations I need. We've strung multi-colored lights along the eaves and set up a decent-sized tree in the corner window. I can see it from my house, and that's enough Christmas for me. K.C. says he doesn't care that we don't have our own tree, although he and the boys strung garland on the stall fronts, so maybe he does.

My mother is coming on Christmas Eve and will stay until after Boxing Day. Reggie, her husband (AKA Wiggles and I guess technically my stepfather) is a sweet guy along with being a decent guitar player. He can be counted on to get everyone involved in a sing song. He's one of the cowboys I got to know the summer I followed the rodeo and is an all-around peach of a guy. As long as Reggie's here, too, I can live through their visit. I hope Mom doesn't insist on sticking her nose in the books, though, because when she gets into that I can count on being interrogated for at least an hour. Now, with our line of credit edging close to the limit and cash flow shrinking, it would really not be pleasant. No ledgers now, though, everything's on computer floppy discs. I wonder if I can refuse to operate it for her. I'd love to! But she's showing signs of computerizing her stores so it's only a matter of time before she knows how to do it herself. I might as well get her started on mine.

I'm in the Bistro early because we didn't finish clean-up after Tire Mart's Christmas party, which went until 2 a.m. We got the kitchen cleared away and sent the staff home while the partiers were still here, but couldn't do the bathrooms and seating area until they were gone, so that's what I'm doing this morning. I swish the yacht mop over the tile side to side, back and forth, bucket, wring, repeat. It's mindless busy work that leaves me free to worry.

No shortage of things for me to worry about, but the big one is the fact Russ and Trina are due back today.

It's been a regular, busy but uneventful day at the Bistro. The freezers of frozen Hutterite chickens and turkeys and our own pies are pretty much empty and we've sold out of the silly little things we got from Butch's inventory: kitschy cartoonish western-themed ornaments and plaques with words to live by such as *Lord give me coffee to change the things I can change and Wine for the things I can't*, and *God Bless this Mess* and the inevitable *Cowboys Stay On For 8 Seconds*. No surprise that one wasn't popular. Still, it sold. Last minute stocking stuffers I suppose.

We're closed now, gathered around the fireplace with most of the overhead lights turned off to give full effect to the Christmas tree in the corner. We share a chuckle at some of the suggestions for who bought that Cowboy—8 second plaque.

"Had to be some girl who divorced her cowboy husband," Kristy says.

"Sure," Jim agrees. "Maybe it's a gift for his girlfriend."

"Maybe the same woman who wrote *Alf has a tiny dick* on the bathroom wall," Red adds.

"Do you guys know anyone named Alf?" Kristy asks.

"Why?" Jim asks. "You want to check to see if it's true?"

"Of course not!" Kristy replies with a snort. "If it said he had a big dick, maybe. But I was thinking we could get the names of his past girlfriends and make her pay for painting that wall," Kristy replies.

"If we find Alf, maybe he'd paint it fer free," Charlie says. I suddenly realize how much he's grown just lately. Now he's in that shadowy no-man's-land between being a kid and an adult and sexual innuendoes no longer go over his head.

"I dunno where they could be," Stu says, breaking into my musing. No one has to ask who he's talking about. "He's usually good at stickin' to his schedule. Something musta happened. Just hope whatever it was, he put in somewhere and found a place to offload the cattle fer the night."

"I'd be just as happy if they never showed up," I grumble. I'm tired, need a shower, and would gladly put off the inevitable confrontation with the two of them for as long as possible. K.C. reaches for my hand. We make eye contact and I wonder if he's thinking about a shower, too.

"Ready to go up?" he asks, and winks.

A second ago I was too tired for anything other than a solo shower and then sleep. Now I'm not so sure.

Headlights in the parking lot alert us to a vehicle coming in. "Charlie, if it's not Russ or Trina, go tell whoever it is the turkeys and pies're all gone and we're closed," Red says.

Charlie gets up and starts toward the door, then says, "It's Dwight. Should I let him in?"

"It's Dwight? Yeah, of course, let him in," Stu says.

Charlie unlocks the door and Dwight, in civvies, comes in. "Hey, guys," he says.

We all say our hellos and Red says, "Come sit. You want a beer?"

"Sure," he says. "Or something stronger if you have it."

"Bring that bottle of Crown Royal and a couple glasses, wouldja, Charlie," Stu says.

"So, Dwight, what makes this a 'something stronger' night?" I ask. "More bad news?"

"Yes and no, I guess. I know you aren't spending time at the Rockin' R, Stu, but don't you at least go into the office once in a while and check your answering machine for messages?"

"No. Why would I?" Stu replies.

"Well, if you had, you'd know Border Services has been trying to get a hold of you for a couple days already."

"Border Services?"

"Yeah. U.S. Marshalls stopped the truck at the border and took Russ into custody."

"What the hell? They sent the Marshalls after him fer a speeding ticket?"

"More than that, buddy," Dwight says. "He's been using North Portal border crossing so often for years, so he knows them all. They usually rubber stamp the paperwork and wave him through. This time he got X-rayed. Long story, but he had quite a valuable undeclared cargo."

We're stunned. K.C. is the first to speak. "Where? How?"

"False floor in the trailer," Dwight says. "Never would've been checked without the X-ray. No one's going to get in there with the bulls."

"So U.S. Marshalls arrested him?" K.C. asks. "Thought it was your task force."

"Well, we've been in contact with the ATF from the start. They'd be happy to keep him. But they'll have to stand in line."

"You mean runnin' guns ain't as serious as a speedin' ticket?" Stu says.

"No, not the speeding ticket. They want him for murder."

Chapter 28

News crews swarm the Bistro again, but this time they're not interested in Wacasko-Wâti. It's just that we're the closest place to warm up and get a hot coffee. The real story is the Rockin' R, across the road and down a little. Like the last time, they make a mess of the coffee bar and might drink us into the poor house thanks to the unlimited free refills. I thought being asked by every second person who comes in about the bones found here months ago was behind us, but no, it's front page news again, so the questions are back. I force a smile, assure everyone that no, we knew nothing and if not for the new building, still would have no idea there were bones below no matter how many times a day we walked over them. It's upsetting, but I tell myself our cash flow is healthy and we haven't had to lay anyone off.

At least this time the media won't be hanging around long. As soon as they realize there's nothing going on at the Rockin' R and the folks who show up to care for the livestock don't know anything, they'll tire of being out in the cold and snow watching cattle doing nothing more interesting than eating hay, and be gone. Especially since the RCMP search of the property turned up nothing.

"They haven't mentioned the boots. Do you think they just won't tell anyone about them, or is it possible they didn't find that secret door?" K.C. and I are having breakfast, discussing the day's tasks. I'm on my third cup of coffee, my stomach too rocky to eat anything yet. K.C. is on his second helping of hashbrowns. He can eat anytime, no matter how stirred up everything is, and how he keeps so trim and fit is beyond me. Frankly, it is kind of annoying.

"I think it's one of those details that isn't made public. You know. Something only the killer knows," K.C. says. "Anyhow, once the dust settles, Dwight might mention it the next time he's off duty and has a couple drinks, just because it's funny."

"Funny? Just funny? You don't think the boots are important?"

"Why would they be?"

"I don't know," I admit. "It's just that I can't figure why anyone would go to so much trouble to hide them, that's all. I wonder if they didn't find them. I think I'll ask Dwight."

"You're going to tell him we broke in?"

"Well, technically we didn't break in. We had the key."

"Okay, but if we tell Dwight what we found, please don't try and convince him us going in wasn't illegal because we found the key. And we admit our reason for being there. We tell him the truth. You made me do it."

"One victim's purse was found in a dumpster," Dwight tells us. We're in Red's kitchen, because the Bistro is crowded and Dwight's information isn't for public consumption, at least not until the RCMP release a statement. "Fingerprints all over it. Once Benson's fingerprints were on file after that arrest for speeding, they had him. He would've gotten away with it if the dumpster had been emptied a day earlier or if the purse wasn't noticed or if the person who found it kept it. In fact, he might've gotten away with all the murders."

"And you thought the killer was my father," I say. It's small of me, I know, but I can't resist rubbing it in.

"Either him or Benson," Dwight admits. "But it could also have been anyone on the rodeo circuit. We could've been chasing our tails for years."

"Well, whaddaya know, that asshole attitude and smart mouth of his finally done him in," Stu says.

"What about our bones?" I ask with a wave of my hand in the direction of the indoor arena, now framed in and waiting for the trusses. "I mean, he killed them, too, right?"

"Well, the pendant could tie him to the one victim. He either won it or stole it from your father," Dwight replies, "he won't admit it, though. He would be happy to let his deceased friend take the blame for that body."

"Creep!" I exclaim. "Even with all the others? How could a couple more matter?"

"Impossible to get inside the mind of a serial killer," Dwight says. "So it's a good thing he took such good care of her boot."

"I wonder how many women he killed," K.C. says. "If he was at it for all those years, there could be dozens."

"Well, one for every boot, that's for sure. There's more boots than victims that we know about at this point. He might cop to more, if we can get him bragging. And we might get stills from the videos to match some missing persons."

"Videos?"

"Yeah. Those movies? The sleeves were for actual movies, but the videos inside were, er, let me just say, graphic."

If I thought there was nothing else that could come out that would shock me, I was wrong. Judging from the sounds everyone is making, we all feel the same. Finally I say, "I guess that explains why there's only one chair in that basement cave."

"But he was killing long before video cameras were widely available," Dwight continues, "so we hope he does confess to more murders. Killers do actually brag, but sometimes not until they've been in jail for years. It's just a good thing someone knew about that secret compartment full of boots or we'd never have tied him even to the ones we have so far." Dwight gives K.C. and me a wink.

"Would've been nice if you'd mentioned that our bones were buried wearing just one boot," I say. "Why did you let me think one of the victims was my grandmother? I seriously doubt she had cowboy boots."

"We didn't know about the cowboy boots, Lindy. With your bones, as you call them, there was a piece of rubber, the plate from the bottom of a boot heel, but you can also find those on shoes and who knows what other garbage people toss in with the manure? So it wasn't a real helpful piece of evidence. The rest of the boot had decomposed in the nearly three decades in the ground. Fortunately we could match the rubber to a boot in Benson's collection. The other female victim was a barrel racer, not in the ground as long, and a boot still, um, that she was still wearing, matches. Nothing unique about it, but a detail only the murderer would know, and something that was never reported. Now we and the FBI have sent out an announcement. A few more victims wearing just one boot have already surfaced, and one was confirmed to be linked to Benson thanks to the red dirt on one of his trophies. It matches the dirt from the girl's farm, just outside of Sedalia, Missouri. They're tracing the routes Benson drove from rodeo to rodeo all over the continent. And they're taking a hard look at that rodeo school in Rocky Mountain House he was part owner of." He looks around the table at all the faces hanging on his every word. "They have a manure pile, too, you know."

"Sounds like he's been really busy," I say. "And Dad generally went everywhere Russ went, and at the same time, like everywhere there was a rodeo. So Dad could still be a suspect."

"That would be true, except for the buckles."

"The buckles?"

"Yeah. Your father and Benson didn't go everywhere together. Didn't you say you hadn't met him before he showed up here? Yet you followed your father for months."

"Well, I wasn't following my father, really. It was a bonus that he just happened to go to the same rodeos as my friends."

"Right. So anyway, the Sedalia victim was last seen at that rodeo. You father won a buckle at the Wenatchee rodeo that weekend so he was a thousand miles away. But Benson supplied the cattle for the Sedalia rodeo."

"So it's been Russ, all these years," I muse. A shiver passes over me. "It creeps me out, thinking how close I've been to a serial killer without having a clue. He's hugged me. Ewww! It makes my skin crawl."

"Well, me too but least now this place ain't gonna need so much smudgin'," Red says.

"That's a good thing," I say. "But there's no connection to the not-church?"

"Well, maybe not directly. We think there's a connection to the bikers, we just can't prove it," Dwight says. "And we think the bikers are connected to the not-church. Besides that, we like them for Daryl Cassidy's murder. Again, can't prove it. Not yet, anyway. Got any thoughts, Lindy?"

"My god, Dwight," K.C. exclaims, "don't give her any ideas."

"Don't be crazy, K.C.," I say. "I am *so* done with criminals. I got enough on my plate with Wacasko-Wâti."

Dwight chuckles. "So there's no use asking if you have any interest in applying to join the force."

Well, that gives me pause. Anyone can do our books. If I joined the RCMP, my paycheck would help the cash flow situation. And I'd always have back up...

"Lindy!" K.C. exclaims.

I'm reminded my face always shows exactly what I'm thinking, give myself a mental head shake and say, "They wouldn't make me a detective right away anyway. Likely I'd be posted to Churchill or Yellowknife or I'd be stuck on traffic or in a desk job. I wouldn't be suitable. I'm not that good at doing what I'm told."

K.C. looks relieved. Dwight grins and gives me a wink. I think Red is about to agree with me on that last point, so I put a stop to that by getting up to get more coffee.

An idea just came to me: there's a job I might like and I could run the business right from my existing office at Wacasko-Wâti. But I guess now is not the time to ask Dwight what a person needs to do to become a P.I.

Author's Notes

I hope you enjoyed this little trip to 1987-88. Computers were just becoming mainstream. The one I had at the time depended on 5-1/2" floppies to do anything so my kids used it for some role playing game—Dungeons & Dragons, maybe? Cellphones were a glimmer on the horizon. Not that I was first in line for tech stuff, but I didn't get my first telephone answering machine until 1989.

The Bones Below is book #4 in my Lindy Larsen series. I thought it would end the series. Then somehow the last sentence appeared on my screen. I have no idea what Lindy will do next, but visions of the lawyer Jesse Bird at his battered army surplus desk keep popping into my head. He looks up at me and smiles. So, here's a look at Lindy's next adventure, *House on the Wrong Side of the Tracks*. *The Woman in the Red Boots* (release date 2027) is next. Both are published by Rowan Prose Publishing.

Enjoy!

Gayle Siebert

House on the Wrong Side of the Tracks

Alphonse Asselstine is boring. I think I'll slip into a coma if I have to surveil him another minute. All he ever does is sit. In his little office. In his truck. In his living room in front of the TV. If nothing pops today, my assignment ends in failure.

It's my first assignment from Saskatchewan Government Insurance, a real feather in my cap. He claims he's too injured do physical work so he can't fix up the old house he was planning to flip, which he says was going to make him a bundle. There goes his early retirement. My mission: to catch him at something he claims he can't do. Video of him sitting on his ample backside won't do it. He moves so seldom I wouldn't have had to go into debt to buy the Camcorder.

The second day, it looked promising. He went to his project house, took something that might have been a tool box inside, and—came right back out with it. I got video of him getting in and out of the truck with no sign of a sore back, but no judge would deny his claim based on that. And every time I've followed him, he does the same thing: leaves his job as dispatcher at Swift Taxi, heads to the old house, goes in, and comes back out half an hour later. Sometimes he stays longer, but whatever he's doing in there doesn't make enough noise to be heard outside. With the windows boarded up, I can't even get a look inside.

At home, he ignores overgrown bushes, lawn grass so tall it's going to seed, and weeds crowding the house. He sits by the window drinking beer until his wife calls him for supper. And K.C. wonders why I call him Beer Belly Boy.

Today being Saturday, I thought he'd spend time at the old house, but his truck isn't there. It's not at his domicile either. I decide to wait in case he comes home, so I tuck my van in beside the neighbor's hedge and settle in. I'm in luck. He drives in, and when he gets out from behind the wheel, he's carrying a twenty-four of Lucky. In minutes, I hear football games on TV. The volume is turned to ear-splitting to drown out the hum of the fan on the window ledge. His wife is either deaf or a saint, putting up with that.

The shadows are growing. It seems unlikely he'll do any work around the place this late and I'm about to give up and go home, when he comes out and gets in his pickup. I duck so if he notices my van, he can't see me in it. After giving him a brief head start, I follow. I get caught on the wrong side of a traffic light, and when the light's green again, I've lost him. In hopes of picking him up again, I drive on, and soon spot his truck pulling into a parking stall at The Stockmen's. I turn into the lot, drive to the far end, and park. With the Handycam stashed in the console bin, I don my Saskatchewan Roughriders ballcap, pull my pony tail out through the hole in the back, and head for the pub entrance.

The Stockmen's smells like every other pub I've been in: stale beer, cigarette smoke, and beef on the grill, with hints of backed-up sewer. The place is busy, the chatter loud, Garth Brooks on the jukebox bragging about his friends in low places rumbling away in the background. The ballcap was a good idea, because I blend right in.

When my eyes have adjusted to the dim lighting, I spot my target on a stool at the bar. There are a couple of empty seats on that side of the bar, including one right beside him, all useless to me. The only other empty stool is on the end, between two guys. I take it. From here, I can covertly watch him in the mirror behind the bar.

I order a glass of house white. The guys on either side of me seem to think my Roughriders cap is a sign I'm a fan, but all I know about the 'Riders is that they won the Grey Cup last year. The cowboy on my right is yammering about their two wins and two losses so far this season and if he was the coach he'd do this, that, or the other, or else 1990 won't be a repeat. He predicts they'll beat the Edmonton Eskimos on Tuesday since they're coming off a win last week against the B.C. Lions. He looks at me and says, "Right?"

"Um ..."

The forty-something guy in the South Saskatchewan Fracking ballcap on my left saves me from answering by disagreeing loudly, and they get into a spirited discussion. I suggest we trade seats so they're not talking over me. They comply.

Another mug of beer is delivered to Beer Belly Boy. It's well past supper time and despite the stench of sewer, my stomach is growling. I'd love to order a Caesar salad, but I'd only have to leave it if that's it for him. I can't sit here nursing a six ounce glass of wine for long, though, so since he shows no signs of moving, I order another. Damn! Two glasses of wine and I've eaten nothing but a sandwich nine hours ago. I'll be too drunk to drive if he doesn't make a move soon. I suppose I could've ordered a ginger ale, but I tell myself since one of our family businesses is winemaking, it's research. When he orders a third mug of beer, I order the salad.

The bartender asks, "Are you sure you don't want to run a tab?"

"I'm sure."

I didn't need to worry about my target leaving when I was mid-salad, because he orders a fourth mug. Before long, a large, heavily-made-up woman slides onto a stool midway down the bar. She orders a glass of house red. When her wine comes, I hear Beer Belly tell the bartender to put it on his tab. She rewards him with a smile. He moves onto the stool next to her and they strike up a conversation.

When the woman is on her second glass, the two of them begin sucking face with abandon. I wonder how I manage to keep my salad down. It looks like a good time for a comfort break, so I put the coaster on top of my glass and go to the ladies' room. When I'm done there and come back, the two lovebirds are gone. At least I can't see them at a table anywhere. I give the bartender a little wave and when he's in front of me, ask, "Oh, hey, where did the two that were at the other end of the bar move to?" When he gives me a quizzical look, I hurry on: "I just realized she used to be one of my teachers, and I was going to go say hi."

"She's a teacher? Really?"

Does he know her? Is the idea of her being a teacher too far-fetched? But it was all I could come up with at the moment. "I think so," I reply, and add, "I mean, maybe. I could be wrong. It's been a few years."

"Whaddaya know," he says. "Well, you missed 'em by two minutes."

"Thanks," I say, swig the last of my wine, and race out into the dark parking lot hoping to see them pressed up against the wall or a car or something. But there's no one anywhere. His truck is still where he parked it. Damn! They must have left in the woman's car. There's no chance I'll find them now.

Defeated, I head for my van, but as I'm passing behind the guy's truck, I notice movement in the cab. Country music? The windows must be open. They haven't gone after all, but are inside, trading spit like a couple of teenagers.

I race to my van and get my Handycam, then slink into the row of scruffy bushes bordering the parking lot and work my way along until I'm right in front of his truck. I was worried I might be seen, but even though I'm mere feet away, I couldn't have a better blind if I planned it. The nearest overhead light isn't far off and the video camera is pretty good in low light. With luck it'll even pick up the audio.

I snagged my shirt on something and the smell wafting up around me suggests I've got dog shit on my boots, but my main problem is stopping myself from laughing. Things in the cab soon progress to the point that I can't see much of either of them, but there's a foot in a wedge-heeled sandal on the dash. Her moans are loud enough to be heard over the radio. "Oh, baby! You make me so hot! That's it! I'm ready, honey!" And more in that vein. She's not much of an actress. Beer Belly Boy would have to be as dumb as a post to believe she's really into it. But he must be that dumb, because he pops up and into view as he climbs on top. They're both moaning and groaning now. He barely gets a rhythm going before uttering a loud, "Gaaahh!"

She says, "Whatsamatter, baby?"

"My goddamn back!" He straightens up and they have a quiet discussion. They must have concluded things would work better if he were to sit up and have her climb on him, because that's what they do. It's a rather tight fit owing to Beer Belly Boy's beer belly, and to call her pleasantly plump would be a kindness.

It's hard work. She plays out quickly. Apparently it's enough, as there's a number of heartfelt *oh gods* and then a loud, lengthy *"Gaaahhh!"* They reposition themselves so they're sitting side by side, and light cigarettes. Clouds of smoke issue from the windows. I imagine they're whispering whatever a john and a hooker whisper at such a time. In a moment, the passenger door opens; she climbs out, straightens her skirt, stuffs her immense breasts back inside her bra, and buttons her blouse. In a voice loud enough to be heard at the other end of the parking lot, she sticks her hand in the window and says, "Next week, Alfie?"

Alfie? She knows his name. He must be a regular. He mumbles a reply but I can't make out what it is. He hands her something, payment I guess, as she tucks it into her cleavage and walks away.

You'd think I'd be disgusted with myself for being a peeping Lindy, but instead, I'm so pleased at getting this great evidence I feel like dancing.

On Monday, I present myself at the office of Jesse Bird & Co., anxious to impress him with the video. I get my Handycam connected to the TV in the lunchroom, and when Jesse and the other half of Jesse and Company, his wife and secretary Eileen, are ready to watch, turn it on.

I give them a running commentary, but mostly let the video speak for itself. Jesse and Eileen are quiet except for low chuckles that could be surprise or humor or maybe embarrassment. When it's finished, I ask, "What do you think? He's able to move around pretty well, at least until she climbs on."

"I dunno, Lindy," Jesse says. "It kind of confirms his back is injured, and—"

"Yeah, I know," I cut in, "he complains about his back, but it doesn't really slow him down. I was thinking more that he wouldn't want this video to come out. I know it's 1990 and people aren't puritanical these days, but he wouldn't want his wife to see him with a hooker. So maybe it's enough to get him to go away?"

"Only one problem. She's Mrs. Asselstine."

"What? She's his wife?"

"Yeah. What you have on video is date night, I guess."

I ponder this news, then ask, "Even so, romping like that in the cab of a truck? Isn't that enough to prove he's faking?"

"Maybe, if we hadn't heard him complain about his back."

When no one speaks for what seems like an hour, I ask, "Can I still submit my bar bill for reimbursement?"

GAYLE SIEBERT

HOUSE ON THE WRONG SIDE OF THE TRACKS
Retailers: https://books2read.com/u/mVlrv2

Don't miss out!

Visit the website below and you can sign up to receive emails whenever Gayle Siebert publishes a new book. There's no charge and no obligation.

https://books2read.com/r/B-A-EAZM-GMSVB

BOOKS 2 READ

Connecting independent readers to independent writers.

Also by Gayle Siebert

Lindy Larsen
Silver Buckles
After The Dance
Katawasis Girls
The Bones Below

Lisa Rogney
Call Me Lisa
Wembly

Secrets
The Bear Mountain Secret
The Spirit Bear Secret
Astrid
The Dark River Secret

Standalone
Where The Mule Grazed
The Feeder

Watch for more at https://www.gaylesiebert.com.

About the Author

Gayle has always loved horses, reading, and writing. She has been a trail rider, barrel racer, and dressage rider. Now retired after more than 3 decades as an insurance adjuster, she lives on a horse farm near Nanaimo, British Columbia, Canada, writes, reads, and yes, still rides.

Read more at www.gaylesiebert.com.

www.ingramcontent.com/pod-product-compliance
Lightning Source LLC
Chambersburg PA
CBHW022011010726
47494CB00003B/996